FRONT RUNNER

WILD CARD - BOOK TWO

NIKKI HALL

Thanks for picking up this copy of Front Runner! If you'd like to go back to where the series begins, grab your FREE copy of Game Changer, the prequel novella for the Wild Card series.

For a FREE copy of Game Changer, go to www.nikkihallbooks.com/signup.

*For everyone who **can**.*

1

Riley

Women can't play football. The refrain played on repeat in my head, matching my steps beat for beat as they echoed off the long, empty hallway.

I'd heard variations of it my whole life, but the thing is... I *can*.

The heavy door of the weight room slammed shut behind me, and I took a second to just breathe. My shoulders relaxed at the smell. The football training center had the same musky undertone that reeked of home—sweat and passion and hard work—though it was almost buried under the scent of cleaning solution.

The university logo reflected back at me a thousand times in the pristine mirrors, a scarlet TU over a snarling cat. Not a surprise since they'd slapped it on every reasonably flat surface. *Go, wildcats!* I wanted to roll my eyes, maintain my stoic distance, but a fissure of excitement traveled through me. Teagan University was a dream. One I hadn't completely accepted yet.

Wide eyes stared back at me from the mirror, and I

forced myself to take deep breaths until my pulse slowed. This place may seem like lightyears ahead of where I'd been, but I'd earned my spot here. All I had to do was show them.

I shook my head. The semester hadn't even started yet, and I was already gearing up for battle. My time would be better used prepping for the grueling practices sure to come. A division one college football program didn't succeed by going easy on the athletes.

And Teagan University was succeeding. Or they had been until the playoffs last season.

Two of their players had orchestrated a take-down of their skeezy coach, which left the team limping into the championship that they ultimately lost. My gain though, since the new coach was the one who'd recruited me.

I began my warm-up as the picture from SportsCenter flashed across my mind. Face impassive, Parker Shaw, the back-up quarterback at the time, had stood on the sidelines as the clock ticked down with sportscasters questioning his actions. I respected someone who'd put doing what's right ahead of winning, but it must have been hard on him.

That same week Coach Gordon had approached me about transferring to TU for my junior year. I'd watched every clip I could find on the internet, and then I spent the next seven months obsessively checking my email to make sure it wasn't a mistake. If I hadn't already committed to a kids' sports camp back home over the summer, I'd have moved as soon as my spring classes ended. Hell, I'd have moved in January if they'd let me.

My dad would have been so proud.

With my heartrate raised and my muscles warm, I eyed the rows of dumbbells and headed for the squat rack instead. All the plates were neatly organized, and I grinned at the distinct lack of dust. Did they have cleaning elves who swept through after every session? Probably some poor intern not getting paid enough.

I was no stranger to late night conditioning, but the stillness and quiet skittered across my nerves, raising the hairs on my arms. Not even the fluorescent lights buzzed above me. I purposely made more noise than normal as I set the bar to the right height and started loading my plates. Next time, I'd remember to unpack my earbuds.

Coach Gordon had warned me the weight room was dead at this time of night, but I wasn't expecting full-on zombie vibes. A loud clang echoed from the big metal doors, and I nearly dropped the weight on my foot. Quiet shuffling from around the corner made me second guess every decision in the last year that had led me here. No amount of playtime was worth getting eaten on my first night.

Instead of the shambling undead my brain insisted on picturing, a tall guy in shorts and a shirt stamped with the TU logo came around the corner. He stopped briefly when he noticed me, but then his mouth widened into a grin.

I recognized him from the months of stalking TU's team. Adam Mackenzie, up-and-coming wide receiver. A junior, like me, he'd earned a spot in the starting lineup last season. Watching him play was a whole different experience from meeting him face-to-face.

Even without all the gear, he was tall and built, but no more than any other guys I'd played with. Football tended to be full of people who were tall and built, even me. I'd dealt with my fair share of attractive teammates, and I hoped he fell on the fun side rather than the douchey, arrogant side.

He eyed me up and down, but it felt like curiosity more

than a come-on. No flicker of recognition, so I guessed the news hadn't hit yet.

"I didn't expect anyone to be in here." He punctuated the statement by dropping a small duffel bag at his feet.

"That makes two of us."

He chuckled. "Yeah, but only one of us is *supposed* to be in here. You must be a rebel, Diana."

My head tilted. "Diana?"

"Prince? Wonder Woman? C'mon, girl."

I smothered a laugh at the utter horror on his face. "I know who Wonder Woman is. What does that have to do with my presence here?"

"You look like her a little bit, and you're not afraid to enter the world of man. This weight room is for football players only, but I won't tell if you won't." He winked, and against all odds, I felt a smile pull at my lips. "Adam Mackenzie. Everyone calls me Mac."

I took his outstretched hand and felt nothing. Thank goodness. He really *was* a good-looking guy. "Nice to meet you, Mac. Riley Jones."

"Need a spotter, RJ?"

RJ. I liked that. No one had ever given me a nickname besides my dad. A quick pang of sadness disrupted the happy thought—there and gone almost before I could register it. Mac's eyes narrowed slightly. Observant. I'd have to remember that.

I shrugged. "As long as you don't plan to offer me helpful advice on how to use the equipment."

He raised a brow at my biceps. "Please. You're cut, and those muscles didn't appear all on their own. I'm too pretty to have you coming out swinging." Mac rubbed his jaw and shuddered.

That earned a full laugh as I finished loading up the

weight and took my starting position. "I'm going light today."

He whistled and moved behind me. "Sure you are."

I worked in silence for the first two sets. To my surprise, Mac's eyes stayed on the bar instead of my ass. By the third set, I was feeling the pull in my muscles, and curiosity got the better of me.

"Do you always come here late at night?"

His eyebrows rose. "I could ask you the same question, but no. I usually come during the day with the team. My nights are reserved for the cheerleaders."

"The cheerleaders?"

"Yeah, I let them use my body for practice."

I pressed my lips together to keep the laugh in and focused on my form—a slow squat down, then back up. "At least you're upfront about it."

He tsked at me with a gleam in his dark eyes. "Cheer practice, RJ. Get your mind out of the gutter."

His answer made me pause. "Like you throw them in the air and stuff?"

"Yeah, they bring the skill, I bring the muscle. At least until they decide what they want to do and call in the professionals."

I could imagine that. Mac had an aura of coiled energy, like he just needed an excuse to let it out. "I suppose it can't be any worse than football practice."

"You like football?"

I focused on finishing my reps before responding, but Mac didn't want to wait. He nodded at my butchered shirt in the mirror.

"SWU football. Plus, you're here in the football weight room."

I re-racked and wiped sweat from my forehead, deciding to go with the simple truth. "I like football."

He grinned with all the enthusiasm of a golden retriever. "Hell yeah, RJ—"

An annoyed voice interrupted him before he could say more. "Dammit, Mac. You can't bring girls in here."

We both turned, and my new quarterback scowled at me. "You can't be in here."

I'd been so focused on what to tell Mac, that I hadn't heard him approach. Parker Shaw stood a few inches taller than my six-foot frame with messy black hair, sharp features, and piercing blue eyes. All my research hadn't prepared me for the intensity I saw there, nor the way my heart suddenly took off.

If Mac was a cute golden retriever, this guy was a wicked guilty pleasure—like a fallen angel that clearly thought very little of my dazed gawking. What the fuck was wrong with me?

His eyes narrowed, and he broke our staring contest to grunt at Mac. "You know better, man. Ball bunnies aren't allowed in the training facilities."

The insult finally knocked my brain free from whatever sleep-deprived lust bubble I'd been trapped in. "Excuse me?"

Parker sighed. "No offense, but there are a million other places you guys could hook up. Try one of those."

I wasn't sure if I should laugh or kick him in the shin. Probably not the second one, since I wanted him uninjured for football reasons. Before I could correct him, Mac slung an arm around my shoulders.

"No hookups this time. I was just doing a little late-night training with my girl, RJ."

Parker's jaw ticked as he stared at Mac's arm. "Then train somewhere else."

His voice oozed with disapproval, but he dismissed us to search around beneath one of the nearby machines. I shrugged off the heavy weight of Mac's arm and started removing plates from the bar to prep for the next exercise. Parker could issue all the orders he wanted, but I wasn't done with my session yet.

Mac scooted closer to sit on the bench next to Parker's crouched form. "You going to the frat party tonight?"

"Which one?" His muffled voice didn't sound excited.

Mac shrugged. "Any of them."

Parker stood and tucked a woven bracelet into his pocket. "You know the deal. If you go, I go."

Mac grinned. "My man."

I moved around the station to put away the last of the plates, and Parker brushed by me on his way out. A shot of sensation traveled up my arm like I'd touched a live wire. His steps faltered for a second, and I wondered if he'd felt the same thing.

He glanced back, his cold eyes skimming over me to land on Mac, who'd moved closer on silent feet. "Text me when you're done, and I'll come get you."

"No need. I'll come with you now, as long as my girl is welcome too."

Parker shook his head and strode out of the weight room without answering.

The second the door closed behind him, I realized I'd only uttered two words in the few minutes he'd been there —and I'd let Mac convince him we were fuck buddies. So much for making a good first impression.

I groaned and put back the last weight with more force than necessary.

Mac grabbed his bag, then turned and walked backward toward the door to waggle his eyebrows at me. "You coming, RJ? Don't worry, I'll keep you away from Captain Grumpyass all night. If you're good, I'll even let you get a feel of these babies." He lifted his shirt to show off a six-pack that probably sent the ladies swooning. Not this lady, though. Still nothing for the gorgeous goofball. The asshole with the attitude problem, on the other hand...

Heat still lingered where he'd brushed my arm.

I shook my head and offered Mac a smile. Captain Grumpyass was a problem for another day. "No thanks. I'm going to finish up here and get some rest."

Mac dropped his shirt and shoved the door open with his shoulder. "Catch."

Out of nowhere, he tossed a phone at me. *My* phone, I realized, as it sailed through the air in a gentle arc. Years of training helped me catch it with ease.

I held it up as Mac's name echoed in the hallway. A tingle went down my spine at Parker's voice, and a sense of foreboding made my tone sharper than I meant. "What the hell, Mac?"

He sent me an unrepentant grin. "I borrowed it during your first set. Call me if you change your mind... or the next time you need a spotter." Mac winked again, then he was gone.

I woke up the phone to see he'd added himself to my contacts under Hottie Mac. Stupid of me not to set up a lock screen, but I didn't like the extra steps involved. It occurred to me that he must not have been doing a fabulous job spotting if he was breaking into my phone. The audacity pulled out another smile.

For a second, I was tempted to use the number and take him up on his offer for the party. He made it hard not to like him, but I still felt out of sorts. The last thing I needed was an early introduction to half the football team, especially after that disastrous meeting with Parker. *Hi, I'm your new wide receiver, and I may or may not be here as a publicity stunt...*

My lips pressed together as waves of nervous energy flooded my system. Even if Coach Gordon and the entire TU administration only saw me as a PR strategy, I'd prove to them I deserved to be here.

New state, new college, new team, same routine. I didn't need wild parties on a Saturday night. I needed to get to work.

2

Parker

What the hell was Mac thinking? He knew the rules. The weight room was off-limits to non-players, precisely to prevent late night hook-ups like that one. I slowed when I realized Mac hadn't been spouting his usual hook-up nonsense.

No woman was worth the trouble of fucking up his scholarship—even one as smoking hot as her. Dark blonde hair pulled back in a messy ponytail with sharp features and full lips. Tall. So tall. Nearly my height and all leg. I had a thing for nice legs, and her stretchy pants left nothing to my imagination.

Mac slapped an arm over my shoulders, yanking me from my thoughts. "Kappa house?"

"Where's your girl?" The question slipped out before I could stop it, but Mac ignored the pissy undertone.

"Not up for a party tonight."

I tried. I really did. We made it to the main lobby before I couldn't hold back the question anymore. "How do you know her?"

Mac sent me a sly look as he stopped to scan out. "Interested? I could introduce you, but you made a shitty first impression."

I eyed him, feeling like maybe I'd missed something. Mac was friends with everyone, but he didn't usually offer to share his conquests. "What would she have to say about you passing her on to me?"

"Thanks?" He shrugged. "Me and RJ aren't serious like that."

"She's okay with you offering her to your friends and hooking up with whatever lady catches your interest at the party?"

"Nah, man. We're just training buddies. For real. Vibe's not right for a hookup. She's all yours."

Relief joined the embarrassment flooding me, and I quickened my pace as if I could outrun the frustrating reaction. It didn't matter who Mac was hooking up with. The game mattered.

"You know my policy." It wasn't an answer, and his snort said he didn't buy my attempt to side-step. "I'm just concerned for the horde of women waiting on you at Kappa House."

"The ladies *do* demand my attention."

We left the facility and headed to my car in the warm night. "Team meeting at eight a.m. tomorrow. You sure you want to party?"

"Hell yes. There's a new batch of freshmen who haven't seen the glory of my physique."

"If you flash your abs at me, I swear I will drop you off at Whataburger instead of Kappa House."

Mac laughed and released the grip he had on his shirt. "Don't play, man. You know I'm addicted to that gravy."

"Better you eat gravy than some girl who'll make you late to the meeting." I climbed behind the wheel and waited for Mac to adjust the seat all the way back. He was all leg too.

"Why not both?" He secured his seatbelt then immediately started messing with my radio. "And I won't be late. Coach would give me that disappointed look I hate."

I shook my head and started the short drive to the "posh" part of our little town. Mostly frat houses now. "At least he won't make you stay for dead practice."

Mac shuddered, and I knew the feeling. Our last coach had believed in beating us into submission. When he wasn't happy with our effort, or someone pissed him off, he'd demand a "voluntary" practice run by the captains with nothing but conditioning, usually in the heat. We called them dead practices because it was a miracle we didn't die.

He'd also apparently been a complete megalomaniac that would do anything to win, including cross a few lines to harass students. I'd helped Soren get him fired last year right before the championship, which we'd lost. Soren and D left for the pros, and the school hired Coach Gordon.

I relaxed my clenched jaw as we turned into the neighborhood of big houses. Coach Gordon was different from every other coach I'd had in that he didn't get aggressive with us. He treated us like colleagues, demanding we give our best for ourselves instead of for anyone else. The system was strange at first, but after working with him all summer and seeing the positive change he brought, I was starting to believe. Not that I had a choice if I wanted to play at TU.

The school had been very clear that I wouldn't get another chance if I fucked up—follow the rules, win games, stay out of trouble. Neither Soren nor I regretted what we'd done, but the team didn't deserve to pay for it. I took full responsibility for my actions last year, and I planned to make it up to everyone by winning them a championship—even if it meant babysitting my teammates at a party.

The street with all the frat houses was packed with cars, as usual on a party night. I parked between a lifted truck and a beater, then turned to Mac. "We could just go home and get a good night's sleep."

Mac laughed. "No thanks, Mom. Have you considered actually coming to the party with me instead of standing in the corner with a scowl on your face? You need to relax. Let go. Have some fun."

Parties weren't my kind of fun at the best of times, but it was hard explaining that to Mac, who thrived on attention. "I'll let go when we win the championship."

"Sure you will," he muttered.

"Besides, the scowl keeps the ladies away. More for you."

Mac rubbed his chin, then nodded decisively. "I'm on board with this plan. Let's go."

He unfolded himself from the car, and I followed with a silent groan. We made it less than a block before a group of four girls in cut-off shorts and bikini tops joined us. Mac flirted shamelessly, but I ignored the sultry smiles aimed in my direction and slowed my pace.

They didn't give me a second glance with Mac ready and willing. I hadn't been kidding about the scowl, just like Mac hadn't been kidding about my position in the corner. A lot of the guys liked these parties, and Mac always managed to corral them to one place. It made my job easier, but I'd have preferred if they stayed home.

Even I wasn't stupid enough to think a bunch of college guys would choose sleep over girls though.

Ahead of me, Mac had each arm around a scantily clad body. I wasn't against sex. Hell, I enjoyed the fame that came with being on an elite college football team, but my hookups were one night with no repeats. And I never picked up a girl at a party. Too much drama.

The girls left us when we reached the sidewalk in front of Kappa House, probably headed for the pool, and Mac nudged my shoulder.

"The redhead kept looking back at you."

I'd seen her, but the short, curvy body did nothing for me. Maybe if she was taller. And blonde. And nowhere near this party.

"One day, you'll stop trying to get me laid."

Mac scoffed. "Not likely. One day, your celibate ass will find the right girl and all this bullshit about not dating will go right out the window."

An image of the girl in the weight room appeared in my mind—the fire in her eyes when I told her in the most asshole way possible she wasn't allowed to be there. I winced as I remembered calling her a ball bunny as if she weren't standing right in front of me like a wet dream.

I pushed it away. She might not be at the party, but she was just as bad. Hanging around the athletes in hopes of getting something from one of us. Maybe Mac wasn't into her, but that didn't make her any less of a distraction. In the back of my mind, I wondered if this one might be worth finding out more.

Instead of defending my sex life, I pointed out the obvious. "You're not planning to date any of those girls."

"I could. I'm just picky."

I snorted. We all knew he had a thing for Eva.

After D graduated last spring, Mac had moved in with

us, and he'd convinced Eva to move into an apartment across the hall. She'd claimed she wanted more room for when we invaded to watch movies, but we suspected she wanted the discount Mac had negotiated for her. Which reminded me...

"Wasn't Eva's roommate supposed to be here this week?"

Mac scrubbed his hand down his face. "Yeah. There was some problem with transportation, but she moved in today."

I frowned. "I thought Eva needed us to help."

"I guess not. When I asked her about it, she told me it was handled and to go away." He held up his hands in surrender. "When she says to go away, I listen."

A loud shriek cut through the party noise, and I tensed. We'd had a bit of trouble at a Kappa party last year. A dark-haired girl I recognized from one of my classes streaked out the door in a tiny dress and bare feet. One of the hockey guys—John? Josh?—chased her outside. I shifted my weight, intending to help, but she had a huge smile on her face.

J-something picked her up and slung her over his shoulder, causing her to laugh her ass off as he carted her back in the house. I shared a look with Mac. He'd been there last year, but he was quicker to recover.

He nodded at the house. "Jaden's gotten slow over the summer if he let her get that far."

Jaden. Right. "Didn't you lose to him in a streaking race last year?"

Always the drama queen, Mac clutched his chest. "You know that race wasn't fair. I was handicapped by holding my massive junk out of the way. Jaden was more aerodynamic."

I couldn't help but laugh. Mac had that effect. "I don't think the girls on the side of the house heard you. Maybe try speaking up next time."

He glanced at the group of giggling women huddled by the fence. "They heard me just fine. Don't forget your promise to Eva. She'll be pissed if you scare off her new roomie, and she'll definitely take it out on me."

She would. Mac was Eva's favorite target. Like every other person she liked, Eva was protective of her roommate. She'd made all of us promise to be nice. I hoped whoever it was lived up to Eva's expectations.

"I haven't forgotten, but what are we going to do if the new girl turns out to be a bitch?"

Mac laughed. "You think Eva can't handle a bitch on her own? She's been a cheerleader for most of her life, and she runs those squads. Besides, Eva handpicked this girl."

"I just don't want to get involved with some roommate squabble when we need to be focused on the season."

Mac rolled his eyes and dragged me down the walkway. "Multitask. Like now. You can have fun *and* make sure Duke doesn't crash through the screen door again."

I groaned. "Duke is here?"

"Where else would he be?"

My head started to pound with the music as we approached the house. Duke was new on the defense this year, a monster on the field, but a teddy bear off. He loved to party like Mac loved Wonder Woman—with a single-minded devotion topped only by football. For such a big guy, he couldn't hold his liquor for shit.

Eva could drink him under the table. Though in fairness, Eva could probably drink most of us under the table. Her metabolism was insane.

If Duke was inside, he was probably already drunk and leaving a jolly path of destruction behind him. Sometimes, I missed the days when D was captain and all I had to do was throw a ball.

I stretched my neck from side to side, trying to relax my stiff shoulders. "I hate this."

Mac gestured at the open door of the Kappa House and threw me a big smile. "Welcome to paradise."

I shook my head and followed him up the walkway, quietly wishing I were anywhere else.

3

Riley

I was going to be late to my first team meeting. With the semester officially started, I couldn't find parking in the tiny lot at the front of the training facility.

After circling for twenty minutes, getting my hopes up every time someone walked out of the building, and cursing under my breath, I squeezed into a spot meant for a much smaller car. It was only after I shut off the engine, I remembered Coach had said something about parking in the back.

The mid-August sun beat down on me as I managed not to hit the truck next to me with my door, making me glad I'd taken the time to put on sunscreen despite the early hour. I'd been warned that Texas was basically the surface of the sun in the summers, but the heat didn't bother me too much. Southeast Wisconsin got hot and humid too.

I hoped there'd be more in common here than the crappy weather and mosquitos. My last team had treated me the same as everyone else playing, but we'd been mediocre at best. I wanted the same respect with a higher caliber of skill. Coach Gordon had assured me I'd find that at TU, but he couldn't possibly speak for every player on his team. My team now.

The encounter with Parker last night didn't fill me with hope.

I stared at the large building in front of me and took a deep breath to calm my chaotic thoughts. Four beats in. Four beats out. I had a spot on the team, at least for now. I couldn't control how the guys would react to me, but I could control how I responded—and I could play my ass off to prove myself.

With a steadier hand, I snagged my backpack and sped through the lines of cars. Other students meandered around the courtyard in front of the building, but I didn't see any of my teammates. My watch said I had two minutes to get inside and find the meeting room.

The lady manning the front desk smiled at me as I scanned in with my ID. Apparently, this system was new after Parker Shaw and Soren Brehm's infamous live that got their previous coach fired. No one in the administration wanted a repeat, so they made everyone scan in and out.

Despite how selfish it felt, I was glad they'd done what they did. Not only because that coach was an embarrassment to the sport, but because I'd never have gotten a shot here without the bad press and Coach Gordon taking over.

One minute past the appointed meeting time, I found the door to the auditorium. My heart raced as I gripped the cool metal handle and pulled it open a crack. I'd trained for this. I was ready. All I had to do was go inside.

An arm shot past my face to slap the door closed in front of me. Goosebumps broke out across my skin, and an unwanted heat rose slowly from my chest.

I turned, not surprised to see Parker leaning into my space. The sixth sense that told me where an opponent was on the field worked overtime with my new quarterback. It would be convenient if only I could stop staring at the angry slash of his mouth.

"You have some balls showing up here. Banging one of the football players doesn't give you an all-access pass."

"Good to know."

My calm response seemed to have no effect on him. He stepped closer, forcing me to lift my chin to maintain eye contact. No way was I backing down, but I'd learned that apathy usually worked best in the face of opposition. Parker didn't respond like I expected. He swallowed his obvious annoyance and lowered his head.

Quarterback or no, I was fully prepared to knee him in the junk if he got aggressive.

Instead, he spoke softly. "I'm going to give you the benefit of the doubt that someone asked you to meet him here. That said, you need to let go of whatever fantasy you have going. Every guy in there puts the game first, second, and third. Whatever he told you, I guarantee he doesn't want to see you in there. Especially when it could affect his position on the team."

I'd heard the speech before—football players were notoriously possessive—but the sincerity in his voice made me pause. The assumption I was a jersey-chaser should have been insulting. I could understand why it would make more sense to him than the truth though. More interesting was the confidence he exuded with the statement. Parker truly believed that not one of his teammates would compromise his position for a woman. It demonstrated the kind of dedication I'd found lacking in my previous team.

Of course, I wasn't going to ruin the moment by telling him that.

I let a small smile slip out. "Noted."

His eyes dropped to my lips for a beat, and I had the crazy feeling he might kiss me. Something deep inside me woke up and took notice before I shoved it back down where it belonged. I didn't fantasize about my teammates. Ever.

Without thinking, I licked my dry lips. Parker's gaze heated, and an answering electricity zipped through me. Oh no. Oh hell no. I hadn't come this far to fall to the temptation of Parker Shaw—no matter how well he could throw a football.

Parker must have had a sixth sense too because he straightened away from me a split second before Coach Gordon turned the corner. The big man with the bigger mustache harumphed as he juggled several file folders, a tablet, a phone, and an enormous travel mug probably filled with his ubiquitous hazelnut coffee.

He spotted us and his heavy brows drew together. "Stop dawdling, Shaw. I expect you to be inside and ready when the meeting starts. You too, Jones."

I wish I could have recorded the shock on Parker's face, but the memory alone would bring me joy for years to come.

The door moved under my hand, swinging out as Mac poked his head through. His face brightened when he spotted me, but he quickly refocused on Parker.

"Saved you a seat," he chirped.

It clearly wasn't what he'd intended to say, but he disappeared back into the room before anyone could call him on it. He'd probably heard the news about me and was intending to warn Parker not to stick his foot in his mouth again. I was so glad he'd been too late. Parker must have come to the same conclusion because he sighed before waving me into the room ahead of him.

I didn't have time to cater to my nerves. One second, I was battling with my quarterback, the next, every eye in the room settled on me. I wiped my hands on my jeans and reminded myself not to show weakness.

Parker followed me into the auditorium, and Mac waved from the second row, dramatically pointing to two open seats next to him. Guess he'd been talking to both of us. I moved toward the stairs, but Coach stopped me.

"Jones, hold up a minute."

Parker passed behind me without a word to claim his seat. I had every intention of ignoring him, but my eyes had a mind of their own. Coach rustled his files on the desk, muttering to himself about bureaucracy, and my gaze slid to Parker's face. He watched me with the same intensity I'd felt in the hallway.

"Jones."

I jumped when Coach called my name. With some effort, I broke the connection and moved to the front of the room. Coach cleared his throat, crossing his arms across his barrel chest.

"I know this year is a departure for most of you, but you've risen to the challenge over the summer. This team has a new head coach and a new starting quarterback, but the same fierce determination to succeed." Mac bumped his shoulder into Parker's as the team cheered, but his blue eyes never wavered from me as Coach continued.

"You're a talented group of athletes, and I expect you to be decent men—" He turned my direction. "And women."

The room quieted, and I scanned the faces staring at me. None of them were outright scowling, though I was pretty sure under Parker's impassive expression he was seething. A few smiled, especially when Mac let out a loud whistle and started applauding.

"Hell yeah, RJ," he yelled as the other guys joined in.

Coach's lips twitched, and he shook his head. "Enough, you bunch of hooligans. As some of you know, this is Riley Jones, our new wide receiver. She's a football player just like you, and I want you to treat her with the same respect you treat each other."

One of the guys a couple of rows behind Mac and Parker snorted loudly. "So none then?"

Someone else threw a wadded-up piece of paper at him, and Coach ignored the outburst. I got the feeling he did that a lot.

"The administration wants me to make sure you're all aware of the new fraternization rule they've instituted. No romantic relationships between coaching staff and players *or* between players themselves."

My head jerked toward him. This was the first I'd heard of a rule like that. The university's brand had suffered after the debacle last year with the coach harassing female students, but it hadn't been sexual.

The rule was an insult to me and to the athletes I played with. Coach didn't look too happy to be mentioning it either. I fought a wave of anger at the school's heavy-handed approach. Their new rule reinforced my suspicion I was only here as a publicity stunt.

Did they think my presence would turn the football team into a salivating horde incapable of controlling themselves? Or worse, that I'd waste this opportunity by sleeping around? What a bunch of horse shit.

"Jones."

I blinked at Coach as he called my name, and the concerned look on his face made me think it wasn't the first time. "Sorry."

"Go sit down so we can get the real meeting started."

Mac nodded at the seat on the other side of Parker, and I smiled at him, thankful for his immediate friendship. I didn't know anyone at this school, not even my new roommate who'd been out when I'd moved in yesterday. Being alone was the norm for me—I'd been burned enough times not to trust easily—but Mac made me want to give him a chance.

Parker spread his legs to make space for me to pass, and I brushed against him as I squeezed by. A shockwave of heat shot up my thigh. From his knee. Dammit.

I took my seat and stared straight ahead. Out of the corner of my eye, I caught Parker rubbing his knee absently. A new source of anxiety reared up as I admitted that something about Parker called to me. Much to my horror, my body reacted to him, but I'd spent years learning to control my body. I'd pay no attention to the flutter in my belly until it went away. Once practice started in earnest, I'd be too exhausted to notice anyway.

Coach started talking about our first game, and I studiously ignored the warmth of Parker sitting next to me. He wasn't the only hot guy on campus. Hell, he wasn't the only hot guy in this row. Mac was attractive if you liked charm and bedroom eyes, and the guy on the other side of me looked like he belonged in a kilt defending Scotland against the English. Dark red hair, a scruffy beard, and shoulders that made me feel like a waif.

He sent me a quick smile when he noticed me looking, and I made a note to do more research because I couldn't place his name for the life of me. Or I could introduce myself when I had the chance like a normal person. Unlike my unsettling reaction to Parker, the big guy's hotness had no effect.

As if he knew I was thinking about him instead of

listening to Coach, Parker shifted, resting his forearm next to mine between the chairs. Goosebumps rose even though we didn't actually touch.

He didn't seem to notice, but I wasn't about to jerk away and give my new team an immediate reason to discount me. I needed to move past Parker's draw and focus on my job. To prove I could sit there unaffected, I left my arm close to his for the remainder of the meeting.

As stupid as the university's new rule was, it wouldn't matter in the end. I didn't date fellow players.

4

Riley

W e didn't have practice the first day of classes, just that long ass meeting. Coach wanted us to acclimate to our new schedules, but he'd only give up one day of training for the cause. As much as I hated to admit it, I needed some time to myself after being on display all morning.

Mac invited me to lunch, but I declined, intending to spend some time unpacking. My apartment wasn't far from campus, and I only had a single class in the early afternoon. Our place had one assigned spot, which another car was currently occupying, so I assumed my roommate was finally home.

She'd offered to help me move in, but I told her not to worry about it. The few things I'd brought with me in my car hadn't taken long to unload, and the rest of my belongings had beaten me to Texas. I'd splurged on movers for most of my stuff since the gap between my contract at the camp and the beginning of school here only gave me a day to travel across the country.

Still, it was sweet of her to offer. Somehow, we still hadn't seen each other in person despite me living here for almost twenty-four hours. She'd been gone yesterday, and her door was closed when I'd gotten home from the weight room last night. This morning, I'd had fresh coffee, but no roommate. I didn't drink coffee, but again, sweet.

From the emails we'd exchanged, I knew she was a cheerleader and close with some of the football players. She'd reached out as soon as she'd heard I was transferring here, and once I got over the weirdness of some random girl knowing who I was, I agreed to move in. Honestly, she didn't give me much of a choice.

I yanked the elastic out of my hair and ran my fingers through the wild length until I felt presentable. Past experience said I was going to make her nervous no matter what my hair looked like. I was a jock who preferred sweats and ESPN to make-up and parties, but she already knew that.

Most of the cheerleaders I'd known were athletes just as much as the people they cheered for. They didn't all worship eyeliner. I hadn't put on any make-up this morning out of habit, but that didn't mean I didn't know how to use it.

Probably a good call considering the heat. My car had become an oven while I wasted my precious free time procrastinating. I climbed out of the car, thankful for a slight breeze that teased my hair, and resolved to wait until *after* something horrible happened to stress about it.

Sweat dotted my brow as I crossed a small patch of grass and paused at the door with my key out. The Midwesterner in me screamed that the polite thing to do was knock, but it felt weird when all my stuff was inside. My hesitation ended when the door swung open before I could decide.

Eva was a blonde, like me, but that was the only similarity. The feelings of being small while sitting beside the giant in the auditorium—Noah, I'd later found out—disappeared while I stood next to this pixie. Her blue eyes widened as she stared up at me, and all the old feelings of inadequacy due to my height rushed back.

Instead of saying hi, I blurted out the first question that hit me. "How did you know I was out here?"

She pointed to a tiny white camera nearly hidden in the eaves. "Mac insisted on a few security measures after last year."

My brows rose. "Mac?" I had the disturbing feeling I'd been hustled.

Eva grinned, then grabbed my arm and hauled me into the apartment. "Yeah, I'll explain, don't worry. I'm Eva, and you must be Riley Jones. Or do you prefer Lorelai?"

My back stiffened at the question. "No one calls me Lorelai."

"Riley it is." She sent me a considering look as she closed the door behind us. "Has Mac given you a nickname yet?"

"RJ. How did you know?"

She waved the question away. "I know everything. You'll pick it up."

I was having trouble following the whirlwind, but Eva didn't stop to let me catch up. She shoved me at the couch— she was really strong for someone so small—and curled up opposite me as I sank down onto the cushions.

"Okay, so Mac is my best friend, well other than Stephen, but since he's not here, Mac gets top billing."

I nodded even though I had no idea who Stephen was, and Eva kept talking.

"I've known Mac most of my life, so I'm pretty close with the football team here. When I heard Coach Gordon recruited a female football player from Wisconsin, I knew it was time to trade in my old place. I watched some of your film, and I can honestly say I'm in awe of your abilities. Not

just that, but your determination to play in a space so dominated by arrogant men."

She paused for breath, and I held up my hand, slightly
overwhelmed. "I have questions before you keep going."

"Right, sorry. I've had a lot of coffee today, and the first
day of the semester always gets me hyped. What are your
questions?"

"Are you always like this?" The question was borderline
rude, but she laughed.

"Yes. Next question."

"How did you hear about my transfer ahead of the football players?"

She tapped her head. "I know everything, remember? I
have spies everywhere. One of them works as an assistant to
the head coach, and he couldn't wait to tell me about
Gordon's choice to recruit you. It was hell keeping the secret
all this time, but he swore me to silence. I take my promises
seriously. Next?"

I shifted to tuck my leg underneath me and face her
fully. "How does that connect to you getting a new
apartment?"

"Mac wanted me to move in here anyway because he
wanted me closer—he lives across the way—and I thought I
could offer you a place to get away from the constant gawking. People can be assholes. You're doing a really brave thing
for women everywhere, challenging the status quo, and I
want to support that as strongly as I can."

She understood. There was no space for mistakes in my
public life. I'd been doing this on my own for years, since
my dad died, and sometimes the urge to quit was overpowering—but every time I got to step onto the field was worth
the pain. Having a place to come back to where I didn't have
to be perfect was a perk I hadn't expected.

I didn't know what I'd done to deserve Eva, but she'd earned my loyalty in less than five minutes.

Hot tears pricked my eyes, and Eva blinked a few times before she cleared her throat. "Good. Now that we've bonded. Tell me everything that's happened since you arrived."

"Wait, Mac lives across the hall?"

Eva hopped up and disappeared into the galley kitchen. "Yeah, with Parker and Noah. Want a drink?"

I groaned, and she peeked her head around the corner. "Everything okay?"

"Yeah..." I paused, unsure how to explain my reaction without compromising the lovely opinion she had of me.

Her expression sharpened, and she leaned against the wall with a slow smile. "Parker or Noah?"

My eyes widened. "What?"

"Parker or Noah? Which one are you hot for? You can tell me. I promise it won't go beyond this room."

She must be a witch. Or a psychic. How had she read me so easily?

"Parker." I slapped a hand over my mouth and stared at her in horror. I'd worked so damn hard to be taken seriously, and within ten minutes of meeting her, Eva had gotten me to confess something I hadn't fully accepted myself yet. "Are you with the CIA? If not, you should be."

"I've heard that before." She shrugged and pushed away from the wall to go back into the kitchen. "I'm not surprised either. Parker is unnaturally beautiful. If I didn't know better, I'd think he was a vampire."

Her phrasing implied she'd tested the theory. I managed to keep my mouth shut this time. Barely.

"He doesn't date, you know. Thinks it will interfere with

his dedication to the team," she said over the sounds of her rummaging in the fridge.

Before I could school my face into polite indifference, she popped back into the room and tossed me a water bottle before taking her spot at the other end of the couch. "We don't have to talk about it if you don't want to, but I *really* want to talk about it."

No one could know. The thought spun around in my head on repeat. I considered trying to backpedal and laugh off the "misunderstanding", but I didn't think Eva would believe me. My bedroom door was only a few feet away. I could plead homework or a headache or any other innocuous excuse and flee.

As if she could read my mind, her face softened. "You're freaked out. I'm sorry. I didn't mean to make this hard on you. Think about this. I've known you were coming for months, and I didn't tell anyone. Not even Mac. I know we just met, but you can trust me."

Her logic calmed my raging fight or flight response. Parker's shock this morning had been one hundred percent real, and I'd bet my lucky Wisconsin Wolves hat Mac hadn't known who I was when he met me in the weight room.

I let out a slow breath, feeling my heart rate start to return to normal. "Okay. Truth? I'm not comfortable with my attraction to Parker. He's my quarterback, and it feels completely unprofessional. To be clear, I'm not against dating—or the occasional hook-up—but never with a teammate. I'd lose all credibility."

She nodded. "I get it. You don't get a second chance."

"Right." I uncapped the water and took a big swig, realizing I knew very little about her beyond the basic facts. "What about you? Any big juicy secrets that will make me feel better about having no control over my mouth?"

Eva laughed and spread her arms. "What you see is what you get with me. I have plenty of secrets, but none are mine to tell."

I narrowed my eyes at her. "Favorite movie?"

"The Princess Bride. Yours?"

"The Replacements."

She shook her head. "I should have seen that one coming."

I raised a brow. "You've seen The Replacements?"

"All the people I hang out with are either football players or cheerleaders, and my best friend thinks he's God's gift to the sport."

We threw rapid questions at each other, and I relaxed into her company. Eva was funny and outgoing and not afraid to voice her opinion. Before I knew it, we'd agreed that Chris Evans was the best superhero Chris, Lucy Score wrote the best books, and Die Hard was *definitely* a Christmas movie. I'd also agreed to let her order dinner from her favorite Chinese place.

My watch buzzed, and I checked my wrist. We'd been chatting for longer than I'd thought and eaten through my unpacking time.

"I have a class soon, so I've got to go. I think I'm going to like you, Eva. Thanks for..." I waved my hand around the apartment. "Everything."

"You're welcome, and I'm glad you're on board because I've decided we're going to be besties. Nadia and Vi will love you."

I'd heard of Vi, Soren Brehm's girlfriend, during my team stalking, but I couldn't place why Nadia sounded familiar. Did they still spend time at TU? I thought I'd read that Vi graduated and moved to another area of Texas.

Eva tilted her head, exercising her mind reading skills

again. "The guys are a tight-knit group. D is in New York with Nadia, but Soren and Vi stayed close in Houston. They're still part of the group text."

I frowned at her. "Seriously, how do you do that?"

"I just understand people and their body language. You should see me at poker night."

My throat closed up unexpectedly at the mention of poker night. The reaction happened sometimes when confronted with a memory of Dad. He taught me to play poker during the long Wisconsin winters when we weren't running drills or watching game tape.

I cleared away the roughness and sent Eva a smile before she could dig out this truth too. "I'll see you tonight."

She waved and watched me leave with knowing eyes.

5

Parker

Mac's girl played football. Riley Jones. RJ. Whatever she wanted to be called. I yanked open the fridge to search for something to eat then slammed it again when I realized it was Mac's week to grocery shop.

As usual, he'd forgotten.

I had maybe ten more minutes to wallow in my bad mood before Mac and Noah got home. They had classes that afternoon, but my professor had emailed to say she'd come down with the flu and cancelled. I'd planned to hit the weight room again. A light workout would help organize the chaos of my thoughts, but the prospect of seeing Riley sent me on a run instead.

Why would Coach Gordon recruit her?

There was a reason women didn't play football at the college level. Kickers, yes—they didn't have to take a hit—but wide receivers were in the middle of the plays. She'd be tackled by guys who had a hundred pounds on her.

My mind helpfully supplied an image of Riley shifting the equipment in the weight room with ease. Her fluid movements and muscular legs made me think she was fast, but speed wouldn't protect her if Duke got ahold of her during practice. He'd snap her in half.

And how was I supposed to focus when all I wanted to do was stare at her as she moved. She'd been hot in the stretchy pants, and she was just as hot in jeans and a tank top. A fact my dick had definitely noticed. That buzz of sensation when we touched would make it impossible to give the game all my attention. None of that was her fault, but it would cause problems for the team.

I shook my head and slumped onto the couch. Even to myself, I sounded like a sexist asshole.

Either I trusted my coach or I didn't. He wouldn't play her if he didn't have a plan. My reaction to her was my own problem, compounded by that damn rule. I couldn't stop trying to find ways around it in the back of my mind, despite knowing the futility of the exercise.

My phone beeped a couple of seconds before keys scraped against the lock outside. After the drama with Vi, Mac had insisted we get a front door camera. It sent a message to my phone every time someone came to our door, which was way more often than I'd thought when I agreed to it. I hadn't figured out how to turn the damn thing off yet.

Mac burst into the room with Noah trailing after him. "Shaw, you aren't going to believe who we saw at the Quack Shack."

My first thought was Riley. Apparently, she was always my first thought now. I frowned and circled my hand at Mac to indicate he should keep going.

"Remember the crazy goth chick from last year?"

I sat up as my thoughts came to screeching halt. "Leticia? Loretta? Something like that?"

Mac dropped down next to me as Noah disappeared into

the kitchen, bound for disappointment. "Lenore. She was ahead of us, and I didn't recognize her until she turned to go into the clinic."

"Why do I care about this?"

"Dude, she was wearing a pink sundress. Her hair was in a ponytail, no dark eye make-up, not a raven feather to be found."

My lips curved up as my mood lifted. Lenore had spent two weeks sending Mac truly horrible love poetry while Mac went through an adventurous phase. "You're sure it was her?"

Noah came back into the room with a frown. "He ran over and started talking before I could stop him. Also, we're out of food."

Mac's head smacked back onto the cushions. "Fuck, I forgot."

"We know," Noah and I said at the same time.

"I'll order pizza tonight and go first thing after the workout tomorrow. Back to my dark little love dumpling."

I groaned. "You need better nicknames."

Mac pulled out his phone and sent off an order for dinner while he continued. "She went to some yoga retreat over the summer and found herself. Retired the angst. Goes by Brighton now."

I faked a gasp. "You mean Lenore wasn't her real name?"

"Ha ha. I figured why not give the new version a chance at all this." He gestured at himself with a wide grin. "She said as much as I rocked her world, she was tragically with someone else now."

Noah snorted. "That's *not* what she said."

"I was paraphrasing."

My non-dramatic roommate crossed his arms over his chest and nodded at Mac's phone. "How long on the pizza?"

"About forty-five minutes. Unless Danny delivers it again. Then add an extra twenty minutes for him to hang around outside the apartment hoping for a glimpse of Eva."

We all rolled our eyes at the newest predicament we'd discovered after Eva moved in. Noah grunted and headed for the hallway that led to our rooms. "I'm going to take a shower. Let me know when it gets here."

Mac nodded once, then turned his full attention on me. "Now that you're not pouting anymore, want to talk about RJ?"

"No." I closed my eyes, but I knew Mac wouldn't let it go.

"I can't believe Coach actually recruited a girl, but after seeing her, I'm a believer."

"You spent twenty minutes pretending to spot for her. How does that relate to her ability to play?" I was proud I'd kept my voice neutral, but Mac nudged me until I met his gaze.

He'd dropped his ever-present smile in an attempt to look solemn, a foreign expression for him. "I am an expert judge of the female physique. She's got the strength and the size to compete. Not to mention the legs of a distance runner. I can't wait to see what she can do on the field."

I shelved the urge to argue with him, or worse, lecture him on how dangerous it could be for her. All he'd hear was my frustration, which wouldn't be helpful. "I guess we'll find out tomorrow. I wouldn't be surprised if the whole thing was Matt Delongio's idea."

Mac's brows drew together. "Why would the athletic director get involved?"

"Riley creates a new media splash the university controls in the hopes of getting people to forget about all the shit from last year. Worst case scenario, she's not that great and spends the season on the bench."

"Best case scenario, she's a prodigy, and you have another weapon in your arsenal for your quest to win the championship that never was," Mac countered.

I linked my fingers behind my head and stared at the ceiling. He wasn't wrong. I didn't have as many elite targets this year after Soren left. Coach Lancaster hadn't expected Soren to enter the draft, so he hadn't picked up a replacement before he was fired.

A couple of the underclassmen stepped up, but none showed the combination of speed, strength, and awareness that had brought us to the championship last year. They needed more time. Riley could be an answer to that weakness.

If we could work together.

No one else seemed to have the reaction I did. Hell, Mac had spent more time with her than I had, and he'd immediately friend zoned her. I frowned at the white expanse above me. He didn't usually skip the flirting phase, which was why I'd assumed it was a hook-up in the first place.

I rolled my head to the side to ask him. "Why are you so taken with her?"

"She looks like Wonder Woman," Mac said in all seriousness.

A laugh burst out of me. "She's blonde."

He scooted closer, clearly excited about the topic. "Other than the hair. Did you see her arms? I'm going to try to convince her to dress up as my future wife for Halloween."

I rubbed my eyes. "You can't keep referring to Wonder Woman that way."

"One day, Gal Gadot will accept me as her love slave."

"I think she's married."

Mac waved that away with a scoff. "Everyone knows

that's a front. She can't have the world realizing her true identity is in actuality Wonder Woman—"

I groaned. "Not this again. If she's your ideal woman, why didn't you call dibs?"

He held up his hands. "Whoa. We don't call dibs, man. They're people."

I raised a brow at him. "Do you remember last week with Gretchen or whatever her name was?"

"You really need to work on your name retention skills. And I didn't call dibs. I just saw her first, so it's only fair I get to talk to her first."

"You looked at me and said 'dibs' before sauntering up to the bar."

He pursed his lips. "Look, it's not important. I could tell RJ wasn't looking for a hook-up. She smacked me down before I had the chance to ease her into loving me. Which makes sense now that I know she wasn't just using the empty room to get her work out on."

Curiosity got the better of me. "And if she'd shown any interest?"

"I'd have tripped your ass on the way into the room." He eyed me. "But it wasn't me she reacted to."

I shook my head. "No. There are so many reasons that's a bad idea. Starting with Coach and ending with the fraternization rule. If she's going to play, I'm not going to disrespect her by treating her like a ball bunny."

"You mean again," he quipped deadpan.

"I hate you."

Mac slapped my back. "No reason you can't be friends then. She's got a wicked mouth on her."

Heat rushed me. I had to grit my teeth to get rid of the image he'd conjured of Riley on her knees in front of me.

From his evil grin, I assumed he'd used those words on purpose. This season was going to be pure hell.

The weak metallic chime of the broken doorbell interrupted us before I could retaliate by smothering him with a couch pillow.

"Pizza!" Mac hollered down the hall, then answered the door.

Noah appeared a second later in sweats with his wet hair a mass of short curls. He detoured to the kitchen as Mac set a stack of three steaming pizzas on the tiny breakfast bar. My stomach rumbled at the scent of tomato sauce and pepperoni.

We ate in silence for a few minutes, and Mac's last comment wouldn't let me go. Not about Riley's mouth, though the image would probably haunt me in the shower later, but about being friends with her.

I didn't have a lot of female friends—mostly just Eva, Nadia, and Vi. Though I'd slacked on the last two after they'd moved away. My social circle was pretty much nonexistent compared to Mac's. Could I be friends with her like I was with my other teammates?

Why not? Riley was hot, but the campus was bursting with attractive women. I could picture any one of them naked instead of her. On cue, my imagination called up Riley tangled in my sheets, wild hair spread across my pillow.

I swallowed hard and carefully tucked the image into a tiny corner of my mind reserved for all the things I'd seen in the locker room. That section was strictly off-limits. I didn't picture any of the other guys naked—I'd seen the real thing enough times that I actively tried *not* to picture it. Duke had an ungodly amount of body hair.

Friends. Definitely. With luck, I'd get over this stupid

obsession by getting to know her. It's not like I had to see her all the time. There were some guys on the team I'd barely exchanged a few words with.

A beep sounded next to me from Mac's phone, then an excited gasp that ended in a coughing fit as he choked on his pizza. Noah got up to—I don't know, do the Heimlich?—but Mac shook his head as he sucked in a rasping breath.

I swallowed my bite and checked to make sure his lips weren't turning blue. "You okay?"

Instead of answering, Mac swiped at the screen then turned his phone toward me. He'd pulled up the door cam app. I recognized our landing, but at a different angle.

I sent him an incredulous look. "Do you have Eva's door cam linked to your phone?"

"Don't judge me," he wheezed. "It's for her protection."

There was no way Eva knew about this. I'd need to have a talk with Mac about privacy and overstepping bounds before Eva de-balled him. Movement on the screen caught my attention. I watched as the door opened, expecting to see a dude come out, or maybe Eva's new roommate.

Nope. Riley Jones stood framed in the doorway. She spoke into the apartment, then Eva slipped past her. Shock dropped my mouth open as I tried to find an explanation that wouldn't lead to my downfall. Maybe they were friends. Maybe they had the same class.

Riley pulled out a set of keys and locked the door before leaving the frame.

Several pieces of information tumbled together into an unfortunate truth. Eva's new roommate was Riley.

Fuck me.

6

Riley

No matter how many times I assured myself this was a practice like any other, I couldn't get my racing heart to calm the hell down. I stood in the shadows at the entrance to the training field and scanned the green expanse. Most of the guys were milling about stretching in small clusters. None of them had noticed me yet.

I wasn't nervous about my skills—I knew what I could do—but the stakes were much higher in this arena. These games would be televised and watched by NFL scouts, not that it made any difference to my future. For me, there wouldn't be a career after college. *This* was my chance, right now, to play.

As long as I didn't fuck it up.

A whistle from the end of the field pulled my attention to Mac, who was doing a handstand in the end zone. His cropped jersey, the same as mine, bunched around his head revealing the tight abs he'd flashed at me a few days ago in the weight room.

Still no response. Thank god. At least my stupid

hormones were only susceptible to Parker's questionable charm. The hairs on the back of my neck stood up, and I straightened my stance.

As if I'd summoned him with my thoughts, Parker stopped next to me at the end of the tunnel. The position shouldn't have been intimate—the space was huge—but in the shadows where no one could see us against the bright sunlight, I felt like we were alone in the world.

He was close enough I only needed to shift a tiny bit to see his face. I risked it and found him watching me with the same intensity as the day of the team meeting. Heat filled my cheeks, and I prayed it was too dark for him to see me blush.

In sync, we both shifted our attention back to the field.

Parker ran a hand through his hair with a disgruntled noise. "You ready for this?"

His question surprised me. After our previous encounters, I'd expected him to try to warn me away. I kept my gaze firmly fixed on the players in the sun and took a deep breath. If he could be civil, so could I.

"Yes, but I like to take a minute before practice to get my head right." I felt his curious glance but didn't elaborate.

He cleared his throat. "I want to apologize for what I said the other day."

"I'm listening."

In my peripheral vision, his lips quirked up. "I shouldn't have said what I did, whether or not you're a teammate. I was an asshole."

No excuses. No shifting of blame. As apologies went, it was pretty damn good.

I nodded and pulled my gloves out of the waistband of my shorts. "Apology accepted."

Silence settled between us as we watched the team. Mac flipped back to his feet and shouted something at Noah.

Parker jerked his chin toward Mac's antics. "He's a good friend to have, but he doesn't understand the concept of quiet."

I snorted out a laugh. "I picked up that much. Why aren't you out there?"

One shoulder lifted in a half shrug. "I like to get my head right too. Sometimes it's hard to see the game past all the drama. Especially when you live with Mac. Music helps."

I glanced at him and noticed the earbuds. So we were doing this. Pretending to be normal teammates. In the interest of my sanity, I tried to put in a little effort.

"What do you listen to?"

The faintest touch of pink hit the top of his ears, confirming that he'd probably seen my blush earlier. Points to him for not mentioning it.

"I have eclectic tastes. We should join the others for warm-up."

Parker had a way of swallowing all of my attention, so I hadn't noticed the guys on the field lining up. I swore under my breath and started forward, but one of my gloves slipped from my hand and hit the concrete floor with a soft slap. Parker snagged it off the ground for me before I could move.

He held it out in his palm, and I stared down at the red lump like it might bite me. "Nice choice. Mac is going to be jealous that you have the new ones. He's been drooling over them since June."

"Thanks." I retrieved my glove, trying desperately to remember how normal people touched each other. My fingers grazed his palm, and the electric jolt sent my heart racing again.

A tiny hitch in Parker's breathing told me I wasn't the

only one who felt it. A little brush of his skin against mine. That was all it took to send my system into overdrive, and now I knew I wasn't alone in the attraction. We were so fucked.

I turned my back on Parker and jogged into the sun. Football. I was here to play football.

The guys grunted in hello as I lined up next to them. Everyone except Mac.

"RJ! About time you got here, girl."

Several pairs of eyes shifted toward me, but Noah, who'd been running the warm-up, clapped his hands. "Laps. Then Coach wants us split for fundamentals."

We took off as one with a slow pace. Luckily, I'd warmed up at home before driving over here. A habit I hadn't been able to kick since high school. I'd been late to practice, missed warm-up, and pulled my hamstring. Never again.

My eyes landed on Parker at the front of the group. He hadn't warmed up with the others because he'd been apologizing to me in the tunnel. I appreciated the effort, but I didn't want him injured.

Sweat dripped between my shoulder blades as we circled the field. My muscles loosened, and a buzz built in my chest. Joy. By the end of the afternoon I'd be aching and soaked in sweat, but I wouldn't trade this time for anything.

Mac bumped my shoulder and waggled his eyebrows at me, then jerked his chin to the opposite end of the field. My gaze followed the direction for a second before I realized the coaches had gathered by our stuff. We had about half a lap left, and if he was anything like me, he wanted to sprint the rest of the way.

I met his eyes and raised my brow. If it was a race he wanted, I'd give him one.

He held up his gloved hand—purple for him—and

counted down from three. When his last finger dropped, I took off. My cleats sank into the grass, propelling me forward in a burst of speed.

A murmur traveled through the rest of the team, and Parker turned as I ran past him. Mac was right on my heels, his breath coming in sharp puffs. I wasn't at max speed, simply running for the fun of it, but as we approached the finish line, Mac pulled up even with me.

I had two choices—push myself all the way and leave him behind or control my speed and come in at the same time. All the coaches had turned to watch our impromptu race, and while I liked the idea of proving myself early, I didn't want to do it at the expense of Mac.

Over the last twenty yards, I pulled my stride to match his.

Mac let out a full belly laugh as we flew past the gear at the same time. I was breathing hard and grinning like an idiot. The problems with Parker faded into insignificance.

We both slowed to a jog, then a walk, and did another half lap before joining the group. Mac slung an arm around me, squeezing me into his sweaty side.

"My girl is *fast*. Damn, RJ."

Coach harrumphed from behind his clipboard. "Mac, get your paws off her and focus."

I elbowed Mac away before he could draw more attention. Coach went through assignments for small group skills practice, and I couldn't wait to get my hands on a ball. Working with kids over the summer had been fun, but they didn't challenge me to get better.

There was only so much I could do on my own. I needed other people on the field to force me to adjust at the last second. Otherwise, I was just playing catch.

I didn't mean to, but I caught Parker's speculative gaze as

I trailed after the other receivers to one end of the field. He dipped his chin in acknowledgement before joining his two backups.

One of them said something to make Parker smile—a dangerous curve of amusement that reflected in his eyes—and I was glad he hadn't unleashed it on me. The last thing I needed was to trip over my own feet in front of my new team. The other backup stood for a second longer as they passed him, and I realized he was staring in my direction.

His face looked indifferent, but I didn't like the cold gleam in his eyes. I turned away, throwing a grin at Mac to shake the uneasy sensation.

"Hey Mac, how did my dust taste?"

He held up both hands. "Whoa now, what's this nonsense you're talking? Do we need a rematch?"

"Anytime."

Mac held his fist out for me to tap. "That's what I'm talking about. I knew I'd like you."

I liked him too. I liked the team, the university, the coach. Dad would have lost his shit at the skill level of these guys. I had two years left to play before the real world intruded, and I intended to enjoy every second of it.

———

WE DIDN'T COME BACK TOGETHER as a team until the very end of practice. Coach wanted us to run a couple of routes. Nothing too complicated, but it would be the first time Parker and I actively played together. A test to see if I could move past my body's reactions and make it perform the way I knew it could.

I guzzled water and splashed some over my head. Most of my conditioning had taken place in humid southeastern

Wisconsin, so the humidity wasn't new to me. TU might have a fancy training facility, but the brutal outdoor practices felt the same as at my D3 school.

Coach motioned us over and explained what he wanted, then set up a rotation between the quarterbacks and the receivers. I took my place near the back of the line and watched the others execute.

We all wore the same shorts and cropped jerseys—I had a tank top under mine—but the difference in ability quickly became obvious. Parker was leagues above the other two quarterbacks in accuracy. They all had the arm strength to get the ball downfield, but time and again, Parker's passes landed right into the receiver's hands. As long as they could make the distance.

By the time my turn came, I knew what to expect. Parker took the pass before mine, and I lined up next to Aidan Williams, the one who'd been staring at me. His balls tended to drift left, so I prepped myself to adjust mid-route.

Coach blew the whistle, and I surged forward. I made it to the twenty-yard line before I zagged left. A prickle at the back of my neck made me turn early, and I had to leap for the ball, well above my head.

My fingers brushed leather, tipping the ball into a crazy spin. The football gods were with me, and it curved my direction. I snagged the football out of the air, tucking it against my chest as I hit the ground on my side.

"What the hell, Williams?"

Coach's brusque question spurred me to move. My hip and shoulder ached from taking the brunt of the fall, but I uncurled from my position and hopped up.

Williams shrugged with his eyes on me as I trotted back. "Sorry, Coach."

He sounded contrite, but I'd seen him make that throw

four times now. The only reason I'd been able to catch it was because I'd expected to have to go left. If I'd run the route as assigned, I'd have missed by inches.

Parker frowned at Williams, then motioned for me to toss him the ball. "Go again. To the endzone this time."

My brows shot up, and I looked to Coach for confirmation. After a considering glance between us, he nodded. Admittedly, I'd paid more attention to Parker's passes than the others. I knew he could throw it to the endzone, and I knew he wanted to see how fast I could get there.

A tiny fissure of nerves wiggled in my stomach, but I squashed it down by tossing shade at Parker. "Let's see if you throw as well as you think you do."

A slow smile spread across his face at the challenge. "Try me, Blondie."

From the group behind us, Mac shouted out a response. "Nuh uh. Her nickname is RJ. I called it already."

Parker's gaze met mine, full of lazy heat. "What do *you* want me to call you?"

I raised a brow and lined up next to him. "You heard the man. RJ, it is."

He made a gravelly sound of ascent that shot heat straight to my core, and I crouched into position, digging my cleat into the dirt. Coach's whistle blasted, and I ran for all I was worth.

7

Parker

I shuffled back a few steps and couldn't tear my eyes off Riley. If we'd been in a game, I'd have been tackled in an instant, but we weren't. This was the end of our first grueling practice, and I'd wanted to see, *really* see, what Riley could do.

She streaked down the field to the endzone, and I almost messed up the timing. Something in me knew the exact moment to let go of the ball though. Riley made her corner and turned, plucking the ball out of the air as if she'd already known exactly where it would be.

Goosebumps raised on my arms at the smooth connection. D and Soren had developed a kind of telepathy with each other after playing together for a while, but I'd never experienced it myself. I certainly hadn't expected to find it on the first pass with a brand-new receiver.

Coach blew his whistle and told everyone to hit the showers. Relieved grumbles joined the thumps of assistants breaking down the gear, but the sounds came from a distance as my world shifted.

Mac had been right. She was the piece missing from the team.

Riley spun the ball in her hand as she walked back to us with a smug smile. "Not bad, Shaw. I think you and I can play beautiful football together."

I felt like I'd swallowed my tongue, so I nodded at her and belatedly caught the ball she tossed at me.

Before I could figure out how to speak again, Mac ambushed her from the side and threw her over his shoulder. Riley squealed as he spun in a circle.

"That's my girl! You're going to show me up, but it'll be worth it."

"Put me down, you idiot. You're going to injure something."

Noah plucked her off Mac as if she were Eva's size, setting her on the ground. "Welcome to the team."

A bunch of the other guys came by to say the same thing until Coach shooed us off the field. I couldn't help but feel pride at the way they accepted her, but inside, I wanted them to leave us alone.

Not that I knew what I wanted to say.

Riley veered off to the women's locker room, and for a fraction of a second, I considered following her. Under no circumstances would my presence in there be a good idea. Just the thought had my dick paying attention, and no one wanted a hard-on while showering with a bunch of dudes.

Besides, I knew where she lived.

———

DESPITE BORDERLINE STALKERISH behavior at the apartment, I wasn't able to catch Riley coming or going. I could have grown some balls and knocked on their door, but that made the gesture feel too purposeful.

As much as I loved Eva, I didn't want her getting involved in anything between me and Riley. I couldn't afford the trouble she'd inevitably cause.

By Wednesday afternoon, I'd stopped compulsively checking Mac's phone after every beep. Mostly because he'd given me access to Eva's door cam app too. Neither of us ever intended to tell her, but Noah started casting suspicious looks our way when we quickly put our phones down every time he entered the room.

I wasn't looking forward to that come to Jesus talk. Noah didn't say much, but he had strong opinions about privacy. Luckily, I had a class on Wednesday afternoon which would keep me busy until practice.

After cancelling on Monday, the prof had sent out assignments for us to complete before today, but I'd been busy watching my phone. I wasn't worried. This class was an easy humanities credit with a sympathetic professor, meaning she'd give me some slack as long as the work got turned in eventually.

The room was in the psych building on the other side of campus from the sports facilities, an older section that hadn't been updated in a while. I didn't spend much time there, but I frowned at the stark differences between the crumbling architecture and the sleek new football training center.

I opened a creaky door on the second floor to a small auditorium. A couple of people waved at me as I walked in, but I didn't recognize any of them. The hazards of being the starting quarterback at a DI school—everyone felt like they owned a part of me.

The warning from last spring floated through my mind.

You're the face of the football team. We expect you to act the part and be a role model for your fellow students. I snorted internally as I waved back. The administration didn't give a flying fuck about role models. They wanted me to be a good little puppet and help them bring in more money.

As long as their stipulations didn't hurt my chances of playing, I'd do as they asked. I had two more years of eligibility, and I wanted to use them. My family was proud of my football accomplishments, but they'd impressed onto me the importance of an education too. I'd graduate with a degree to prepare for the day—hopefully a long time from now—when I'd have to hang up my cleats.

Like so many things on this side of campus, these rooms weren't meant for football players. Tiny seats sat practically on top of each other with a joke of a desk attached. I picked a spot in the back row so I could stretch my legs into the aisle without getting in anyone's way.

The prof hadn't arrived yet, so I pulled my hat low over my head and people watched. After the initial interest in my entrance, the other students had gone back to chatting with each other. I recognized a few of them from other sports teams, not surprising since this class was well known as the easiest way to fulfill the requirement.

No other football players though. Unusual since the class was only offered in the fall semester. Mac and Noah had taken it already, but I'd put it off until this year when I knew I'd need an easier load.

Right as the clock ticked over to start time, a slim woman in a pencil skirt and heels strode into the room. She was maybe mid-forties with short ashy blonde hair and a very pale complexion, probably from the flu or whatever she'd had. I could see the dark circles under her eyes from the other side of the room.

"I'm Professor Declann. Welcome to Human Sexuality." She paused and smiled at the giggles from the front row. "I apologize for Monday, but when your body says to rest, you should rest. You didn't miss much because the first day is usually about getting to know each other anyway. We'll skip the awkward ice breakers and jump into the syllabus I asked you to read. You may want to take notes."

I didn't bother getting anything out of my backpack. The syllabus had been one of three attachments to her email that I'd ignored. About half of the class seemed to be of the same mind because they didn't move. I was pretty sure the guy in the corner buried in his hoodie was already asleep.

She continued as if she didn't notice the lack of interest. "This semester we'll be discussing—"

A loud squeal interrupted her sentence as the door swung open. Professor Declann frowned at the latecomer, and I got that same buzz I'd had at practice. I sat up straighter in my seat with a good idea of who had just shown up.

As expected, Riley slunk into the room with a mumbled apology. She'd piled her hair onto her head in a messy bun that defied gravity. A black tank top hugged her slight curves, and her long legs were on display in cutoff shorts. For once, I was thankful for the Texas heat. The prof didn't respond other than to shake her head and launch back into her lecture.

Riley's eyes scanned the room, then widened slightly when they landed on me. I wasn't sure my half-assed apology would be enough to change my bad first impression, but I hoped so. At practice, I'd been able to mostly separate Riley the receiver from Riley the woman, but she didn't look like a football player right now. She looked like my deepest fantasy come to life.

When she started in my direction, I told my dick to calm the fuck down. Friends. We were supposed to be friends.

She scooted past me to take the next seat and sat angled away from me to stretch out in the space beside her. Unlike me and most of the class, she immediately pulled several sheets of paper, a notebook, and a pen from her bag.

I leaned closer so my voice wouldn't carry down to the prof. "Is being late a regular thing for you?"

"Only since I moved to Texas," she muttered back.

"Did you read that already?" I nodded at the syllabus and assignments in her hand.

Her dark eyes flashed to me for a second, and I felt the impact in my chest. "Yes. After I showed up on Monday to an empty class."

"Good, then you can talk to me and you won't be missing out on anything."

She matched my position. "Who says I want to talk to you?"

We hadn't been this close since before the meeting, and I had a hell of a time not stretching my arm across the back of her seat to play with the ends of her hair. Instead, I pulled my phone from the front pocket of my backpack and set it in my lap. If nothing else, I could pretend to take notes.

"Maybe I want to talk to you," I said.

Her lips pressed together briefly, and I got another quick glance. "About what?"

"I try to get to know everyone on the team." It wasn't a complete lie. I *did* want to make a connection with everyone, but with over a hundred people on the roster, it was mostly a nod and fist bump situation. "You weren't here over the summer, so I'm doing it now."

She finally gave in and met my eyes. "Why do I feel like

the universe keeps throwing us together? I've been here for less than a week, and you're *everywhere*."

I shrugged. "Just lucky, I guess. What were you doing over the summer?"

Riley picked at the edge of her paper. "I was a counselor at a summer camp back home."

My brows rose. "That was more important than camp at TU?"

"I told them I'd come, and I don't break my promises." Her lips curled up in a slight smile. "And I signed a contract."

"Was it fun?"

She tore tiny strips off the syllabus as she thought about it. "Yeah. I like working with kids, especially since I was in charge of the sports. There's nothing like teaching little girls they can throw and catch just as well as the boys. Well, almost nothing."

Her gaze sharpened, and I knew she was thinking of that last pass at practice—the perfect moment when we were in sync and everything fell into place. Did she feel the same connection I did?

Riley blinked and moved away. "I answered your questions. My turn."

Despite the setback, I grinned. At least she was still talking to me. "What do you want to know?"

She nodded at the phone in my hand. "Tell me what's on your playlist."

After a quick glance at the prof to be sure she was busy with the rest of the class, I pulled out my earbuds and handed one to Riley. "Hear for yourself."

"Am I going to regret this?" she teased.

God, I hoped not. My gaze lingered on her lips for a beat too long, then I shook myself out of my own stupidity and cued up my music. Not the Chill the F* Out playlist, that one was reserved for before practice and games. We weren't there yet.

"This is my Study Now or Pay the Price playlist."

"You name your playlists?"

"Doesn't everyone?" I hit shuffle and electric violin filled my head.

Interest lit her face. "What else is on here?"

"Mostly Lindsey Stirling and video game soundtracks, a couple of trip-hop songs."

I hit the skip button to give her a sample, and the opening drumbeat of "I'll Make a Man out of You" made me swipe frantically at the screen.

"Fuck," I muttered as the song got louder. I'd forgotten Mac had added that one.

Riley tried to smother her laugh, but she was loud enough to draw attention from the rows around us. I closed the app and shifted to accommodate my sudden hard-on. She looked up at me with a real smile, one I'd helped create. My chest filled with the need to make her laugh like that again.

When I looked away, Professor Declann was glaring at us. No, not us. Riley. My stupid grin dimmed a notch, and Riley straightened in her seat, surreptitiously removing my earbud.

She slipped it to me, and this time, I was prepared for the thrumming sensation of her touch. I wanted to close my hand over hers, just to see if this reaction was an every time thing or if regular contact would make it less powerful.

Professor Declann turned back to the white board she'd been scribbling on, and Riley's hand landed next to mine on the armrests between our seats. What would happen if I crossed that half an inch and closed the distance?

On cue, the memory of Coach laying down the no fraternization rule slipped across my mind.

Getting caught goofing off in class hadn't completely erased the little smile from her face, but I had a feeling she wouldn't risk her spot on the team for anything more. And she shouldn't. *I* shouldn't.

Even if we were only friends, Riley could be a problem for me if I couldn't get out of my head about her getting hurt. How much worse would the urge to protect her be if I crossed that distance?

There couldn't be anything between us, no matter how much I was drawn to her.

8

Riley

"**C**an you take a hit?" Parker's eyes blazed a path down my body, bulked up by pads for practice. When he landed on my face again, heat had burned away the frustration.

I crossed my arms—both an attempt to regain some control and to keep from stupidly reaching for him. "Can you?"

A chorus of *ohhhs* surrounded us. I'd forgotten there were witnesses to our little battle. Coach had waited until two weeks into practice to require full pads, a huge departure from the usual, but I wasn't going to complain.

We'd been suffering under a heat wave, and most of the players had dressed out in as little clothes as possible, me included. Today, that ended because Coach wanted a "thud" scrimmage, meaning shoulder pads and helmets with limited contact.

Parker was in a pissy mood when he found out there'd be no special compensation for me. I admit, I was a little disappointed in him. In a miracle of restraint, we'd gotten friendly over the past weeks without any inappropriate touching. It helped that I'd managed to avoid him except for class and practice.

I'd thought he'd accepted my position as his teammate.

Now, here we stood, facing off while the team snickered around us. I didn't have the patience to pander to his delicate sensibilities. "This is stupid. Get your head out of your ass and throw me the ball before Coach lectures both of us."

I pulled on my helmet, and most of the guys around me did the same. Mac shoved Parker's shoulder and sent him a commiserating look.

"Don't you start too," Parker grumbled.

He called the play and counted it off. I knew the route—we'd done it repeatedly—but my attention wasn't on the field around me. It was on the sliver of hurt he'd delivered with his outburst.

I turned my head, and like every other time Parker passed to me, the ball was exactly where I thought it would be. We could be so *good* if he'd just get over his issues. None of the other guys treated me like I was weak. I needed Parker on my side too, but he stubbornly refused to see past my vagina.

Screw him.

The tackle took me by surprise. Both because I hadn't seen Duke coming and because no one should have been tackling. I curled my body around the ball, holding on with both hands as he took me to the ground.

Somehow, the impact wasn't as violent as I expected. Duke's hand positioning helped cushion some of the force, and he caught most of his weight on his knees. Still, there was enough to nearly knock the wind out of me.

Duke lumbered up, and I untucked, tossing the football to one of the assistants hovering out of the way. With the chaotic thoughts cleared from my head, I noticed the hush on the field. All the attention was on me, waiting to see how I'd react.

Parker took a jolting step toward me before catching himself, and I hoped no one else noticed. I didn't need his doubts to catch on. He should have known the answer to his question earlier. Thanks to my dad, I'd been playing tackle football since I was a kid—I knew how to take a hit.

Duke held out a hand, and I let him haul me up. "Sorry, RJ. I got a little excited."

I tilted my head at him. "Do you apologize every time you make a tackle?"

He laughed, a quiet, rumbling noise. "No, but I usually get the ball out if it goes that far. You have a grip like duct tape."

"Sounds like we're even then since I shouldn't have let you catch me."

"Duke!" Coach barked from the sidelines. "We've talked about this. Light contact only. Save the ground tackles for the dummies and the other team."

Duke lifted his hands in acknowledgement and returned to his side of the scrimmage line. "Sorry, Coach."

"You okay?" Parker asked quietly as I walked past him.

I paused. "Do you check on Mac like this when he gets tackled?"

Parker's jaw twitched, but he shook his head. "No. You're right."

"You have to trust your team. We know what we're doing."

He nodded slowly and jogged back to the group without answering. I hoped this little demonstration would be enough to convince him, but Mac's enigmatic shrug didn't inspire a lot of confidence.

————

"I CAN'T BELIEVE you convinced me to come out here." I tried to stifle my yawn, but I'd only left practice a couple of hours before. My body desperately wanted to be horizontal and unconscious.

Eva shimmied in place as if I'd given her a compliment. "It's not even a big party, and I promise we won't stay long."

After the crap with Parker today, I wasn't in the mood for coddling, so I waved her off. "I don't need you to hold my hand. Go have fun. If I want to leave, I'll call a rideshare."

She eyed my jeans and tank top, a vast departure from her cute little sundress and sandals, then sighed. "Okay, but text me when you leave. And don't take a drink from anyone. And stay away from Duke if he's drunk, he doesn't know his own strength."

I smirked at her. "Yes, I'm aware of Duke's strength."

Eva sent me a playful glare, but her attention had already been claimed by a guy at the beer pong table. "Text me if you need me. I don't mind hand-holding."

She sounded distracted, but I'd learned with Eva, her friends came first. "Go." I nudged her toward the guy and made my way toward the kitchen.

The house stank of beer and weed, and my head throbbed with the deep bass beat of the music. I wanted a water and somewhere to be relatively alone, preferably in the fresh air. Plastic cups littered every surface, along with chips and pizza crusts, but no one else was in the galley kitchen.

Liquor bottles sat in a sticky puddle on the counter next to half empty juice containers. None of the drink options looked appetizing, and I sure as hell wasn't going to take my chances with the keg. House parties weren't known for their discriminating beer tastes.

I grabbed a cup that looked clean and filled it at the sink. Most of my headache was from stress. The constant pressure to never show any weakness unless I wanted it broadcast across the university's social media network. A tiny bit was probably because I'd skipped dinner in favor of soaking in the tub until we ran out of hot water.

Fine. That was probably the larger portion, but stress played a part too. Parker's angry face flashed across my mind, and I had to agree with my subconscious. I blamed Parker too.

In lieu of nasty table scraps, I chugged my water and refilled the cup. By the time I'd finished a second glass, the throbbing had abated. Usually, I took better care of myself. TU had a fancy nutritionist on staff that I planned to visit, but I hadn't made time.

My stomach grumbled, and I searched the pantry for anything even slightly edible. More chips, Pop-Tarts, a package of toaster waffles that definitely should have been in the freezer—nothing I wanted to eat. As I stood in the gross kitchen and eyed the chips, I realized I'd made a poor choice.

I should have convinced Eva to grab dinner with me. She'd have caved if I promised a rom-com movie marathon. A cheer went up from the other room, and I decided to humor Eva by being social for a few minutes so I could leave to get food with a clear conscience.

The living room was packed with bodies, but I was taller than most of them. At one end, lights had been doused and furniture shoved against the wall to create a dance floor. Not that anyone was dancing. People grinded on each other in the shadows, and at least one girl in there was topless.

Fantastic.

At the other end of the room, Eva lined up a shot at the beer pong table, her guy of choice long gone. Instead, Mac stood next to her, and Noah hulked in the background behind them.

Mac met my eyes over a sea of heads. "RJ!"

He threw up his arms, jostling Eva during her release. She missed and speared him with a glare, which he ignored while beckoning me forward. I shook my head. This was too much socializing. Eva would forgive me.

Beyond the beer pong, I spotted a sliding glass door open to the warm night. Eva elbowed Mac in the stomach, and he forgot all about me to take his shot. I made a beeline for the relative quiet of outside.

It wasn't until I'd closed the screen door behind me and glanced back that I realized Duke was at the other end of the table. No wonder Eva had chosen this party—it was full of football players. Or maybe Mac and the others were here because of Eva.

The door led to a backyard that barely qualified as such. A set of concrete steps led down to a patio ending in a three-foot drop-off. There were no outside lights, no bonfire, nothing to draw drunk college students, and it was perfect.

I sat at the edge of the concrete with my legs crossed and leaned back to stare at the sky. One more week before our first game, and I was worried about the team. We had talent, but there was still too much second-guessing. Skill came from reps and muscle memory... and trust. I wasn't sure we had time to foster the last one.

Maybe I'd made a mistake in missing the summer training camps.

Pine-scented air filled my lungs, and a familiar shiver ran over my skin. The screen door snicked closed. I didn't move as Parker levered himself down next to me, propping his arm on one upraised knee.

"I didn't know you were the partying type," he said.

On some level, I'd known he was in the house, but I hadn't expected him to seek me out. "I'm not. Parties tend to suck when you're the sober one."

"You don't drink?"

I shook my head, keeping my eyes on the stars.

"At all?"

I sighed. Always the same reaction, disbelief followed by the snap decision that I must be a prude or a bitch. I'd had plenty of practice ignoring the haters, but Parker's undertone of shock brought my eyes crashing down to his.

"It's not worth the potential problems. I have to work twice as hard for twice as long to get half as much recognition that you and your boys get. One stupid decision could ruin that, and I don't make smart decisions when I'm drunk. Plus, I hate the taste of beer. Warm, shitty beer? No thanks."

The corner of his lips tipped up. "You're not wrong, especially about this beer." He wiggled his cup at me then set it on the stone next to him. "Why football?"

The question surprised me, though it shouldn't have. Parker had been putting a significant effort into getting me to talk. His persistence the last couple of weeks paid off because I didn't immediately get up and leave.

I didn't like to talk about my dad, who'd shared his love of football with me. He'd played professionally, and the sport never left his blood. I kept his name to myself because people tended to overreact. I didn't want to be known as Jed Jones' daughter—I wanted to be RJ.

Especially to Parker. My time with him in class was mostly spent telling horrible dad jokes, but we'd built a sort of friendship that made me want to open up a little bit.

Trust had to come from both sides. Practice today proved my point, but I got the feeling Parker didn't want to talk about his outburst.

Probably a good short-term plan since I was still salty about the whole thing. He was shrewd, both on and off the field. I brushed my hands on my jeans, and he watched me, waiting for an answer I wasn't sure I would give.

To buy myself time, I deflected. "I could ask you the same thing."

Parker inclined his head once. "You could, and I'll answer whatever you want to know, but I asked first."

Maybe I could share a generic version of my past. "My dad was really into football, so I grew up immersed in it. He started me playing, but I love the game."

His brows drew together. "Was?"

"Yeah, he died during my senior year of high school."

This was the part where people usually pushed, but Parker nodded and changed the subject.

"What are you doing here if you're not into partying?"

"Eva convinced me to come then got distracted by the beer pong table. She gave me a list of rules to follow in her absence."

He laughed. "Like what?"

"Like don't take open drinks from random guys, but I haven't been given any."

"Here." He offered his cup to me, and I raised a brow.

"You seem to have completely missed my last comment."

Parker looked out toward the trees as a smile crept across his face. "I heard you. Normally I'd agree with you one hundred percent, but I'm not some random guy you met at the party."

"That's what they all say." My joke fell flat, even to my own ears.

He shook his head. "We have to learn to trust each other some time."

I grunted at the echo of my earlier thoughts. Normally, I'd politely decline, no matter how many times he told me terrible jokes in class, but this was Parker. He didn't seem like the kind of guy to go around messing with a girl's drink, and he definitely wouldn't fuck with a teammate.

With a grimace, I took his proffered cup and stared down at the clear liquid. Not beer, thank god. Probably vodka, though I hadn't pegged him as the hard liquor type. A shrieky laugh from the house reminded me we weren't alone. The backyard felt like a bubble of solitude, but on the very off chance Parker was the secret villain of this story, I could be inside within seconds.

He shifted to watch me instead of the trees, so I met his gaze and swallowed deep.

Water. He was drinking water.

I took another deep swallow, suddenly thirsty. "Your turn. Why aren't you drinking? Not that I think you should be, but..." I waved in the general direction of the house.

He blew out a breath and ran a hand through his hair. "Babysitting duty. I take my role as the captain seriously. My guys are here, so I'm here. I don't drink during the season, and I want them to know they can always count on me for a ride."

My eyebrows crept up my forehead. "You can't possibly come to *every* party someone on the team might show up to. Even you must have to sleep sometime."

Parker scrubbed his face with his hands. "Tell that to them."

I tilted my head. "Why don't *you* tell them? Those guys practically worship you. I'm sure they know you'll have their backs when they do stupid shit. Trust works best if it goes both ways. You're not solely responsible for the team."

A considering look crossed his handsome face, and a warm flush had me staring down at his drink. He glanced over his shoulder at the two big guys still clearly visible playing beer pong in the kitchen. "Mac."

The goofball held up one finger and finished his throw, sinking the ping pong ball into the last cup. Chaos erupted as Duke lifted Mac off the ground and spun him around.

Once on his feet again, Mac sauntered out to us. "What's up, Shaw?"

Parker nodded his chin at Duke, still celebrating with anyone unlucky enough to be in arm's reach. "Can you make sure Duke doesn't end up passed out in the yard?"

Mack's eyes danced back and forth between us before he saluted. "On it, Cap'n."

Parker plucked the cup out of my hand and set it on the other side of him. "Let's go somewhere."

My pulse picked up, and I surprisingly wasn't tired anymore. Anticipation lit my blood. A stupid response considering he hadn't given one indication that he'd act on the heat between us.

I met his eyes, and the intensity there made me question my assumption. Parker hopped up and extended his hand. "Come on, I want to show you something. I promise to have you home at a decent hour."

Curiosity won the battle for him. "Okay, but I'm going to haunt your ass forever if you murder me."

He snorted out a laugh as he pulled me to my feet. "And miss you being flattened in practice? Never."

9

Riley

Parker didn't let go of my hand. He linked our fingers together and led me around the side of the house, through a gate I hadn't noticed on the way in, and down the street to his car. I felt like I'd swallowed a balloon. I couldn't catch my breath.

He opened the door for me, and I stared into the dark interior as he circled to the driver's side. Parker kept his car clean. It was the only thing I'd let myself think. No fast food trash or empty sports drink bottles, just us together—alone —in air that smelled faintly of leather and grass.

I could change my mind. Go back into the party. Call myself a ride. I had any number of other options, but this hesitation felt like fear. The wind blew my loose hair into my face, and when I brushed it away, Parker rested his arm on the roof, watching me. Sharp blue eyes waiting to see if I'd take a chance with him.

He didn't scare me. My reaction to his gaze scared me. I liked the way he looked at me with all of his focus. I wanted to believe he had just as much to lose as I did, but reality didn't work that way. Nothing could happen between us.

Maybe if I repeated that mantra enough times, I'd stop thinking about it.

Parker arched a brow. "I can take you home instead."

The challenge burned me. I didn't need an out—I needed to get a grip on my thoughts. And maybe I needed to get laid. It'd been a while, since before the summer at least. Parker was temptation incarnate, but nothing stopped me from finding another outlet for my needs.

If I'd let fear rule me, I wouldn't be here at TU. This wasn't any different.

"You can take me home later." I slid into the car, and the words echoed in my head. *Take me home later.* When he dropped me off, I would *not* invite him inside.

A satisfied smile curved his lips as he took his seat and drove us away from the party.

I remembered at the last second to text Eva that I was leaving. We'd taken an Uber to the party at Eva's insistence, so I wasn't worried about leaving her stranded. Mac would make sure she didn't make any bad choices.

Parker plugged his phone into the aux cable, then turned the music down to a low murmur as we hit the highway. Over the sounds of the road, I recognized Brandon Urie's distinctive voice, though I didn't know the song.

"Is this another one of your playlists?"

He glanced at me briefly, and his fingers twitched on the wheel. "Yeah."

"What's this one called?"

"Stop Touching the Radio, Mac."

I laughed and turned it up a little. His shoulders relaxed. Was he nervous at all about being alone with me or did he not feel the pressure in the air between us?

Parker nodded at his phone sitting on the dash. "Why don't you look through the playlist and pick something?"

I liked the music already playing, but if this whole trip was about getting to know each other, I could play along. At least it would distract me from staring at him while he drove. I reached for the phone without really looking and knocked it off the dash with a glancing blow.

Lightning fast, Parker reached out to save his phone at the same time I did. We both missed. The phone clattered to the console, and he caught me instead.

His hand wrapped around mine, like before but so very different. A flush warmed my cheeks, from both my clumsiness and the contact neither of us rushed to break. When he'd held my hand earlier, it had felt like an afterthought—a means to make sure I followed him. This time was different, a conscious choice to prolong the contact.

I stared at our entwined hands, mine cradled in his, and told myself to pull away. One second passed, then another. He didn't move, and neither did I. My gaze shifted to Parker's face. I don't know what I expected, but it wasn't the struggle evident from his tight jaw.

His thumb stroked a line of heat across my wrist, then he let go. My arm dropped back into my lap, and he retrieved his phone to hold it out for me.

"Pick a song," he repeated. If I'd had any doubts before, his husky voice cemented the truth in my mind.

He felt it.

I shook off the heady effects of Parker's touch and tried to steady my erratic breathing. Parker's playlist was extensive, but I didn't have the mental bandwidth to play the game anymore. I hit shuffle and let fate decide.

Out of the corner of my eye, because I was decidedly *not* going to look his way again until we were out of the car, I saw a smile flash across his face. Something told me he'd gleaned a lot of information out of that exchange.

Several seconds passed as the random song played, then Parker shook his head and launched into a story about Mac at karaoke. We drove back toward campus, chatting about Mac's need to sing along to every song, before Parker slowed and turned onto the road behind the training facility.

Like that first disastrous day when I'd been late, my heart raced as we approached the parking lot. The same exhilaration fired my blood—this time caused by the man sitting next to me rather than a roomful of strangers. Parker pulled into a spot on the far side next to the thick line of trees. He got out and opened my door before I had unbuckled my seat belt.

I couldn't think of anything I hadn't already seen at the facility, but Parker knew it much better than I did. At least I wouldn't have to worry about anyone making assumptions about seeing us together. We were both here so often no one would think twice to see us like this.

Mac knew we'd left the party together, but despite his love of hearing himself talk, I didn't think he'd tell anyone.

Instead of heading toward the building, Parker stepped off the concrete toward the trees. Once again, I considered changing my mind. I wasn't a hiker on the best of days, and it was dark under the pines. The lights from the parking lot didn't reach much past the edge of the grass, but Parker seemed to know where he was going.

With heavy reluctance, I followed him into the forest at a slower pace. "If you're not going to murder me, where are we going?"

He grinned over his shoulder. "You'll see."

We walked for maybe five minutes in relative silence. The branches creaked above us in the slight breeze, and something skittered in the underbrush, making me draw closer to Parker. I could handle angry linebackers, but rodents freaked me out.

He glanced over at me, and his arm twitched like he wanted to reach out then stopped himself. Brambles caught at my jeans, making me glad I'd opted for comfort instead of fashion. The fleeting thought of Parker bringing girls out here made me frown, but I couldn't imagine someone making this trek in stilettos and a short skirt. Then again, jersey chasers did a lot of crazy things to get the attention of football players.

While I was mentally scolding myself for thinking about Parker's potential hook-ups, he stopped abruptly, and I smacked into his back. He twisted to steady me, and I got my first look at what I assumed he wanted to show me.

My mouth dropped open in shock. Moonlight reflected off the shiny exterior of a tiny camping trailer parked in the middle of the woods. It sat at one end of a small clearing next to a handful of cheap patio chairs and a rudimentary firepit.

Maybe I hadn't been that far off after all. My first, third, and fourth thoughts involved how perfect this place would be for a sneaky booty call. Heat coiled inside me at the possibility, and I had to remind my lady bits to calm down. We weren't about to get any action.

I turned my raised eyebrows on Parker and went with thought number two. "Is this where you keep your victims?"

He laughed and ran his hand through his short hair, making me want to do the same. "Not as far as I know, but Noah can be scary quiet sometimes."

My eyes narrowed. "Creepy hook-up spot?"

"I can see how it would look like that, but this is for our crew only. No girls allowed. Except for you." He sank into one of the chairs scattered around the cold firepit and waved me to another. "The pressure is hard on all of us. Sometimes we want to get away. Mac, Noah, and I pooled our money, then Soren found this beauty."

I cast a disbelieving glance at the dents and rust and sat next to him. "Whose land is this?"

"Technically, the university's. It's part of the section allotted for the training facility, but no one ever comes back here."

"So we're squatting?"

He shrugged. "It's easy enough to move if the school finds out. I was out of line earlier, at practice. I'm sorry I doubted you, but I'm probably never going to be able to treat you like the guys on the team."

I wasn't sure how to take his comment. His abrupt subject change made my head spin, and I wanted to dismiss him as another narrow-minded asshole. The problem was… I knew Parker, and he wasn't like that.

"What does that mean?" I asked as neutrally as I could.

Parker tapped his fingers against the plastic arm of the chair in a complicated rhythm, staring at the trees across from us. "You're so fucking talented. I've never had to factor gender into my game before, and if asked, I would have said it didn't matter as long as the player was good. I want to think with any other player that expectation would be true. But not with you."

He met my eyes. "On the field, I trust you to make the play, but I never forget who's under the helmet. You don't have to be one of the guys to be good at football. I cleared it with the others, and we wanted you to be able to use the trailer too. You'll probably need it more than any of us."

His admission cracked open something deep inside me that I didn't want to examine too closely. My last team had accepted me as a player, but they never put much effort into seeing me as a person. On some level, it was easier that way.

Parker saw Riley. Not a football player who happened to be female.

The understanding in his eyes was too much for me to handle, so I looked away, searching for anything to distract me. My gaze landed on his hand, still tapping away, and the woven bracelet he wore.

I pointed at the red, black, and white design wrapped around his wrist. "I remember this. You came back to the weight room looking for it."

Parker turned his arm to show off both sides of the intricate pattern. "It's from my little sister. She made it for me when I got into TU."

I didn't like imagining Parker as a doting older brother, part of a family. He needed to stay firmly in teammate territory. I should steer the conversation back to football where I wouldn't be imagining him relaxed and smiling.

My mouth went rogue though. "How old is she?"

He slanted an amused look at me as if he sensed my inner struggle. "Sixteen. She was a surprise for all of us, but my parents are the best. Jaina isn't into football, but she expects me to join the NFL so I can buy her a goat."

I tilted my head at him. "That's an interesting request."

"Jaina's an interesting kid. She loves reading about everything, and she remembers all of it. It's scary sometimes, but you learn not to argue with her. She's always right." Affection softened his voice. "I miss her, and my parents. They can't come out often, but they'll be here for the first game."

He'd given me the perfect opportunity to change the subject, but curiosity ate me up. "Where are they now?"

"West of Denver, in the same little town where I grew up.

They joke that the council is ready to erect a billboard with my face on it as soon as I get famous enough. What about you? Where do you call home?"

"Wisconsin." Unlike him, I didn't throw out any cute bonus details. My hometown wasn't really home anymore.

He shifted to study my face. "You don't sound like you're from Wisconsin."

"Maybe not, but I still love a good batch of cheese curds."

"What the hell is a cheese curd?"

I schooled him on the different forms of fried cheese, and we talked as the moon moved across the sky. Parker was funny and charming... and he listened. All those threads of friendship we'd created over the last few weeks melded together into a tight connection.

At one point, he raided the tiny kitchenette and brought me snacks to make up for the dinner I'd missed. Without power, they couldn't keep anything cold, but I appreciated the pita chips and peanut butter.

Long after I should have been in bed, Parker and I slouched in the chairs and watched the stars. I yawned, tired but content to stay there with him. A new feeling for me.

Parker ruined the moment by mentioning our impending early morning workout.

"We have to be back here in four hours."

I groaned. "Why would you bring that up?"

He laughed and stood, offering his hand again. "Ready to go home?"

This time, I took it immediately. We'd spent hours together, and neither of us had jumped the other. Clearly, we had the capacity to be friends without benefits. Parker led the way to his car for the short drive back to our complex.

No one was around as he walked with me to our shared hallway, not surprising considering the hour.

Instead of heading to his door, he lingered next to mine, like he was just as reluctant as I was for our evening to end. "With all respect to Mac, I like Riley better than RJ."

"Riley's not my real name." I slapped a hand over my mouth, appalled at my absent-minded admission, but it was too late.

Parker's face lit up like I'd given him the Heisman. "What is it?"

I hesitated, doing some quick calculations. My name was one of my more harmless secrets, and if I asked him to keep it to himself, he would. If he dug for my name on his own, he might discover who my dad was, which could cause all kinds of problems.

"It stays between us."

Parker laid his hand over his chest. "I promise."

"Lorelai. My real name is Lorelai."

"Lorelai," Parker repeated slowly, drawing the sounds out in a way that should not have sounded sexy. "I like it."

"So glad you approve."

He grinned at my sarcasm. "I like Riley too. They both fit you."

I shifted, uncomfortable being associated with my birth name. "My mom picked it out. Two years later, she decided parenting wasn't for her and left without looking back. Dad called me Riley ever since."

He surprised me by wrapping an arm around my waist and dragging me into a hug. "Your mom is an idiot, and you should own your name."

My heart fluttered, pressed against Parker's chest, but for once it wasn't proximity causing my reaction. He had a way of slicing right through to the center of me.

I let my head fall against his shoulder, and we both exhaled, relaxing into the embrace when we should have been pulling apart. Gradually, Parker's light comfort shifted into something darker, hungrier. Tension built, a slow and steady climb, until his chin tipped toward me.

A tiny movement, but I couldn't take a breath without sharing the air with him.

"We can't do this, for so many reasons," I whispered.

"I want to touch you." His quiet admission made my breath hitch.

My hands curled into the cotton of his shirt as the words tickled the hair at my temple. His fingers already pressed against my back, but I knew what he meant. Parker wanted to cross the line we'd been toeing all night. Neither of us dared to move, unwilling to disrupt the delicate balance between friends and something more.

I knew what would happen, but I lifted my face anyway, giving him access. Parker trailed his fingers down my cheek, over my jaw, and along the side of my neck. His thumb stroked my lower lip, and my mouth opened instinctively.

He dropped his head to whisper into my ear. "Would you let me kiss you?"

I shivered, unsure if he was taunting me or asking permission.

"What else would you let me do?" His lips grazed my throat, and I may have moaned.

My lungs burned for air, but I couldn't seem to draw in any oxygen past the throbbing need that had taken over my body.

"Parker..." I tilted, just a little, just enough for him to swipe his tongue against my erratic pulse.

"Tell me what you want, Lorelai."

I wanted the blinding pleasure he promised with his

teasing touches. I wanted to shove him against the door and ride him until we both collapsed. I wanted it bad enough that I hesitated another long second with his body close to mine, imagining spending the rest of the night with Parker.

But then I leaned back because I also wanted to play football, and I couldn't have both.

Parker let me slide away from his touch, then flattened his hands on either side of me against the door. "We can't ignore this."

"We have to. The team looks to you for leadership. You can't be seen messing around with me, for both our sakes. The athletic director was very clear about the rules." Despite my words, I didn't make any effort to leave.

Shadows cut lines onto his biceps as he leaned closer. "And if I don't care about the rules?"

"I do." I ducked under his arm. "I'll see you in the morning, Shaw."

He pushed away from the door with a pained smile. "What happened to Parker?"

I shook my head. We were already well beyond the line of friendship, and I desperately needed to reestablish some distance.

"Goodnight, Shaw."

Parker nodded and backed away toward his apartment. I closed the door, then leaned against it in the dark space. Eva had texted to say not to wait up. A blessing considering the show we'd just put on in the hallway.

I wasn't sure how this fiasco would affect our relationship on the team, but I had a feeling Monday's class would be *interesting*.

One thing was clear—I couldn't let myself be alone with Parker anymore.

10

Parker

Fuck the rules. I wanted Lorelai Jones in a way I'd never wanted anything before—and she'd clearly decided I was off-limits.

I stood in the chaos of the tunnel, minutes before we had to run out onto the field, and let the noise blur around me. My Chill the F* Out playlist hadn't been able to touch the churning in my chest. I wasn't worried about the game— week zero was never competitive so we used it as a warm-up for the season—but Riley had shoved me so far into the friend zone I could probably braid her hair from my apartment.

Seeing her multiple times a day in class and at practice without being able to touch her was slowly killing me.

I kept replaying that night outside our apartments. After having her in my arms, hearing that breathy noise she made, I couldn't think about anything else. I faked it well enough that Coach didn't notice, but Mac kept sneaking me concerned glances.

He knew I'd left the party with Riley, then come home way past my normal time. I'd managed to deflect all his questions about what went down when I showed her the camper. He clearly didn't believe we'd sat and talked for hours—the truth, incidentally—but he didn't think we were hooking up.

Riley helped out his confusion by teasing me at practice like everyone else while refusing to move from her spot on the fringe of our friend group. Mac and Eva had both invited her to lunch, but she always had an excuse. No matter what she told them, I knew I was the real reason.

"There you are!" My mom's excited shout rang across the tunnel, yanking my thoughts away from Riley.

She pushed her way through the wall of players with my dad trailing along behind her, grinning like an idiot as he watched. I knew the feeling. When Riley turned her attention on me, I couldn't stop smiling. Except I didn't want to be thinking about Riley in my tight football pants with my mom coming in fast.

I winced at my own choice of words and surreptitiously adjusted myself before she got too close.

Mom rushed up and hugged me, then stepped back to let my dad have a turn. The rest of the team ignored them. They'd all met my parents by now.

"I'm so proud of you, honey. Not that I ever doubted you'd be starting as soon as D graduated. I'm just excited for the first game of the season with my baby as the captain."

Over her shoulder, Riley came out of the women's locker room. I tried not to stare, but I couldn't help myself. Watching Riley had become an involuntary reaction whenever she was in the vicinity.

Like the rest of us, she was dressed out in full pads and carried her helmet. Her long hair fell in an intricate braid over one shoulder, and she smiled at Mac when he bounded her way. For a long second, I couldn't take my eyes off her.

Once we left the tunnel, I'd need to focus on the game, but I had this moment where I could pretend she was smiling like that at me.

Mom's hand on my forearm grabbed my attention, and I cursed inside when I saw her face. She looked at Riley, then back at me with a knowing smile that I dreaded. Fuck. I needed better control of my facial muscles.

"You'll have to introduce me to the woman on your team. She's been all over SportsCenter."

I was totally screwed. Mom didn't take no for an answer. "Sure. I can introduce you to Riley after the game, but you guys should go find your seats." I frowned as I realized I didn't see a dark-haired teen with her nose buried in a book. "Where's Jaina?"

Mom rolled her eyes. "Lecturing the guard on letting random people into the tunnel."

I frowned. "But you guys have permission to be back here."

"I know, but he didn't check our passes, just waved us through. Jaina's newest obsession is forensic pathology, so she's been reading a lot of police procedurals."

Dad clapped me on the back. "Good luck out there. We'll meet up with you after. Italian okay?"

They always insisted on buying me and my crew dinner after the game. I perked up. That crew included Eva... and now Riley.

"Sure. You know we're not picky."

Dad nodded and ushered Mom away. She bumped into Riley on the way out, and immediately started talking. I shook my head. The woman must have been a spy in another life.

Riley offered her a smile and glanced around in confusion until her eyes landed on me. A silent message passed between us, questioning why this strange woman was in the middle of our pre-game ritual.

Mom said something that drew Riley's interest, most likely introducing herself as my biggest fan because Riley's dark eyes sparkled with laughter when they found me again. The amused, intimate look hit me square in the chest.

Noah sidled up next to me and crossed his arms. "I like her."

He wasn't talking about my mom. I already knew he liked *her*. He'd caught me ogling Riley, exactly as she'd warned me about.

"Me too," I muttered, watching as she shifted her smile to my mom.

Noah grunted, and I forced myself to focus on my roommate instead of my fantasy girl.

The music changed, signaling our entrance, and Mac joined Noah and me to lead the team out of the tunnel. Fan noise was nothing new, but the stands exploded several seconds after we emerged. They must have seen Riley.

She'd been all over TU's social media leading up to this game, and it warmed my chest to see our fans embracing her.

Time to focus and give them something to cheer about.

———

"You have a thing for RJ." Mac had the worst timing. He'd waited until we'd scored again and sent the defense onto the field before cornering me.

I crossed my arms and refused to meet his eyes. "You don't know what you're talking about."

Mac scoffed and moved to block my view of the game. "Please. You've been making eyes at her all week."

"What does that even mean?"

"You're hot for each other."

"So what? Riley is hot, no question. You said yourself you'd have hit on her if she hadn't burned you right away."

"But I didn't... and you *did*."

I checked the area around us to make sure no one was within hearing distance. "She's not interested in risking her career for a quickie with her teammate."

Mac laughed so hard he had to put his helmet down. "Boy, there's no way you offered her a quickie."

"I was paraphrasing. No one offered anything. We're just friends."

He glanced at the field, then raised a brow at me. "I've seen the hungry looks you keep sending her way. That's not the face of someone who only wants to be friends."

Frustration had me picking at the tape around my wrist that covered my bracelet. "It doesn't matter what I want. Or what looks I'm sending her way. She's not sending them back."

"Trust me, she's sending them back. She's just better than you at judging when no one is looking." Mac shoved his helmet into my chest when my eyes wandered back to the field. "It's not like you to give up. I'm not saying chase her when she straight up tells you no, but I don't believe for a second she told you no."

I scanned the sidelines again, this time searching for Riley's slightly smaller build. She was deep in conversation with one of the assistant coaches, so I let myself look my fill. Mac was right. She hadn't told me no, only goodnight.

The whistle blew marking the end of the other team's drive. They'd gone halfway down the field only to have to punt it away.

Mac bumped my shoulder as we strapped on our helmets. "You know I've got your back, whatever you need."

I nodded and forced my attention to the game.

―――――

ONE QUARTER and two touchdowns later, we'd blown OSU away. They had a field goal and a touchdown in garbage time, but we couldn't have asked for a better first game.

The locker room was crazy with music blasting and guys shouting back and forth. Everyone rode the high of a good win. We'd been so far ahead Coach had pulled me at the end to give my backup, Aidan Williams, some reps.

He'd thrown exclusively to Mac despite Riley being open several times. One that cost us an interception and the single touchdown OSU had scored. I tried not to put any extra meaning behind it, but I couldn't let it go. Part of my responsibility as captain involved sussing out any problems between my players.

I let the room clear out a little, taking a shower and dressing in fresh clothes while I waited on Williams to finish getting cleaned up. He took his time primping, which meant only me, Mac, and Noah remained when he grabbed his bag.

"You need to do a better read before you pass."

Williams' head snapped up. "My reads are just fine."

The pushback didn't surprise me, but I'd hoped he'd take the criticism and improve without argument. "What about the interception?"

"I had to make a gametime decision." He tried to shrug past me, but I sidestepped to stay in front of him.

"Then it was a shitty decision. Riley was open, and Mac had two defenders."

Williams' jaw clenched as he stared over my shoulder. "Riley's only here because the school needed good publicity, and she's looking for a sap to take her with him to the pros." His gaze shifted to meet my eyes. "You better watch out before she gets her hooks into you."

"I don't give a fuck if she strips naked and dances in the quad. She earned her place on this team with her skill, just like everyone else here. You show her the respect she deserves or you're insulting all of us."

Mac and Noah lined up next to me with similar serious expressions.

Williams gave a tight nod and slunk around us out the door. When I turned, Riley stood staring after him with her brow furrowed.

She'd changed into sweats and a tank top, and her wet hair meant she'd showered like the rest of us. I hadn't expected to see her until dinner, but she had her duffel slung over her shoulder like she was ready to go. After a second, her face cleared, and she took a couple of steps into the room to join us.

"You need a ride, RJ?" Mac slung his arm over her shoulders, and I had to check the sudden urge to shove him away from her.

She did it herself, elbowing him and sliding away. "Yeah. Eva dropped me off before the game, but she had other plans tonight."

My mood soured. Without Eva to pressure Riley into dinner, she'd probably go straight home. We'd just played an entire football game together, but I wanted to spend some time with her without all the pads and pressure between us. Even if that meant I had to share her with my friends, parents, and little sister.

Her eyes flitted back and forth between the three of us.

"You guys know *which* Italian place we're supposed to be eating at, right?"

Just like that, the night was saved. "You're coming to dinner?"

Riley sighed. "Your mom is a force of nature. I was going to say no, but before I had a chance, she'd discovered my love of garlic bread and used it against me. Apparently, we're sharing an order, so I have to sit next to her? It must have been challenging growing up with her knowing everything." Riley eyed me up and down. "Actually, this explains a lot about your personality."

I burned from that quick glance, but for once, I made sure not to telegraph my inner struggle all over my face. "She *did* teach me the value of effective blackmail."

Riley laughed. "I'll keep that in mind. Let's go eat. I'm starving, and your mom owes me garlic bread." She hooked her arm through mine, and I let her drag me out of the locker room.

I got my wish. Riley spent dinner sandwiched between me and my mom, and she quickly warmed up to my family. Mom's heavy-handed interference paid off like it usually did. I'd have to thank her later.

As if she could read my mind, which wasn't entirely out of the realm of possibility, Mom pulled me aside after the meal as everyone gathered their leftovers and said goodbye.

She cornered me in the alcove by the restrooms and didn't waste time. "When were you going to tell me about her?"

I leaned back against the wall, suddenly tired of having this conversation. "There's nothing to tell."

She arched a brow. "Don't lie to me. You may be able to fool your friends, but you've never been able to keep a secret from me. I know what I saw."

"There's nothing between Riley and me other than friendship. Even if we wanted it to be more, the university has a rule against players dating each other."

She crossed her arms. "Well that's a stupid rule."

I barked out a laugh. "She doesn't think so."

"You've talked to her about it?"

"Yeah, and she wasn't willing to take the risk. Riley has a lot more to lose than I do. In other circumstances..." I shook my head.

Mom's face softened. "This must be hard for both of you then."

"Mac says to try anyway."

She chuckled and sent an affectionate look his way. "Bless that boy, he's a romantic at heart, but an idiot in the head. If Riley asked for friendship, give it to her. Show her she can trust you to put her needs over yours."

I nodded. The advice echoed what I'd already decided on my own after the game.

Mom hugged me, then patted my chest. "One more thing to think about, you're not players once the season is over."

With that mic drop of information, she turned and caught up to the rest of my family as they walked out the door. Three more months, then the playoffs. Suddenly, my drive to return to the championship seemed a lot more complicated.

11

Riley

I'd never had the hatred for Mondays that my friends did. My weekends were busy with football, both personal and professional, which was how most of my weekdays went as well. I didn't have down time to lament the end of the weekend. Hell, I didn't have a weekend.

Mondays meant practice and training and recently, Parker's wicked smile in class. Today, he arrived with an iced chai, leaning close to set it on my tiny excuse for a desk.

"Morning, Lorelai," he murmured, low enough no one else would hear him.

After I'd let my real name slip, he'd only called me Riley if there were other people around, which I'd made sure was always. He still managed to work Lorelai in at least once a day.

In truth, I liked when he said my real name. Something about the way he formed the word made my chest pull tight —a caress on a part of me only he knew.

"Morning, Shaw." I took a long, slow sip from the cup, not surprised in the least he'd figured out my favorite morning beverage.

This particular Monday also meant we got our first test back in Human Sexuality. One that Parker aced, and I nearly failed.

I frowned down at the red mark on my paper. School had never been a huge priority for me, but I made good grades. Better than a D at least. Professor Declann bustled around at the front of the class as the students passed the stack of sheets down the rows.

Not only had I gotten a shitty grade, most of the class had probably seen it. I fought the rising embarrassment as several female students in the front row looked back our way. It was entirely possible they weren't talking about me. According to Eva, Parker was a popular topic of conversation around here even before he was the starting quarterback.

The professor caught whatever they said and met my eyes with a frown. Yep. Definitely talking about me. She shook her head and dismissed me to speak to the girls in front of her. I didn't know what her problem was, but if I dared to say anything in class, I only got negative responses.

Parker glanced over and pried the crumpled paper from my hand with a low whistle. "Damn, Riley. You know you have to maintain a B average to play, right?"

"Yes, thank you," I responded through clenched teeth.

Between learning TU's playbook and being behind from missing summer practices, I'd let my classes slide down my list of priorities. Professor Declann didn't make me want to put in the effort here if it was going to be wasted.

He shoved the offending test into his backpack where I couldn't glare at it anymore. "I could help you study."

When he faced me again, Parker had adopted an inno-cent expression which immediately made me suspicious.

"Is this some excuse to get an invite into my apartment?"

"I was in your apartment last week for movie night. Eva

burnt the popcorn, and you yelled at us from your bedroom for being too loud."

Right. I'd forgotten about that. I was trying to read for one of my classes, and I'd kept imagining what would happen if I joined them. In my head, Parker pulled me down on his lap and whispered naughty things in my ear while his fingers traced fire along my thigh.

What else would you let me do to you?

Real life Parker bumped me with his shoulder, and I sucked in air. The professor was lecturing about how humans used body language to signal enthusiasm for sex, and I realized for the first time how dangerous this class could be with Parker sitting next to me.

I catalogued every movement I made over the next hour, trying to be sure I didn't give away my thoughts. Parker didn't say anything more until the professor's wrap-up when she glared in my direction while encouraging tutoring options.

He stood with the rest of the class, blocking my sight of the front with his broad shoulders. "Let me help you study. I'd offer the same thing to any of the guys. Eva, too."

I stared up at him, debating the intelligence of his idea. If any of the other guys offered to help with a class where I was struggling, would I automatically say no? If they asked for help, what would I do?

Dammit.

Parker must have read the answer on my face because he nodded decisively. "I'll come over after practice this afternoon if you're free."

Of course I was free. I made it a point to not be social, which he knew. At least Eva would be home too. Parker and I could study in the living room, and her presence would help me control my baser instincts.

Professor Declann may hate me, but my poor grade was on me. I was behind in the reading, and I had trouble focusing in class. Parker's fault, naturally, so the least he could do was help me bring my grade up.

"Okay. You can help me study after practice—once—so it better be good."

His slow smile lit a fire between my thighs. "You're going to want more than once."

Fuck, I was going to combust if he ever actually tried to seduce me.

———

PRACTICE WAS A MESS. The apartment was a mess. My life was a mess. Nothing new to see here. I rushed home after showering to find Eva lazing on the couch with a sink full of dishes in the kitchen.

As I frantically cleaned—when did we become slobs?—I informed her of my impromptu study session. Being the brat she was, she refused to give up the TV so we could study in the living room. Her exact words involved putting on my big girl panties and then taking them off.

Before I could argue, Parker knocked on the door. At least, I assumed it was Parker. Eva turned her attention back to the cheer videos she was watching, and I sighed. My bedroom was definitely worse than the living room, but at least Eva would be here to act as chaperone. With the door closed.

Yeah, that was going to be super helpful.

I yanked the front door open before I could talk myself out of it. Like me, Parker had showered and changed after practice. He wore sweats and a faded TU shirt that should have made him look like a hobo, but I'd yet to see Parker wear anything that took away from his sheer masculine beauty.

His jaw ticked as his gaze traveled down the length of me. I'd changed into my favorite SWU shorts and a tank top as a nod to the heat. Usually, I was comfortable in this outfit, but with Parker staring at me, I suddenly felt every inch of exposed skin.

With a start, I moved back to let him in. "We have to use my bedroom."

"Fine by me."

Eva snickered and waved at Parker as he strode through the living room. I glared at her as I closed the door and followed. She pretended not to see me, but I'd exact revenge later.

Parker had never been in my room—I didn't let many people in there—so I expected him to take advantage of the opportunity to look around. I would have. He scanned the room with a cursory glance, then his gaze landed on me again, hovering by the closed door.

Why was I so jumpy? Eva was right outside, and our apartment wasn't exactly soundproofed. Worst case scenario, Parker would ruin my opinion of him by hitting on me. I promised myself I'd kick him out, but it felt weak. If he made a move, I couldn't guarantee my body wouldn't mutiny and go rogue.

Ugh. I was tired of second-guessing everything. Parker was here to help my failing ass study. End of story.

I collapsed on the bed next to my backpack, utterly exhausted from my own mental gymnastics. "I need to change before we start."

Parker grunted. "Don't be a prude, Lorelai. I've seen you in less at practice. Scoot over." He maneuvered his big body next to me on the double bed and stretched out his long legs.

I balked. "This is a bad idea."

He tilted his head at me. "Nothing is going to happen. I wouldn't do that to you. Now, open your book to page eighty-four."

I fought a smile at the pedantic tone he adopted, and the nerves melted away.

To my surprise, Parker was a good tutor. We discussed the topics from the first two weeks, and he quizzed me on the concepts. My stubborn brain refused to retain anything until he made little inside jokes to help me remember.

When we got to week three, I had to retrieve my laptop to watch the video Professor Declann had assigned. Parker took a break to use the bathroom, and when we settled back onto the bed, we were pressed against each other from hip to shoulder so we could both see.

The nerves didn't return, and he didn't make a single move. No unnecessary touching, no double entendres, only his eyes betrayed how much he wanted a different afternoon on my bed.

In a quiet corner of my mind, something shifted. The tight part inside me relaxed at last. Parker had said nothing would happen, and I believed him.

The video droned on, a throwback from several decades ago, and I couldn't focus with the warmth of Parker seeping into me. My eyes got heavy, and the last thing I remembered was letting my head fall to his shoulder, just for a second.

By the time I woke up, the shadows had lengthened, leaving the room mostly in darkness. I didn't have the energy to lift my head and check the clock, but sunset was several hours after the end of practice.

I'd curled around Parker in my sleep, legs entwined with

his, the strong sound of his heartbeat under my cheek. His arms wrapped around me, holding me in place. As if I wanted to go anywhere else.

All the reasons I had to stay away from him faded under the languid weight of my sleepy body. I breathed in the scent of dryer sheets and Parker, absently wondering which of them did the laundry.

His fingers stroked my hip where they rested, brushing over the inch of skin where my top had ridden up. The shock of sensation made me squirm, bringing his hand closer to where I wanted him.

Parker murmured something too low for me to catch and turned his head to nuzzle my hair. The quiet twilight made it easy for me to pretend this was a dream. If I didn't move too much, I wouldn't have to wake up. I could lay there with him until morning.

The slow burn of a building ache wouldn't let me sink back into sleep though.

I tucked my hand under his shirt and splayed my fingers across his stomach. If I was going to wake up next to him, I could at least indulge a little. The relief of not fighting the urge to touch him made me giddy. Stupid, too. I brushed the waistband of his sweats and hesitated.

Under my fingers, his abs tightened, and he laid his hand over mine. "Not today, Lorelai."

"Sorry." Heat burned my cheeks, but when I tried to pull away, he held me in place.

"I want you. I'm not going to try to hide that—not from you—but I promised nothing would happen. Nothing will. This was just a little nap while studying. Gives the brain a break."

With my ego soothed, I relaxed against him again. "Do you always nap with Mac when you're studying?"

He laughed, the sound low and rough from sleep. "No. He starfishes as soon as he's out. Horrible cuddler."

"What's this then?" I whispered.

Parker linked our fingers on his stomach. "Sometimes it's nice just to be held."

"I like napping with you." The truth was easier to hedge when I wasn't staring into striking blue eyes, so I pulled away and sat up to face him. "But that's not all this is. I wouldn't do this with anyone else."

"Me either, but it feels right with you. If I had my way—"

I laid my fingers over his lips to stop him. Whatever he was about to say would add another brick to the weight of my own need. I was strong, but everyone reached a breaking point eventually.

He gripped my wrist, holding me still for a moment before lowering my arm, like he was fighting the same battle not to cross another line. "Do you remember the point of the homework reading from the first day of class?"

I searched my memory, and a filmy thought solidified. "Human touch is necessary for comfort."

Parker flattened my hand on his chest. "We're not doing anything wrong. It's human touch. Mac slaps my ass way more than necessary. Duke gets handsy when he's drunk. And I can hold you when it feels like the pressure is going to bury us. We deserve comfort."

He wasn't wrong. Our lives were hard on our bodies, and I hadn't slept this well in ages. Part of me recognized I was reaching for the handy excuse he'd provided, but I didn't care.

"No one can know about this. If anyone asks, we studied and that's it."

He nodded solemnly, and his agreement finally pushed me over the edge. We'd already spent hours wrapped around each other. Nothing had happened because Parker had stopped us. I trusted him more than I trusted myself at this point.

And I wanted that warmth again.

"Come back tomorrow?"

Parker took a deep breath, and the hint of a smile crossed his face. "I'll be here."

12

Parker

I didn't know what was happening between Riley and me, but I didn't want it to stop. If we were caught, both of us would pay the price. Riley would lose all the respect she'd earned, and the athletic director could follow through on his threat from last year.

I couldn't make myself care. Not when Riley had finally opened up to me.

We didn't meet every day, but several times a week, she let me into her space—let me hold her while she slept.

Sometimes we actually studied—Riley had a fucking smart mind to go with her fucking fast feet—but more often we watched a movie or talked. She balked whenever I tried to ask about her family or her past, so I'd change the subject and she wouldn't ask me to leave.

Riley insisted Eva had to be home whenever I came over, but I barely saw her. She'd give me a raised eyebrow and a salute when I walked through the living room, as if she saw something we didn't.

I saw it.

Hell, I felt it. If Riley weren't my teammate, I'd have

broken my rules against dating in a heartbeat. She fit with me so perfectly, and for once, I was counting the days until the season ended.

In the meantime, I'd take whatever Riley could give me. Which meant making time for "study sessions" whenever Eva was willing to babysit.

This week, fate intervened by sending Eva out of town for a competition. No studying of any kind, and by the time we returned from our away game, which we lost, I was frustrated as all hell.

The atmosphere on the bus was somber as we returned to the school. We'd expected this game to be tough, but we'd prepared for it. Or I'd thought we had. Something had felt off the whole game, like we'd forgotten how to work together. To make it worse, I made a bunch of stupid mistakes that would have made freshman me cringe. I wouldn't be leading us to a championship with that level of play.

I knew part of the problem was my inability to get my mind off of Riley. If she was on the field, I tracked her. If she was on the sidelines, I felt her watching me. Even on the bus, I'd picked this row halfway back because it offered the best view of the front seats Riley preferred.

The ease we'd developed over the last weeks in practice had disappeared during the game today, entirely my fault. I'd let the frustration of not spending alone time with Riley build, thinking I'd be able to handle it.

Pride was a sneaky bitch, and I'd been a cranky bastard today.

I slumped in my seat, music quietly playing in my ears, and tried to work through the problems I'd had on the field. As usual, my thoughts immediately returned to Riley. Early on in the first quarter, she'd taken a hard hit. I'd controlled myself at the time, but every play after, the image of her going down had frozen me for a split second.

The other team took advantage of my hesitation. With every mistake, the frustration built on itself. I closed my eyes and let my head fall back to the padded seat. This was why I never dated, never took the chance that someone could become large enough in my mind to eclipse everything else.

I'd been a detriment to the team today, and the failure twisted in my gut. Maybe I needed a break. Not from football, but from Riley. I could limit our interactions until I had a stronger grip on myself.

We'd fallen into our current pattern by accident, and Eva's departure had jarred us out of it. This was my chance to pull away without risking drama in the team—except I didn't want to. Everything in me rebelled at the thought.

I wanted Riley closer, not farther away.

The bus jostled, and I opened my eyes to see we'd left the highway for the small roads in town that would lead to campus. Low grumbles about plans for the evening came from the guys around me as we started gathering our stuff from the ride. I wasn't in the mood to party, and thankfully, it sounded like neither was anyone else.

Out of habit, or sheer obsession, my gaze returned to Riley at the front. She felt the loss as keenly as the rest of us. Knowing her, she'd work off her frustration in the weight room, but Coach had forbidden us from moping around in the facility until tomorrow.

Would she go anyway? I didn't think so.

She respected Coach and his "requests". Most likely, she'd go back to her apartment—alone. Temptation began to creep into my mind, but she'd been clear about her boundaries. We hadn't discussed the reason why. I hadn't asked. If I knew, I might try to change her mind.

As it was, I might try to change her mind anyway. If Mac weren't sitting between me and the aisle, I might make my way to the front of the bus and take the seat next to her. Might offer to share my They Can't All Be Winners playlist. Might lean closer and ask her to leave the door unlocked for me.

I didn't. Mac's long legs blocked my way, and Riley had been giving fuck off vibes since she boarded the bus. As soon as we'd hit the highway, she'd put in earbuds and closed her eyes. She wasn't sleeping though.

I knew what she looked like asleep, knew she liked to tuck her hands between us where it was warm, knew she mumbled about plays as she dreamed.

Mac bumped me, his warning that I was staring again. I dragged my gaze away and stopped my music. No parties tonight, but I didn't want to be alone. Too much temptation to show up at Riley's door.

I rubbed my face. "Camper tonight?"

Mac studied me for a second, then nodded. "Yeah, man. I'll let Noah know."

With my roommates on board, some of the pressure in my chest eased. We could all use a break. The bus slowed as it turned into the training facility parking lot, and Riley stretched her arms above her head.

We could *all* use a break.

I could leave Riley to a night alone, knowing she'd be without her favorite pressure release and Eva would be gone… or I could invite her to the camper with the rest of us.

No contest.

I elbowed Mac. "Let Riley know too."

———

I HALF EXPECTED her to politely decline. If I'd asked her, there would have been subtext, but Mac was hard to deny. We piled off the bus, saying our goodbyes, and I did my best to keep my concerns separate from the team. They didn't want a frustrated quarterback—they wanted a leader. I took that role seriously.

Mac and Noah followed me to my car where we all stored our gear for the ride home. If we went home. We'd crashed in the camper more than once. Riley thought I'd been kidding about Mac being a horrible cuddler, but the bed inside was only big enough for two of us... as long as neither of the two was Noah.

Riley peeled off to her car, then joined us. "Is this how you guys usually shake off a loss?"

Noah shrugged. "Better than drugs."

I started down the nearly invisible path, speaking over my shoulder. "Not always. Sometimes we watch film for the next game. Sometimes we get massively drunk. Depends on the night."

"*You* don't get drunk."

Her quiet words reached me over the crunching sounds of us tromping through the underbrush. She was right. I didn't get drunk—I watched over the guys who wanted to blow off steam for a while.

We reached the camper in silence. Mac headed inside to grab drinks from the cooler, while Noah started the fire—leaving Riley and me alone at the edge of the clearing. She met my eyes, and I jerked my chin at the chairs stacked by the door.

"Grab a seat."

We arranged the shitty patio furniture a decent distance from the rapidly growing flames. The warm evening meant we didn't need the heat, but the light was nice. Mac returned and distributed the bottles in his hands, beer for him and Noah, water for me and Riley.

By the time we'd all settled down, the harsh memories of the game started to fade. I would have been fine sitting in silence, but Mac couldn't handle it.

He raised his bottle. "To all the poor suckers who don't get to play college ball."

We all lifted our drinks, and Noah grunted. "Amen."

Riley took a long swig, then kicked her feet out in front of her. "I know we can't win them all, but damn... losing sucks ass."

I set my water down in the dirt, ignoring the sharp prickle of guilt. "Belcourt is a good team this year. We knew that going in."

Mac shrugged one shoulder. "We had a few unlucky plays that cost us the game."

Riley snorted. "Bullshit. We lost because of us. Belcourt is a good team, but we're better. Our mistakes cost us the game. It's not all bad though. We can fix mistakes. Losing helps us find where we're weak, so we know where to put our focus."

Her gaze stayed locked on the fire, seemingly oblivious to the three of us staring at her. I couldn't tell if she was talking about me specifically or not, but her assessment eased some of my foul mood. Her take sounded like something Coach would say, and she'd included herself in the effort to improve.

After a long second, Mac drained his beer and started pestering Noah about the grocery rotation. I ignored them to watch Riley. She picked at the label on the water bottle, her eyes far away. What was she thinking about?

Probably her efforts during the game, ways she could improve, action plans to hit her new goals. Things I should be thinking about but wasn't. I suspected there would never come a day when Riley Jones didn't intrigue me.

She had no fear. None. She'd built her body into a weapon—an elite machine capable of amazing feats—and she knew how to use it. Unlike some of the guys wary of injuring themselves before they reached the draft, Riley gave all of herself to every game, every practice.

I wanted to know everything about her, and I was tired of waiting.

I kicked a pebble toward her, and it bounced off the metal frame of her chair with a ping. "Where'd you learn to play football?"

The flickering shadows made it hard to read her expression as she reached down to pick up the rock. "I don't like to talk about myself."

"Not even to your best friend?"

She sent me a sidelong glance. "Eva isn't here."

I winced. "Ouch. That one hurt. Here I was thinking I'd earned bestie status with all the time we spend together studying."

Even in the dim light, I saw the flush move across her cheeks. I'd hoped to remind her she trusted me during our purely platonic naps, but her reaction spurred a different train of thought. For a second, I was lost in the memory of her ass snuggled against me, with her warm and relaxed in sleep.

I missed her, and the loss sliced through me.

Riley met my eyes for an instant, and I saw the same longing there. Then she blinked, and I wondered if I'd imagined it.

Mac's chair scraped through the dirt, reminding me we weren't alone in the woods. I glanced over to see both Mac and Noah looking our direction. Mac raised a brow, silently asking if I wanted them to head out, but I shook my head at him.

Better if he stayed. I hadn't wanted to come to the camper for a chance to be alone with Riley. Her presence was a bonus.

I spread my hands. "Look, we tried Google, but you're surprisingly absent on the internet for someone who was recruited by a D1 football coach. You don't have to tell us anything, but we're curious because we care about you. Nothing you say will go beyond us if you don't want it to. Right, guys?"

Mac mimed zipping his lips, and Noah crossed his heart with his finger. Both wore giant shit-eating grins.

Riley rolled her eyes. "Fine. What do you want to know?"

All three of us scooted closer, and I ended up with my chair arm nearly touching hers. "Where'd you play before this?"

She pointed to the dark green shirt she wore. "Southern Wisconsin University. The Beavers. D3 school, not a bad coaching staff, but focused more on the run."

We all stared at the large angry beaver splashed across her chest, and Mac spoke up first. "TU Wildcats are kind of an upgrade. Beavers don't really inspire fear."

"We could be the TU Christmas trees for all I care. The mascot's only a symbol. The power comes from the team."

There she went again, surprising me with her insight. I wanted to ask her how she could say that with such authority. What had given her the confidence I found so sexy?

Noah leaned back in his chair. "You should tell that to the rest of *our* team."

She pursed her lips. "I'll leave the motivational speeches to Shaw. Feel free to use it though."

"You grew up in Wisconsin, right?" Mac asked.

Riley nodded, and I hoped she'd tell Mac more than she'd told me.

He shifted to the edge of his seat, resting his elbows on his knees. "What was it like?"

Riley laughed. "Great—if you enjoy cows, cheese, and a cult-like obsession with the Wolves."

"You don't sound like you miss it."

"I don't. Living in Wisconsin is really fun in a lot of ways, but I was ready to move on."

Mac sent me a pointed look, but for once, I couldn't decipher his meaning. "Well, we're definitely more fun than cows and cheese. No comment on the Packers. Not going to jinx my chances by bad-mouthing any team."

Riley tilted her head at him. "Are you going out for the draft after this year?"

"Nah, girl. I'm playing out my eligibility and getting my degree. My mama would kill me if I left school early. If I get picked up by a team after that, it's all good, but I'll have a back-up plan in place."

My brows drew together. This was the first time I'd heard him mention anything other than the draft after college.

"What about you?" he asked.

She shrugged. "That depends on what happens over the next two years."

I noticed the evasion, but Mac didn't.

He whooped and pointed at her with the lip of his bottle. "That's my girl."

"Not your girl," she muttered.

"Close enough. You're one of us now, RJ. I'm getting another beer. Want one?"

A smile crept across her face. "No, thanks."

Mac hopped up and disappeared into the camper, and she yawned. It wasn't late, but game days were exhausting. Before I could suggest we head back, Noah surprised me by asking her a question.

"What's your plan after you graduate?"

"I want to work with kids, especially young girls, who are interested in sports but don't have the means to pursue being on a team. In Wisconsin, I used to work for a camp that set up a summer football league for low-income kids. That's why I couldn't be here for the summer practices." Her voice softened, and my heart did a funny little flip at the thought of Riley surrounded by a bunch of hero-worshipping little girls.

Noah's eyes sharpened. "No plans for the draft?"

She laughed dryly. "I know it's a miracle I'm playing football *now*. No matter how good I am, a professional team won't use one of their few draft picks on me. I like the idea of molding the next generation of female athletes, encouraging each of them to push a little farther past the barriers."

He rubbed the dark stubble on his chin and nodded. We all knew she was right, but I still wanted to argue—she deserved the same opportunities as the rest of us.

Noah snorted, probably all he'd say on the topic, though I knew he agreed with me. "Will you go back to Wisconsin?"

Riley glanced my way. "No reason to go back."

I knew why. I also knew she didn't want to talk about it. Her long fingers rubbed the stone she'd picked up, turning it around and around in her hand, and I searched my mind for a topic to distract Noah. Once he had his hooks in, he was hard to deter.

Riley didn't need me to rescue her though. A fact I kept forgetting.

She turned her smile on Noah. "Where did you live before TU?"

He blinked. "California. Bay area. TU offered me a scholarship, but I almost went to a UC school. My counselor insisted I'd be stupid to pass up the opportunity, so here I am."

"Here we are," she repeated quietly.

Mac returned with a second round and quickly changed the subject to Eva's competition that week. We stayed another hour talking about everything except football, and though she was contributing, I didn't think Riley paid much attention.

She mumbled the right responses, but her eyes were far away. I had to fight the urge to touch her—to break her distraction and make her focus on me just one more time before we had to go our separate ways.

Instead, I waited until Mac and Noah moved around the fire to start cleanup, then leaned into her space. "If you were done with Wisconsin, why SWU?"

She threw the pebble into the brush. "They let me play."

13

Riley

"Fixing the car is more expensive than fixing your attitude," I muttered to myself as I fought the urge to slam my door closed.

A lesson from my dad I hadn't thought about in years. He'd been popping up in my thoughts a lot lately—since I moved to Texas to play for a D1 football program, which had always been his dream for me.

I took a deep breath that didn't really help and stared up at the sky. Clouds mercifully blocked the heat of the sun, but I was still rage sweating. Thunder rolled in the distance, warning of the incoming storm Eva had mentioned before I left for my appointment with Professor Declann more than an hour ago.

The woman refused to join the digital age and required me to drive to her office for the meeting. I'd done as she'd asked, then sat quietly while she snidely listed all the ways I was wasting university resources. *No special treatment in my class simply because you're playing off your gender to gain attention.*

The attitude was nothing new, but Parker, Mac, and the

rest had lulled me into a false sense of belonging. Not everyone wanted to see me succeed. I let the car door click quietly shut and vented my anger by strangling the living fuck out of the paper she'd given me.

Suggestions for ways to improve my grade—except all she'd put on there was the stuff I'd gotten wrong. I was pretty sure the university required her to have a meeting like this where she attempted to help before letting her fail someone. It wasn't a reassuring thought.

After that first D, I'd been doing better up until last week. Coincidentally, the week I'd refused to let Parker come over for our study naps. Also, the week we had our second test in the class.

I'd turned in A-level homework for weeks, but a second D on the test brought my grade right back down. Professor Declann had tried to look sympathetic, but she didn't put a lot of effort into hiding the smug surety that I was going to fail.

We had two more tests and a final in addition to the homework. I had time to bring the grade up to a B, but the damn paper informed me I wasn't meeting the classroom requirements for participation either.

Red hot rage made me want to punch something, but I knew better than to use anger to fuel aggression. Another lesson from my dad.

Instead, I started the hike to my apartment, hoping Eva wasn't home so I could sneak off to the weight room without her giving me the judgy eyes. Technically, I didn't have training today, but I needed a release.

Besides, Parker and the others would be crowding onto our tiny couch for movie night soon. I wasn't angry at Parker. Despite pushing the boundaries of friendship, our study sessions had helped.

I'd been the one who stupidly decided I didn't need them anymore. My steps slowed as I approached our hallway. The real truth was I'd given in to my fear. This last week I'd pulled back from Parker because I looked forward to my time with him all day. More than practice. More than playing.

No matter how much I told myself we were just friends, my heart didn't believe it. I'd had two weeks of no studying, no cuddling, no comfort, and I hated it.

I needed his help, but I was afraid I'd make a stupid decision if I spent enough time with him alone—like asking him to stay the night, in the naked, non-friend zone way.

The apartment was dark when I entered, but something thumped in Eva's room. Either we were being robbed, good luck there, or Eva was home. I tried to sneak through the living room, but she burst through her door before I could make it to safety.

"There you are. Come on, we're going to be late."

I sighed and dropped my backpack on the couch. "I'm not in the mood to go out tonight."

"Good. We're going in. Mac insisted on hosting movie night because they got some new streaming service they wanted to try out."

"I don't do movie night."

She crossed her arms. "There's a first time for everything. That douchey professor probably got your panties in a twist again, and you need something besides lifting weights to release steam."

"Can a female professor be douchey?"

Her mouth snapped shut for a second and her head tilted. "I'm not sure, but you're not changing the subject on me. We're going across the hall to spend time with our friends."

"I spend time with them all the time," I muttered.

Eva hooked her arm through mine. "Well, I don't, and I want you there too. It's more efficient to see all my friends at once."

I groaned. "Fine. Give me two seconds to change."

She studied my leggings and tank top, then shook her head. "Nope. If I let go, you'll try to escape through the window."

I narrowed my eyes at her, but she didn't relent. Despite her creepily accurate prediction—yes, I was considering crawling through my window—her presence was taking the edge off my anger. It was hard to be mad around Eva or Mac.

"Can I at least grab my phone?"

She hauled me to my backpack so I could shove my phone in the thigh pocket of my leggings. I could always use it as an excuse to leave if I needed to get away. Not that she wouldn't follow me, but at least the others would probably stay put.

Eva beamed up at me. "Okay, let's go. I'm starving, and Mac promised pizza."

To no one's surprise—at least not mine—movie night was awkward. The guys' place smelled like bacon and burnt popcorn, but it wasn't too bad. The giant couches were a nice touch, as was the giant flat screen on the wall, but I couldn't focus on the movie.

Stuffed with pizza, I sat stiffly in one corner of the couch next to Parker, trying not to inadvertently make sex noises every time his fingers brushed my hair. He'd stretched his arm out behind me, and I wanted to curl into him the way we had countless times before in my bed.

By the time we made the halfway point in the movie, I'd given up and let myself relax against him. A slow burn warmed me from the inside out, reminding me why I'd distanced myself from him in the first place.

I liked him too much. My mind jumped from memory to memory of Parker in my room, insisting on a montage of happy moments I'd thrown away just to tank my grade again.

In the middle of my internal struggle, my cell phone buzzed against my leg. I fished it out and frowned down at the unfamiliar number with the Wisconsin area code. There were a few people back at SWU that I'd consider friends, but they were just as busy as me during the season.

I thought about letting it go to voicemail, but I'd feel guilty if I blew off my old coach. He'd taught me a lot about how to deal with the haters. The movie was loud, so I slipped past everyone to find some quiet.

The weight of Parker's gaze followed me until I turned the corner into the galley kitchen. I took one last look at the number I didn't recognize, then shrugged and answered.

"Hello?"

"Hey there, Lola girl."

My whole body clenched at the raspy voice.

"How'd you get this number?"

"Is that any way to greet your favorite uncle?"

"You were Dad's step-brother. That doesn't make you my uncle."

"The law disagrees with you there, Lola girl."

My teeth ground together with enough force to make my jaw ache. "Don't call me that."

George laughed and devolved into a coughing fit. "When are you coming home? The shower in the big bathroom is leaking something fierce."

I switched the phone to my other ear and ventured farther into the kitchen, leaning against the sink. "I told you.

I'm not coming back. You were the one who insisted on living there—figure it out for yourself."

My throat nearly closed on the words. He didn't give a shit about the plumbing. "Uncle" George called me every couple of months to try to get me to return to Brookville, Wisconsin for the express purpose of locking me down as his golden goose. His entitled ass thought he'd earned it by acting as my dad's manager in the early years of his career. Unfortunately, a state judge agreed.

As the beneficiary of Dad's estate, I was ordered to pay support for George while he burned through several other high-profile businesses. Except I didn't have full access to my dad's money until I turned twenty-five. Our solution was to let George live in my old house and give him most of my trust stipend until the rest of the money was released to me.

I had enough to cover the rest of my college expenses after my scholarship, but it was a paltry amount compared to what he got.

"I could call a plumber, but he's going to charge a godawful amount. I'd hate to have to report to the authorities that you're not fulfilling your end of the deal," he wheezed.

He could easily afford a plumber, and nowhere did it say I had to personally respond to his every need. This phone call was harassment, pure and simple.

I closed my eyes and rubbed the building pressure at my temples. "It's the middle of football season. Even if I wanted to come home—which I don't, to be clear—I couldn't get away right now."

He laughed again, this time with an edge of mockery. "C'mon now. Aren't you a little old to be chasing that fantasy? Girls can't play football. Your team will survive without your fine ass cheering them on from the bench."

"Listen, you sexist parasite, I've followed the court order to the letter. I'm not your property manager. Call a plumber or don't. I'm not coming back."

I couldn't choke out the word home one more time. The house where I'd lived with Dad had stopped being home after he died. When George had moved in, he'd destroyed any remnants that remained. Hot tears pricked my eyes, both at the sharp memory and at my inability to do anything about the situation.

George laughed on the line, but I stabbed at the screen to end the call. If the asshole really did call the case worker, I'd deal with it then.

A telltale shiver of awareness raised the hair on my arms a second before Parker spoke from behind me.

"You okay?"

His quiet presence should have surprised me. Booming explosions and Mac's chatter came from the living room, so I knew the others were still watching the movie. Parker had known though. Somehow, from the other room, he'd known I wasn't okay.

The question was a courtesy. I swiped at my cheeks before turning, but the effort was in vain. Parker could read me from across a football field. The two-foot gap in the kitchen was nothing.

"Yeah, I'm fine. I just need a minute alone." I didn't wait for him to respond, simply walked past him out of the kitchen and down the hallway toward the bedrooms.

It figured Parker would come looking for me when I was at my weakest. I hated feeling out of control, and everything was spiraling that direction. The stupid Human Sexuality class, our shaky football game, now George—I should have told Eva no tonight and gone to the weight room. At least there no one would see me break.

Parker didn't waste any time. I'd barely made it to the closest door before he caught up to me. "Not that one."

His words halted me with my hand on the knob, but I didn't dare look at him. "What's the difference?"

"That one is Mac's room. Mine's at the end. No one will bother you in there, and I have my own bathroom."

Dim light from the living room cast shadows across his face when I turned away from the door. Parker didn't move closer, didn't try to take control or insert himself into my issues. He waited to see what I'd do.

I could escape to my apartment, but that would get Eva's attention. I could try to suck up the helpless anger coursing through me, go back and fake my way through the rest of the movie. Or I could stop fighting so hard.

The choice was easy. I didn't actually want solitude. I wanted him.

"Show me."

Parker took my hand, linking our fingers together as he led me to the door at the end of the hall. His room was bigger than mine, and cleaner, dominated by a giant bed on the far wall. The lock clicked behind me, almost drowned out by the rain spattering against his window.

I wondered if he was keeping the others out or keeping us in. I didn't bother to turn, but Parker answered my silent question.

"Mac doesn't respect closed doors. You can leave whenever you want."

The room smelled like fresh linens, which was weird because I'd never associated that smell with actual linens before. I took a couple of steps, examining Parker's inner sanctum without actually seeing anything, but my momentary distraction didn't alleviate the knot in my chest.

When I stopped, my bravado crumbled. I sucked in a

shuddering breath, unsure of what I wanted now that I was here.

Parker squeezed my fingers, then circled me. He didn't push, only slid his hand around the back of my neck and into my hair to pull me close.

I buried my face in his chest and held on tight. We both took a deep breath, and everything relaxed. This was home. *He* was home for me—the safe space I'd lost all those years ago. I didn't know how it had happened, but I was done denying the truth.

After the last few weeks, I wanted nothing more than to pull him down onto the convenient bed and take advantage of the locked door until we had to go back to school. I clutched Parker's shirt as he trailed his fingers up and down my back.

"Talk or sleep?"

It was the question he always asked at the end of our study sessions. Until I'd stopped letting him in.

"Both?"

He chuckled. "Okay, you decide which you want to do first."

I nodded, but neither of us moved. This time was different than all the other ones before. I wasn't trying to fool myself into thinking we were indulging in a harmless nap. If—when—I crawled into bed with him, it would be because I wanted Parker, not sleep.

14

Riley

"My dad had a lot of money..." I trailed off, unsure if that was the right place to start.

Parker drew away enough to lift my chin until I met his eyes. "You don't have to tell me."

I wanted to. The urge bubbled up inside me with all the words I couldn't say—the secrets I wasn't willing to share with most people. But Parker wasn't most people.

He searched my face, then led me to his bed, flipping back the covers. "Don't worry. The sheets are clean. I wash them every Sunday. My mom would murder me if I brought someone in here with a mess."

A giggle slipped out, and I slapped a hand over my mouth. "I believe that. Your mom is awesome and terrifying."

"She is." He smiled and pulled me down with him onto the mattress. We settled into our usual position with Parker on his back and me curled against his side. I tucked my feet under the blanket and let him take some of the weight I'd been carrying.

"I'm the beneficiary of his estate, but all the assets are held in a trust for me until I turn twenty-five."

"Who was on the phone?"

"My dad's stepbrother, George. He showed up less than a year after Dad died, claiming he should have been included in the will. I was a freshman at SWU at the time, living in our old house and trying to ignore all the ghosts haunting me around every corner."

"And playing football."

A smile slipped out despite the depressing topic. "Yes, and playing football. George sued the estate, and a sympathetic judge ruled in his favor. He was awarded part of the house, and a monthly support payment. I didn't care by that point. I was going to sell the house as soon as I turned twenty-five anyway, and there was more than enough money in the estate. Except I couldn't change the terms of the trust."

Parker tensed. "What happened?"

"He claimed I was withholding his rightful assets and tried to sue me for all of it. I may have lost my temper and lunged at him, which his PI conveniently caught on film. He threatened to have me arrested for assault, and he made it clear he'd take the story to every journalist who would listen."

"Lorelai, please tell me you didn't give that asshole your inheritance," Parker said through a clenched jaw.

"No, we came to an agreement through mediation. George preferred to use the legal system as much as possible to manipulate me. I'd give him most of my stipend, let him live in the house with me, and agree to an environment free of threats."

"What the fuck does that mean?"

"I had to be nice to him or he'd tattle. The bullshit

assault charge would go forward, and my coach at SWU wouldn't have had a choice but to suspend me while they investigated."

He threaded his fingers through my hair, tugging gently. "And by then it would be too late. Your reputation would be trashed."

"Yeah. I just wanted to play and be left alone. George made my life a living hell until I gave in."

I hated that part of the story—where I wasn't strong enough to defy him. The storm worsened outside, sending flashes of lightning streaking across the sky, but I felt safe with Parker. Cocooned in his dim room, in his bed with him wrapped around me, the shit with George seemed like it had happened to someone else.

Parker tugged on my hair until I raised my chin to meet his gaze. "Your transfer to TU was about more than playing football."

I propped myself up on his chest. "Don't get me wrong— I'd have jumped at this chance no matter what. But after two years of dealing with George's constant demands, I couldn't pack my bags fast enough."

Parker grunted in assent, subtly shifting his hips away from me. We'd done this enough that his hard-ons were nothing new.

"Why does he want you to come back?"

He'd nailed the part I still didn't understand. All evidence pointed to George being better off with me gone, but he kept searching me out.

I shook my head. "I honestly don't know. My best guess is that he likes having me under his control. Maybe he's hoping to find some other way to weasel himself into the estate. He can't truly get in my way because he loses his leverage if I stop playing football."

"Has he ever..." Parker didn't need to finish the sentence for me to understand.

"No. He's a horrible human being, but he's never crossed that line."

His shoulders relaxed, and he pulled me back down to kiss my forehead. "Want me to sic my mom on him?"

A laugh burst out of me at the unexpected threat. "Thanks, but I don't want your mom involved in my sordid past."

"Nothing sordid about it. He took advantage of you when you were grieving."

Tears threatened again, and I cursed the emotions hiding just under the surface. I needed them to burrow down so I could enjoy Parker's soft bed and hard body.

"I'd make it better if I could," he whispered into the dark.

"You already are."

His lips brushed my temple. "Go to sleep, Lorelai."

As if he'd flipped a switch, my eyes became heavy and lethargy seeped into my muscles. I hadn't been tired when we came in here, but telling him about George had exhausted me. I didn't think I'd given him enough information to make him suspicious about my dad, but the potential for discovery was always in the back of my mind.

Would it be so bad if Parker found out? Not any worse than someone discovering that we couldn't keep our hands off each other in the most frustrating way possible.

I was almost asleep when Parker grazed my ass and trailed his hand down my thigh. Before I could stop it, a moan slipped out as my half-dreaming brain screamed *finally*. Under my fingers, his abs clenched, but I didn't get the result I wanted.

He paused, then pulled my phone from the pocket in my

leggings and set it on the bedside table next to him. I slipped back down into sleep, disappointed and horny, as he covered us both with the blanket.

———

THE ROOM WAS dark when I opened my eyes. For a long moment, I looked around at the strange configuration with confusion. The window was on the wrong side of the room, and the air smelled way too fresh.

Parker made a gruff noise behind me, and the last few hours came rushing back. He was plastered against my back, arms banded around my middle where my tank top had ridden up. His fingers grazed back and forth across my stomach, igniting a slow burn.

My phone chimed with a message, probably what had woken me up, but I couldn't see it anywhere. Another chime, and the light flashed in the room from behind me. Right. Parker had put it on his table when I'd thought he was groping me.

I started to extricate myself from Parker's hold, but his arms tightened.

"Don't leave," he whispered.

Not asleep, then. "I'm not leaving. My phone is going off."

He found my hand and laced our fingers together over my stomach. "Ignore it. Everyone who matters knows where you are."

And who I was with. Which was the problem. I needed to do damage control before Eva or, god forbid, Mac blabbered to the wrong people.

"They won't say anything, Lorelai." Parker nuzzled my hair. "Stay with me."

This was my favorite Parker—warm from sleep, voice rough, and not afraid to touch me. I didn't bother questioning how he knew what I'd been worrying about. We had the same concerns.

I trusted him to know what our friends would do, but a prickle of guilt made me try again. "I need to check if it's Eva. She might have an emergency."

"She'll call Mac in an emergency."

"Still, I'd be a shitty friend if I didn't check. I'd think you'd appreciate my friend skills."

Normally, he backed down when I teased him about being friends, but tonight, he wasn't playing. His arms didn't loosen one bit.

"I don't want to be your friend," he said quietly into my ear. "I want to be able to touch you." His lips skimmed my neck, and my breath hitched. "Kiss you." A shiver ran down my back as he rolled his hips against my ass. "Fuck you."

Hell. Yes. My body was instantly on board, but admitting the truth didn't change the circumstances.

He slipped a leg between mine from behind and did that dirty roll again. "I want to wake up tomorrow with you curled around me in my bed."

My eyes closed for a long beat as I tried to remember my weak protests. "We can't. The university—"

"We can. They don't get to dictate my feelings or who I have them for."

"If this got out, the press would jump all over themselves to prove every stereotype of female athletes correct. Even if the administration looked the other way, any hope I had of being taken seriously would be gone."

His movements stilled, and he loosened his hold enough to let me turn and meet his eyes. "I know. That's why it won't get out. What we do in private is for us. No one else gets a say, and no one else needs to know."

I frowned. "You want me to be your dirty little secret?"

Parker dropped his forehead to mine. "Lorelai, I want you however I can get you. For now, we have to keep our relationship a secret to protect both of us, but one day, the world will see me kiss you on SportsCenter."

A secret relationship with Parker. I won't deny I'd considered it once or twice before, but the idea had seemed crazy. Why would he want to go through all of that when he could have his pick of hook-ups?

Parker could take a five-minute walk through campus and come away with a dozen numbers simply from existing. None of those girls would involve risking his future. Or mine.

My phone chimed again, and Parker sighed, then moved away to snatch it off the nightstand. He held it out to me without checking the screen. I took my phone from him and set it face down on the bed. Whatever messages I'd gotten weren't as important as the conversation we were having.

"We can't let anything that happens in private affect what happens on the field. Promise me."

His gaze sharpened. "I promise. Are you going to be able to hold back when Courtney throws herself at me again?"

I pressed my lips together to keep from smiling. Courtney was a cheerleader—one Eva had trouble control-ling. She had a bad habit of launching herself at Parker after every game. Last week, I'd "accidentally" gotten in the way.

She'd bounced off my shoulder, then stood around looking lost for a few seconds before heading back to her squad. The timing had been spectacular.

I lifted my chin. "You could try stopping her yourself. I know she's half your size, but I think you could take her."

Parker planted a palm on either side of my head, blocking my view of anything but him. "I don't want to take *her*."

"Probably for the best since I don't share."

"I'm all yours, Lorelai."

The possessive streak I didn't know I had came to life with visceral satisfaction. He was *mine*, and I didn't want to keep pushing him away because of what other people would think. "Okay. I can keep a secret if you can."

"For you, I can do anything."

"Are we crazy?"

A wicked smile curved his lips. "Yes. No take-backs. Now lose the pants."

I feigned shock. "On the first date?"

Parker chuckled. "Oh, this isn't our first date."

"Are you referring to the time you tried to kick me out of the weight room and called me a ball bunny?"

He winced. "At least I didn't accept when Mac offered to share you with me."

My mouth opened then closed again. "I'm not sure how to feel about that."

"Flattered. Definitely flattered. And I was referring to the night I almost kissed you outside your apartment."

My knee-jerk reaction was to argue. I wouldn't consider staying up late talking a date. Up until he walked me to my door, he could have been with any of his teammates. But the ending... that brief moment in Parker's arms was seared into my memory.

I curled my fingers into the neck of his shirt and pulled him down to me. "Just because you wanted me doesn't make it a date."

His nose brushed mine. "Agree to disagree. Do I get to call this a date?"

"I could be convinced," I murmured.

"Does this mean I finally get to kiss you?"

I didn't answer him with words. My hand curled around the back of his neck as I closed the distance between us. I kissed him softly, slowly, savoring the feel of his mouth on mine.

Parker's weight came down on me inch by inch until I was pressed into the mattress. His thumb skimmed my jawline, reverent and gentle. Warmth spread like honey everywhere we touched, and he still wasn't close enough.

I'd been with guys before, but Parker set a different mood. There was no rush to the finish line. He kissed me like we had endless time, with no destination or motive. In the dark, there were only hands and lips and tongues building a sweet ache.

"Stay the night," he whispered again.

A lust-infused fog had taken over my brain, but I mumbled a yes before hauling him back to me. The slow rhythm we'd built incinerated in a rush of need as the excuses keeping us apart became irrelevant.

Our mouths fused, taking and giving, with no space between us. I curled one leg around Parker's waist, and he groaned at the extended contact. My hips moved with my mouth, pressing myself against the hard length of him. I was hot and wet, and I wanted him inside me.

Parker stroked my leg, then broke the kiss to lean back. He hooked his fingers in the waistband of my leggings and undies, dragging them down until I could kick them off. On the way back up, he trailed his hand along my calf, my thigh, my hip, before circling around to my pussy where I wanted him.

He kissed his way down my neck and plucked at the fabric of my tank. "Take this off."

I sat up enough to yank the shirt and sport bra over my head, tossing it somewhere in the room, but he didn't follow me back down. Instead, he slowly pushed two fingers inside me while his thumb circled my clit.

A whimper escaped me, and I clenched around him, reaching for the bulge in his sweats. "You're wearing too many clothes."

He caught my hand, raising it above my head to grasp the headboard. "My clothes are staying on this time. I've dreamed of you naked underneath me, and I'm not going to rush this."

I lost the ability to speak when his head lowered to my breasts. With one hand holding mine in place above us and the other fucking me, he sucked a nipple into his mouth, making me arch up off the bed.

"That's it," he groaned. "Let go for me."

Parker knew exactly how to touch me—when to be rough and when to tease. I lifted my hips to meet his movements, quickly climbing as I grasped the sheet next to me.

Tingles built in a tight spiral, and I gasped for air. So close.

At the last second, his mouth took mine, swallowing my cry when I came. White stars burst behind my lids as ripples of pleasure swept over me. He didn't let up after the first crushing wave, taking me higher and stretching out the orgasm into an endless moment of euphoria.

His mouth left mine to press against my ear. "You're fucking beautiful when you come."

Parker pulled his hand away, and I floated down from the high, completely spent. I met his gaze as he sucked his fingers into his mouth. Despite having the best orgasm of my life literally seconds ago, a jolt shot through me at the sight, urging me to climb on for round two.

His sinful smile returned as if he could read my mind, and at that point, I wouldn't be surprised if he could. I shivered at the promise in his eyes.

"Not bad for a first date," he said.

I made a contented hum and threaded my fingers through his on the headboard. "I'm never leaving your bed."

Parker used our linked hands to gather me against him, tucking his rock-hard cock between my ass cheeks. "I can live with that."

I reached back to stroke him through his sweats. "To be clear, I'm naked and willing."

"A fact I will forever be grateful for, but you ended up in my bed because you were upset. I didn't bring you in here for sex."

"My orgasm says otherwise."

He smiled against my neck. "That was just to take the edge off. I wasn't going to push, but now that we're here, I want to make sure it sticks. Give me one night, and if you still want to be with me in the morning, game on."

I rolled over so he could see the sincerity on my face. "I'm not changing my mind."

"Good, because the only way I'm keeping my hands off you at practice is knowing you'll be back here afterward."

The mention of practice brought me down from my post-orgasm high. "Pretty cocky for a guy who's turning down sex."

"Temporarily, Lorelai. Tomorrow, you're mine." He kissed me, rolling us so I could curl up with my head on his shoulder—my preferred sleeping position.

I was already his. Now that I'd had a taste of Parker, I couldn't go back. His breathing deepened, though I could still feel his erection against my thigh. Intellectually, I understood why he'd stopped us, but I was ready to dive in. I didn't need more time to think about it.

We hadn't talked about the future—what we'd do after the season, next year, after graduation—but I didn't need to look that far ahead. Parker made me happy now. I'd take him for as long as we could make it work. He rubbed his lips over my hair in an absent caress, and my heart turned over.

What else would you let me do to you? Apparently, the answer was everything.

15

Parker

When I woke up, Riley was in my shower. My aching cock insisted we should join her, but a quick glance at my phone showed we'd slept in. A lot.

The morning workout started ten minutes ago, and Coach hated when we missed training. Riley hated it too, but she hadn't woken me up. As much as I wanted a repeat of last night, I'd promised our relationship wouldn't affect the team.

Other than immediately making us both late. Fuck. We couldn't show up late together. For that matter, why was Riley showering *before* getting sweaty in the weight room.

I rolled out of bed and got a whiff of Riley's soap, some kind of spicy orange thing. It had to have been from her since I didn't stock her soap in my bathroom. Yet. I lifted my shirt to my nose, and sure enough, I smelled like Riley.

Normally, I'd take it as a win and move on with my day, but the guys in the weight room might notice. The water shut off, spurring me into action. I changed into clean clothes, weirdly sad to toss the ones from last night into the hamper, and grabbed my gym bag.

Riley came out of the bathroom in a cloud of steam— fully dressed, much to my disappointment.

She scrubbed her wet hair with a towel and grimaced. "I'm skipping the weight room today, but you need to go."

I frowned. "Coach will make you run laps if you miss a session."

"I can handle a little cardio. We can't show up together."

I'd come to same conclusion, but the restriction still pissed me off. Riley didn't seem bothered at all, and I had an uncomfortable moment of doubt. Last night, I'd held myself back because I wanted her to be absolutely sure. But what if she changed her mind?

I crossed my arms, trying not to go full asshole. "So you're just going to bail whenever there's a chance we could be seen together? I thought you were dedicated to the team."

She raised a brow. "You don't get to talk to me like that. You *know* why we can't show up together, and you agreed to it last night. If you don't think I'm putting the team first by sending you off to be their fearless leader, you can fuck right off."

Clearly, I'd missed the mark on not being an asshole. I approached her, then stopped short at the violence in her eyes. "That's not what I meant, and I'm sorry. I know how important the team is to you."

"Do you think maybe you're cranky because only one of us got off last night?"

My cock screamed yes, but I shook my head—the attitude wasn't crankiness, it was fear. "I have zero regrets about last night, but if you've changed your mind, say so."

Her face softened, and she dropped the towel to wrap

her arms around my neck. "I told you I wasn't going to change my mind. I'm all in."

Relief washed through me, sweeping away the rest of the frustration and anger. "All in," I agreed.

I cupped her face, bringing my mouth to hers. Kissing her reset all the fucked-up emotions clawing for space in my chest. Despite me doing my best to screw everything up, she didn't run. Riley wouldn't give up on something she wanted, and thank god, she wanted me.

———

I SPENT the morning stuck in my head. My reaction to Riley and her push back to my stupidity was the first experience I'd had with a relationship in a long while, not that I'd ever dated someone secretly before. Riley had handled my mood swing pretty well, but I needed to get a grip on myself.

We'd both agreed to the boundaries, and it wouldn't be fair to her if I got pissy every time we ran into one of them.

Mac picked up on my mood and played interference while Noah spotted me. The guys circling Mac laughed at his antics as I racked the bar after my second set. Noah glanced their way then eyed me.

"Want to talk about it?"

I did, but talking about it didn't seem like a great way to keep things secret.

Noah tilted his head at my extended silence. "You know I live with you, right? I'm fully aware of who stayed over last night."

His quiet words made me scan the room to be sure no one was in earshot. "I can't discuss it in here."

"Use general terms."

I sat up on the bench and stretched. "Why are you pushing this? You hate talking."

"I don't hate talking. I choose to speak when I have something to say. *You* have something to say."

The location could have been better, but Noah wouldn't repeat anything. He barely talked to *us*. Still, I hesitated. Was this something I was supposed to run by Riley? Relationships were confusing. The truth absolutely couldn't get out, but I trusted Noah.

"I may be making a horrible mistake, and I can't seem to stop myself from pushing forward."

"Do you want to stop yourself?"

"Fuck no."

Noah's eyes flicked to the others before landing on me again. "Why do you think it's a horrible mistake? Are you worried about her?"

I didn't want to have this conversation facing him, so I laid back down to finish my last set. "It's a concern—a big one. We both have a lot to lose."

"What do you have to gain?"

Air filled my lungs as I breathed deep. Everything. She felt like everything. The thought of seeing her later made me giddy, even if all we did was talk. I purposefully steered my thoughts away from what we'd probably do later because I didn't want to show off my dick in a room full of my teammates.

Being with her felt right—as if everything subtly clicked into place when I didn't even know the world was sideways. We were halfway through the season, and I felt like I'd known her all my life.

What did I have to gain?

"Her," I finally answered him.

Noah nodded in my peripheral. "Regular sex can be worth it, but that's never been a motivating factor for you."

I gritted my teeth as my tired muscles strained. "It's not about sex."

He laughed. "It's always about sex on some level. What's the difference between what you had before and what you have now?"

Sex. Sort of. But that was only a difference as of last night. I frowned up at him. "How did you know things had changed between us?"

Noah raised his hands in surrender. "It was an assumption. You're not usually late for training, and she's never stayed the night before." He didn't mention Riley's absence from the weight room, but he didn't have to. She hadn't missed a session until today. "Have you thought about why she's willing to risk so much to be with you?"

I hadn't, not really. I'd thought a lot about the risks themselves, but her motivation hadn't factored in. Something else I should probably talk about with her.

"What do you think about the risks?" I asked him.

"I think it's none of my business what you do with your free time. It shouldn't be anyone else's business either. If Duke can bounce from ball bunny to ball bunny, certain concerns are a little more pointed than they need to be."

"Amen," I muttered.

"But..." He glanced at the other guys again. "Respect is hard to earn back once it's lost."

I wanted to argue that whoever Riley decided to fuck should have nothing to do with her spot on the team. Like he'd said, Duke had a new lady every night. No one questioned his man whore habits.

I didn't.

We both knew that wasn't how it would go down if the

public found out about me and Riley. It would be hot news across the college football world. Playing was Riley's life, and I refused to make her choose between me and something she loved. Mostly because I'd probably lose.

Talk about complicated motivations. As long as she played for this team, she should be off-limits, but I couldn't stay away.

My thoughts dredged up guilt I wasn't sure how to deal with, so I changed the subject.

"Why didn't you come get me this morning?"

Noah snorted. "I know better than to mess with a locked door. Remember that time D's sister came to visit for the weekend? I knocked on his door to remind him about training on Monday, and Chloe answered in nothing but a t-shirt."

I grunted as I slowly moved the weights up and down. "I remember Chloe visiting, but D wasn't late for training. He was never late for training."

D had been a great captain. He'd really cared about the guys, not just the team, and I tried to live up to his legacy. He'd also been a hardass about things like showing up on time and putting in maximum effort.

"That's because he was at Nadia's. Chloe decided to take advantage of having the room to herself to invite some asshole from the hockey team in for a sleepover."

Noah sounded pissed about the hockey guy, but I couldn't work out why. We didn't have a rivalry with the hockey team. It was a little insulting that she'd chosen a guy from a different sport, but D would have kneecapped anyone on the team who messed with his sister.

I couldn't imagine Noah getting in the guy's face when we'd given Chloe free reign of the apartment while she stayed with us.

"What'd you do?"

Noah helped me rack, refusing to meet my eyes. "Nothing."

Bullshit. Something had happened, but I'd have remembered Noah beating the shit out of a hockey player in our apartment.

I wouldn't ask, though. He'd tell me if I needed to know.

Noah wiped his hands on his shorts and took my spot on the bench. "Think about it, Shaw. Football isn't everything."

I frowned at him as he lifted the bar off the supports. My gut said Riley would disagree, but my heart hoped last night meant she'd made space for me next to the game she loved.

————

THE REST of the day dragged by. I was stupidly excited for my Monday afternoon class with Riley. We'd only been apart a few hours, but I was jonesing like an addict to touch her. With practice after, I needed to get the twitchy impulse out of my system before then.

My heart sped up when Riley walked through the classroom door. Her lips pressed together as she confronted Professor Declann at the front, slapping a paper down on the professor's desk.

From somewhere deep in the back of my mind, I remembered she'd had a meeting about this class on Sunday. Things had changed so quickly I'd forgotten, but she'd been pissed off at movie night before George had called her.

A second later, she looked up at me with a half-smile. My damn face went rogue again, and I grinned. I knew I was supposed to treat Riley like any other teammate, but I was just so happy to see her. With her chin high, she marched past Professor Declann's desk, gaze locked on me until she sat down.

She pulled out her notebook and sent me an innocent look that was anything but innocent. "Are you up for studying later?"

I adjusted the perpetual hard-on I'd had on and off since I'd left her this morning. "Yes, but we're going to actually study. What did the prof say in your meeting?"

Riley slumped back in her chair, rolling a pen through her fingers. "I'm not applying myself, I'm behind on the coursework, and I'm a distraction to the other students. She also warned me my grade is currently a low C."

I was cruising along with an A, and I'd done the same amount of work as Riley. "How are you behind on coursework?"

"I hadn't turned in the last assignment yet."

My gaze shot to the professor, neatly stacking the pile of papers on her desk. "She said we had until today to turn it in."

"Apparently, that was a suggestion, and she really wanted it last week." Riley's dry tone didn't hide her frustration.

"That's some bullshit," I muttered. "We need to get your grade up. Did the prof offer extra credit?"

She sighed. "Yes, but the way she offered it was so damn smug. I hate meeting her low expectations."

"Fuck her expectations. Your goal is to hit that B average so you can keep playing. It has nothing to do with her."

Riley's lips twisted into a sardonic smile. "I'll try to keep that in mind while I'm writing a paper on blow jobs in my abundance of free time."

I tried not to stare at her mouth as an image of her on her knees in front of me flashed into my mind. The heat in her eyes told me she knew exactly what she'd done to me. I'd make her pay for that later.

"She assigned you a paper on blow jobs?"

"Yep." She scowled at the professor. "And implied that it should be easy because of all my experience."

Fury burned away my little fantasy. "What the fuck?"

Riley glanced at my face and laid a hand on my arm. "Don't. I don't need you to defend my honor. I've had worse insults from middle school kids. I'll write the stupid paper, and she can kiss my ass when I earn a good grade."

The fierce determination in her gaze went a long way toward calming me down. I'd never had a professor act so unprofessionally. Then again, I was the quarterback of an elite college team. Soren had told me last year he suspected the professors were ordered to go easy on the players.

Riley was a player too, but no one seemed to take her seriously.

Not even me at first. The memory of my reaction when I'd found out she was the new receiver churned in my gut. But blow jobs? I crossed my arms and glared at the woman standing in the front. Sure, we were in a class called human sexuality, but I'd bet Professor Declann wanted all of us to take the subject seriously.

Screw her and her double standards. Screw the university too, while I was at it. I might not be able to shield Riley from the double standard, but I could help her with this class. And then I could fuck her into next week.

I nudged Riley's leg. "Come over after practice and we'll write a kickass paper."

She rolled her eyes. "*I'll* write a kickass paper. You can watch film while I do research."

"Are you sure I can't help with the research?" I managed to get the whole question out with a straight face.

She smacked me lightly on the shoulder. "Stop it, or I'll go straight back to my apartment today."

I leaned closer, careful to keep my eyes on the front. "No, you won't."

"No, I won't," she admitted quietly.

16

Riley

P ractice went smoothly for once. I'd had years of training in shutting out the rest of the world when I played. For those two hours, I could push Parker to the back of my mind, but the second Coach blew the whistle, I became immediately aware of him.

As we headed to the locker rooms, Mac slung an arm around Parker and Noah kept pace beside me. A hotshot and a human wall stood between us, preventing me from doing something stupid, like licking the droplets of sweat off Parker's neck.

I bit my lip. That wasn't my usual kink, but I could almost taste the saltiness on his skin.

Noah bumped me with his shoulder as we entered the tunnel. "Got any plans for tonight?"

My eyes narrowed at his easy smile. "I have a feeling you already know the answer to that."

He shrugged. "You could do worse."

Heat filled my cheeks. "Thanks."

The guys peeled off to their locker room, and I felt the weight of Parker's gaze on me. I met his eyes as he backed through the door, and he quirked an eyebrow. A challenge not to dawdle. As if I wanted to waste any more time.

I'd be happy skipping the stupid paper completely and diving crotch-first onto Parker's lap. First, though, I needed to stop by the apartment and have a talk with Eva.

The flood of texts had indeed been from her, but she'd been gushing about a cheer award TU had won. I was happy for her—they worked hard for their competitions—but part of me was glad she'd been distracted.

When I came home to change this morning, Eva had already left for her classes, but there was no guarantee she knew I'd been missing all night. Most Mondays I left before her to clock some extra time in the weight room.

Two nights in a row, she'd notice. I didn't want her to worry—or worse, ask the other guys about it.

As expected, Eva had planted herself on the couch to review video of her squad. She was scarily similar to most of the good football players I knew in her obsession with improvement. I plopped down next to her and watched the screen for a minute.

I didn't have a lot of experience with competitive cheer, but they looked good. Really good. I couldn't imagine tossing a whole person around the way her teammates did without someone ending up with a concussion.

The view panned to the side, and there was Eva. A black guy with the same build as Mac launched her into the air, catching all her weight on one hand. Eva didn't wobble once. She lifted a leg all the way up, popped back to the first position, then spun down in a dizzying dismount, where the guy caught her.

"Damn, Eva. Why don't you do stuff like that when you're cheering for our games?"

She paused the video and shifted to face me. "We do. I

forgive you for not noticing though, since you're playing in the game. What's the plan for dinner tonight? Or have you finally forgiven Shaw for whatever he did to piss you off?"

I tucked my legs under me and hugged one of the throw pillows to my chest. "He didn't do anything. I just needed some time apart."

"I'm getting a coffee. Want one?"

I shook my head. "Still don't drink coffee."

"I'll convert you one day." She disappeared into the galley kitchen to grab a Frappuccino out of the fridge and raised her voice. "So what's going on? You usually do your own thing after practice unless our illustrious quarterback shows up."

"You and I eat together almost every night," I reminded her.

"And you ignored my question about food to answer the one about Shaw, so that's what we're talking about."

I silently cursed. She'd used her evil mind powers on me again. "I wanted to warn you I'd be gone tonight. Again."

The fridge door slammed shut, and Eva skidded around the corner fighting to get the lid off her glass bottle.

"You spent the night with Shaw!" Her high-pitched squeal made me wince.

"It wasn't like that," I lied.

She scoffed so hard she nearly spilled her coffee. "Yes, it was. Though I appreciate the stone-cold lie to my face. You and Parker disappeared halfway through the movie and never returned."

I pinched the bridge of my nose as she joined me on the couch again. "I spent the night with him. We didn't have sex. We probably will tonight. You can't tell anyone."

She composed her face and took a delicate sip. "You know I'd never spill your secrets... but I am going to demand all the details. He has big hands. Is the rest of him proportional?"

"I don't know. We didn't have sex, remember?"

"There's a lot of things you can do with a penis that don't involve sex."

"Well, in this case, he kept his pants on." Not through lack of trying on my part, but I wasn't going to mention how he refused my very generous offer.

Eva rolled her eyes. "Figures Shaw would be a good boy. I have a bet with Mac that he was a boy scout as a kid."

I jumped on the chance to change the subject. "Couldn't you just ask him?"

"Where's the fun in that? The deal is we have to get *him* to bring it up."

I stared at her pixie-like face, sharp with amusement, and narrowed my eyes. "This is how you develop your dark magic, isn't it?"

"If you're referring to my ability to get people to tell me things… yes. You have to practice a skill to keep it sharp. Speaking of skills, at least tell me Shaw got you off."

For once, I desperately wished I'd accepted the coffee so I'd have something to do besides talk. Warmth bloomed in my cheeks, but it wasn't from embarrassment—it was from anticipation. She'd reminded me that Parker was probably waiting across the hall right now.

Eva's gaze skimmed my face and she nodded. "He's good with his hands."

I dropped my head back with a sigh. "So fucking good."

"I knew it," she muttered. "You can report back about the rest tomorrow."

"I'm supposed to be over there right now. Studying."

She laughed. "Mhmm. Studying. Sure."

"For real." I explained about Professor Declann and the

problems with my grade. "I agreed to work on the paper and study before the fun times."

She whistled. "You're a stronger woman than I am. Shaw is so pretty. If he offered, I'd ride his face until dawn. And don't worry. If anyone asks, you spent the night here."

I reached over to hug her, careful not to jostle her drink. "You're a good friend, Eva."

She squeezed me back. "That's what they tell me. Now go enjoy Shaw's talented... parts."

––––––

Parker answered his door with a frown. "I thought I told you to come on in."

I brushed past him, doing a quick scan of the living room. "At any given time, there's at least a fifty percent chance Mac is lounging on the couch in his underwear."

He shut the door and opened his arms to encompass the empty room. "Not today. He's really proud of his underwear collection, by the way. Noah keeps finding him these crazy designs."

"Are they here?"

The air thickened between us, but Parker didn't move closer. "No. They decided to grab pizza at Johnny's. Noah said they'd bring us some back."

Pizza sounded good, and I suddenly realized I hadn't eaten since lunch. "Are we sure Mac won't inhale it all on the way home?"

Parker laughed. "He likes you, so he'll at least put in a little effort. We can always order more."

Silence descended, and we stood there, a room apart, staring at each other. I didn't understand the awkwardness.

Things were never awkward between us, and we were finally alone in a private space.

Was I supposed to kiss him? Did I want to? Why was he so far away? What should I do with my hands?

I chewed on my bottom lip, absolutely hating the indecision. "What's happening right now?"

He shoved his hands in the pockets of his sweats and leaned back against the wall. "I'm trying like hell to remember your grade is important. I haven't been a boyfriend in a while, but I'm pretty sure I'm not supposed to jump you the second you walk through the door."

Just like that, the awkwardness disappeared. I dropped my bag at my feet and approached him.

"Is that what we are?"

His heated gaze skimmed down my body. "As far as I'm concerned, that's what we are. I guess you have a say, but I should warn you I can be very persistent when it comes to getting my way."

I stopped short of his legs, and he widened his stance. "I haven't been a girlfriend in a while either. Guess we'll have to muddle through together."

He sucked in a breath as I slipped my hands under his shirt. Lifting it to reveal an expanse of warm skin and stacked muscle.

"Take this off," I murmured.

Parker lifted his arms, letting me pull the material over his head. The shirt fell to the floor, and I wondered why I'd never dated an athlete before. His gray sweats hung low on his hips, and I wanted to lick the ridges of his abs, following the V down until he lost control.

I leaned into him, feathering kisses along his jaw as his hands settled at my hips. "I think it's my turn to have a little fun."

"Lorelai," he said reverently.

Parker tilted his head to kiss me, and we both sank into the release. A different tension built with every taste, a slow, thorough exploration of what it meant to belong to him. I threaded my hands through his hair and tried to pull him closer. The length of him pressed against my lower belly, but his hands stayed locked tightly at my waist, as if his grip was the only thing holding him back.

"What about your paper?" he finally asked.

"I'll write it after," I promised against his mouth, then dropped down to my knees.

His head thudded back against the wood, and he reached out to lock the door. I pulled his sweats and briefs down past his ass, allowing his cock to spring forward.

I raised my brows, definitely proportional. Eva would be pleased.

My fingers barely wrapped around him, and I decided to save the V for later. I swept my tongue across the bead of moisture on his tip while I looked up at him.

Parker fisted his hands in my hair. "Fuck. This isn't going to last long. I've been hard for you for days."

I grinned. "Better enjoy it then."

Contrary to the assumption of our professor, I didn't have a lot of experience with blow jobs, but I was a fast learner. Parker let me know what he liked, groaning or guiding me with his hands.

His grip tightened until he took over completely, slowly thrusting into my mouth. To my surprise, he wasn't hard to accommodate despite his size. I glanced up again, expecting to see his eyes closed, but his gaze was locked on me.

"I could watch this all day. Seeing my cock slide in and out of your mouth. Will you be a good girl and swallow?"

Challenge accepted. I scraped my fingers down his thighs, then reached around and pulled his ass toward me.

He didn't last much longer. Parker moaned my name when he exploded down my throat, and I swallowed every drop. I licked my lips and stood, impressed that he was still half hard.

Parker dragged me forward for a quick, violent kiss, then brushed my nose with his. "Give me two minutes," he panted.

My lady parts cheered at his recovery rate. By that point, I was so hot I could probably come from a single touch. Parker tested the theory for me by dipping his hand into my pants and sliding two fingers inside me.

I shuddered—hard—and my knees gave out. Parker's arm around my waist held me upright, but he chuckled as he nuzzled my neck. He stroked me a few more times, then retreated.

"Think you can make it to the bedroom?"

I let him hold my weight a second longer, then pulled back with a sly grin. "I don't know... we're supposed to be studying."

His once-again hard cock twitched between us at my threat. "Take my word on it. You don't need to do *any* research on blow jobs."

I laughed, stepping back to fix my top and grab my bag from the middle of the floor. "Well then, I guess I'm ready for the advanced course."

He'd yet to pull up his pants when I turned and bolted for the hallway. I was fast—I knew I was fast—but Parker was motivated.

I barely got his door open.

Parker caught me at the threshold, and his hands were everywhere. Somehow, we maneuvered into the room, and he kicked the door shut behind us, taking a second to lock it. My bag ended up somewhere by his desk, and his pants lost the battle with gravity.

He kicked them off, completely comfortable being naked in the lengthening shadows of dusk and yanked mine down before grabbing two handfuls of my ass. To my surprise, he lifted me, spinning to pin me against the wall. My back hit the plaster with a thud, and my drenched panties nearly incinerated. I wasn't a small woman, but Parker had no problem holding me up.

I sent a quick prayer of thanks to the years of weight training football players endured. Most guys couldn't handle my height, but Parker and I lined up perfectly. I locked my legs around his waist and moaned when he sucked on my throat.

"Don't leave any marks," I mumbled.

He made a rough sound of assent and moved lower. The tank top I wore didn't offer much resistance to his mouth. In seconds, he'd shoved the material and my sport bra aside to expose my breasts.

I'd never been self-conscious about my body—I accepted small breasts and subtle curves in exchange for the power to play football—but I was intimidating to a lot of guys. They couldn't dominate me, and I rarely surrendered.

Parker didn't try to dominate—he worshipped me. He held me like he'd die if he stopped touching me, and I couldn't get enough. We wriggled my shirt and bra off until the only thing between us was sweat and a scrap of cotton.

He shoved the material aside, fucking me with his fingers while his thumb applied pressure to my clit. My nails dug into his shoulders, and I hissed dirty nonsense at him. He withdrew to line up his cock at my entrance, then stopped.

"Protection?" he asked.

"IUD, and I'm clean."

"Me too, but I have condoms..." He groaned as my hand closed around him again. "Bedside drawer."

In any other circumstance, I wouldn't take a guy's word on his health, but I knew the extensive testing we went through with the team. And I trusted Parker.

"I don't need them if you don't."

He raised his head to meet my eyes. "Are you sure?"

I stroked him. "Yes."

Parker didn't need to hear more. He plunged into me, nearly bottoming out, and we both gasped. Shivers chased themselves up my back as he started to move. He withdrew slowly and pushed forward again.

"Fuck, baby. You feel so good."

The leisurely pace didn't last long. Hunger took over, and he gripped my thighs as he slammed into me.

He swiped his tongue across the sensitive bud of my nipple, then sucked it into his mouth. I whimpered at the sharp burst of pleasure. My heels dug into his ass as I lifted and dropped to meet his thrusts.

"That's it, baby. Ride me until you come. I want to feel your sweet pussy squeezing my cock." Parker whispered the words into my ear, sending me over the edge.

The orgasm came up on me fast, and all I could do was hold on during the free fall. My inner muscles clenched down hard, and Parker's shoulders tensed as he buried himself inside me and held there.

"Fuck, Lorelai," he breathed.

My legs were jelly. If he let me go, I'd slide to the floor in a puddle of happy goo.

Parker shook slightly as he carried me to the bed, but he managed to drop me somewhat gently on the mattress.

"Be right back." He dropped a kiss on my forehead, then strode into the bathroom.

I rolled my head to watch him, but the rest of me was content to lay in a boneless heap. A few seconds later, he returned with a wet washcloth and cleaned me up. A sex god and a gentleman. Fuck, I'd have to marry him.

He tossed the washcloth back into the bathroom and pulled a clean shirt from his dresser, holding it out. "Here."

I raised a brow. "I have my own clothes, and how do you still have use of your legs?"

"I don't skip leg day. To be clear, I'm happy to spend the rest of the night naked with you, but it's going to make studying really hard." He nodded down at his dick, and I laughed.

Parker's shirt was tempting, but it wouldn't cover much of me. Since I wasn't yet comfortable walking around his apartment mostly naked, I took my chances with my wobbly legs and dressed in my own clothes from my bag. He shrugged and pulled the shirt on himself.

A thud and laughter came from somewhere else in the apartment, and my gaze shot to Parker's. Mac and Noah were home. My presence wouldn't be a surprise to them, but nerves suddenly made my stomach churn. We'd officially crossed the line, and I wasn't sure I was ready to test our friends' reactions.

Parker, doing his mind-reader deal, wrapped his arms around me. "Don't worry. They'll treat you exactly the same as before. Mac has been on board with this since the beginning, but if we don't get out there soon, he really will eat all the pizza."

He reached out to unlock and open the door while keeping one arm around me. The spicy smell of pepperoni and cheese wafted in, and my stomach gurgled.

"I could eat."

Parker laughed at my dry comment. "Food first. Then studying. Then rounds two and three."

"Two *and* three?"

"I have high expectations for your stamina." He grinned at me, and my heart did a curious flip in my chest.

For a second, I considered pretending Parker hadn't just fucked me senseless, but Mac and Noah weren't stupid. They'd know. I'd already broken all my personal rules about teammates, might as well lean into the part I got to enjoy.

"There better be pepperoni left for me," I yelled down the hallway, then linked my fingers with Parker's and led him out of the room.

17

Parker

"Mac, get your head out of your ass," I snapped at him across the circle of players.

Sweat dripped into my eyes despite the chill in the air. He'd dropped two passes, but he was my only option. Riley couldn't get free from her double coverage.

"Sorry, Shaw." His lips pressed into a thin line, and the lack of a smart-ass nickname let me know he was taking the game seriously.

I got it. Sometimes, we had off nights, but I needed him to get back on. Or I needed Riley to be faster. She wiped her mouth and nodded at our running back.

"Give it to Holbrook. He can get us the first down. Mac can use the reset." She held my eyes for a long moment, and a terrible, sneaky idea formed in the back of my mind.

Could I make Riley run just a little faster?

She left her whole self on the field, but in the last weeks, we'd been forced to build a barrier between our public and private relationships. Strictly business when football was involved. I'd promised not to let my feelings for her affect the team, but this was a gray area.

Riley lived in my thoughts constantly—it took concentrated effort to treat her like one of the guys. What if I shifted that focus to the game by breaking down the wall?

Either she'd react the way I thought and put that effort into her play, or I'd have a very pissed off girlfriend after we lost. Maybe both.

I sent a look to Coach, who signaled a run play that I planned to ignore. At this point, he trusted me to make my own decisions, though I doubted he'd approve of my methods in this case. The seconds ticked down on our timeout, and everyone looked to me to make a call.

My gaze landed on Mac, and I gave the order for a pass option. He'd understand, and if my plan backfired, I could still pray Mac would hold on to the ball.

He nodded, and the huddle broke apart. I waited a beat, my heart in my throat, to call Riley's name.

"RILEY." Parker barked my name as the rest of the offense spread out.

I slowed next to him, acutely aware we had maybe ten seconds to get moving. "Yeah?"

He leaned closer, practically whispering in my ear. "When we win tonight, your ass belongs to me."

The shock of his comment made me miss a step. We

didn't even stand next to each other in the huddle to prevent a slip, and here he was with the mother of all distractions. I loved his dirty talk—when we weren't about to lose a fucking game because I couldn't get free.

My body didn't care where we were. I was instantly wet and ready for him. For a split second, I entertained the fantasy of coming up with a reasonable excuse for leaving at the end of a game. I could drag him into the empty women's locker room with me. Hell, the tunnel would probably be good enough.

As quick as the thoughts flashed through my head, I regained my stride. Instead of making a huge mistake because my boyfriend needed a refresher on the concept of *secret*, I nodded as if he'd called a play and took my position. With Parker's words circling in my mind, I forced myself to watch the defense. Two guys on me, like they'd been playing all game, but the coverage on Mac's side was lax. The defender kept glancing my way.

The easy move would be to let Holbrook, our running back, eke us out the couple of yards we needed for the first down then stop the clock. Parker was right not to take the easy choice though. With less than a minute left for us to make it down the field, inches wouldn't win us the game.

We needed a big play. Parker would throw to Mac, which meant I had to draw the defenders my way. If I could split Mac's coverage, he'd have more space to catch the damn ball. Better convince them I was the intended target.

Parker rubbed his hands together, like he always did before calling the signals, and the memory of those same hands holding my thighs open that morning sent a shot of adrenaline through my system. *When we win tonight...*

Our center snapped the ball, launching all of us into motion. I grunted as I pushed off. Explosive speed was my superpower, and I used every bit of what I had to push myself farther, faster.

Run. I wanted it to be the only word in my head, but Parker's voice wouldn't be silenced. A tingle started in between my shoulder blades, and I turned my head in time to see Parker let loose with a deep throw.

To me.

I'd shaken one of the defensive backs, but the other was only steps behind me—and the end zone was only steps in front of me.

Mac's guy gunned for me in my peripheral, but he wouldn't make it in time to stop the catch. I pivoted laterally, then spun around the last defender. Parker's pass was high, but I jumped and caught the football with one hand, pulling it in against my chest.

As expected, both defenders hit me while I was still airborne. I curled around the ball as we crashed to the ground. They attempted to knock it loose, but I sacrificed trying to soften my landing in favor of maintaining my death grip.

We hit hard and slid on the grass. Pain exploded across my hip where I took the brunt of the fall, and I gritted my teeth against the smaller jabs from elbows and knees and helmets. A whistle blew, and a few seconds later, a horde of football players surrounded us.

Someone pulled the defenders off me, and Mac offered me his hand. I wanted to lay there until my whole body stopped throbbing, but I couldn't afford even the slightest hesitation. With the world watching—or at least the people in our stadium—I wasn't going to show any signs of weakness.

Mac pulled me up, and the stadium exploded with noise. I held the football up, then let it fall into the endzone at my feet. The team surrounded me, jostling to slap my back, my helmet, anything they could reach.

My heart pounded out a drumbeat as wild as the crowd as we vacated the field for the kicking team. Mac nearly bowled me over to shake my shoulder.

"Yes, RJ. Boss. Ass. Bitch. The world's going to be talking about Riley Jones." He didn't wait for a response before taking off again down the sidelines.

I unstrapped my helmet and smiled at the praise from my teammates, but one voice was missing from the chorus. Parker stood deep in conversation with Coach near our end zone.

The rest of the game passed in a blur. We made the extra point, and the other team couldn't rally. Final score 13-10, and another win in our column, maintaining our unde-feated streak since the Belcourt game.

I watched Parker surreptitiously as we shook hands and headed to the locker rooms. As far as I could tell, he never looked my way. After his ambush, he'd gone back to playing with cold precision.

Anger mixed with confusion and pulsing need as I slammed through the double doors. I should have been celebrating a hard win, especially considering I'd earned the only touchdown we made after two field goals.

The strong floral scent of perfume surrounded me as I headed toward the showers, but my steps echoed dully in the empty room. No one else was in the small space with me, as usual. The cheerleaders came and went while we did the sportsmanship bit. They stored their personal stuff in the lockers for convenience, but since they didn't need to change or anything, it only took them a few minutes to clear out.

I left my gear in a heap near the showers, peeling off my

sweaty underlayers with relief. Once I stopped moving, they'd gotten clammy and cold. This locker room didn't offer separate stalls, opting for a long, open row instead.

The guys' showers reportedly had a few stalls with multi-jet heads, not that I'd ever use them. I had a locker assigned to me on their side, but I didn't want to make anyone uncomfortable or give the wrong idea. Naked, I let my forehead rest against the cold white tile. Why was it always my responsibility to control the way people saw me?

I'd thought Parker understood why I needed to separate the boyfriend from the quarterback. When steam bathed my face, I stepped under the spray, hissing as the water hit the dark purple bruise blooming across my hip. Stiffness had already begun tightening up that leg, but I knew how to take care of the injury.

I'd had worse.

Normally, I'd consider the pain worth it for the win, but was it? Bruises were a part of the playing cost, and I usually wore my injuries with pride. The potential to lose everything from a stupid slip-up was considerably less appealing. *When we win this game...*

Parker's taunt had been distracting as all hell, but it made me stop trying to fight the part of me clamoring to think about him. Turned out all my parts could work together just fine. I'd read the defense and found the speed I needed to create a hole.

He'd done it on purpose. It was the only explanation that made sense. Parker had risked someone overhearing to try to goad me into getting around the defense.

And it had worked.

That part pissed me off almost as much as the risk he'd taken. His stupid penis shouldn't be a factor in my gameplay.

I soaped up, ignoring the urge to run my hand between my legs.

Parker would love to know how strongly he'd affected me, but I wouldn't give him the satisfaction. A quiet, deep part of me questioned why getting myself off in a dark locker room—alone—had *anything* to do with Parker.

I brushed the loofah over my nipples and groaned as the light touch made my inner muscles clench. These days, getting off had everything to do with Parker. He'd know, and I'd have to smother that smug smile with a pillow at the first opportunity.

My head jerked up at the sound of the metal locker room door closing. The cheerleaders had already changed and left, so I should have had the room to myself. Then again, Lizzy was always forgetting something.

Slow footsteps approached, and I considered diving for my towel.

Parker came around the corner, and my heart jumped for a different reason. His eyes followed the path of the water running down my body, then met mine again with a matching hunger.

"Nice catch."

I turned my back on him to wash off the soap. "I can't decide if you're insane or just that good."

"I knew you'd get free."

The soft smack of clothes hitting the ground behind me sent a thrill up my spine. A second later, his hands smoothed across my stomach. Parker kissed my shoulder and pulled me tight to him.

"I'm sorry."

His warmth covered my back, rivaling the hot water, and his stupid penis snuggled against my ass in a hard line. I was so lost in the feel of him it took several seconds for his words to register. When they did, I stiffened. His apology confirmed he'd been manipulative on the field.

"You got what you wanted. We won." I tried to move away from him to turn off the water, but he held me in place.

"We both wanted that win, and I'm not sorry for saying the words I'd been thinking all game. I'm sorry for ignoring you after."

I hadn't let myself put much thought into his actions after—mostly because I didn't want to dwell on the way he could turn his feelings for me on and off. My biggest struggle the last few weeks had been to narrow my focus to my job. Run and catch. Nowhere in there could I afford errant thoughts about the cut of shadow in Parker's bicep as he released the ball.

Duke took great joy in tackling me whenever my attention wavered, though he remembered to keep it easy in practice.

"We're *supposed to* be ignoring each other. That's the deal." I tugged away again, and this time he let me go.

The water cut off, allowing cool air to seep in past the steam. I took a deep breath, shoring up my defenses before I turned to face him. Parker stood only inches away.

He caged me in with his arms, leaning down to brush my nose with his. "Lorelai, I think about you whether you're on the field or not."

"I didn't think I could do that," I whispered. "Focus on the game and on you at the same time."

"You can. This connection is what makes us so dangerous. Use it." Parker knelt in front of me, palming my ass and shifting my hips forward.

I dug my fingers through his hair. "What are you doing?"

"Taking the edge off." He grinned up at me for a brief second. "I just want a taste."

My eyes rolled back in my head with a whimper as his tongue stroked a long line up to my clit. I was so ready for him it didn't take much effort on his part. He growled his approval when I moved my hips in time with the thrusts of his fingers and yanked his face closer.

The low, rough noise raked my nerve endings, sending me over the edge. My legs shook with my release, but I managed to keep my groans quiet by biting my lip.

"Good girl," he murmured, nipping at the inside of my thigh.

So much better than getting myself off.

I slid to the ground in front of him, and he brushed wet hair away from my face to kiss me. Slow and decadent, like we had all the time in the world. I tasted myself on his tongue and scooted closer to straddle his lap.

He flexed upward, rubbing his cock through my folds with sinful precision. The move ignited my sated lull into a burning need. I wanted Parker. Right now. All I'd have to do was lift myself a little to feel him inside me. When I leaned into him, though, he gripped my hips to stop me from sinking down.

With a curse, Parker set me aside and stood to grab my towel. "I have plans for you tonight that don't involve hard tile floors and the chance of being outed."

My heart took off as I realized how precarious our situation was. Anyone could have walked into the locker room and seen us. Granted, they'd have to come around the corner into the shower area, but I hadn't tried all that hard to be quiet.

He held my towel out for me with a lift of his eyebrow. "Unless you want to take our chances here?"

Before I could answer him, Mac burst through the main locker room door calling my name. I lunged for the towel, wrapping it around all my pertinent parts. The timing couldn't have been better because I was on the verge of saying to hell with caution and jumping Parker.

Since I didn't want either of the guys to figure out how close I'd come, I yelled to my inadvertent savior. "Dammit, Mac. I'm naked in here."

"Don't worry. I can't see shit from this side of the wall."

I shared a look with Parker, whose face split into the smug grin I'd expected. He started pulling on his clothes, but mine were still in the locker I used.

"Go away," I yelled, though I wasn't hopeful it would work. Mac had selective hearing when people gave him orders. Only Coach, Parker, and Eva could get him to do anything.

"I wanted to catch you before you disappeared like you always do."

"By interrupting my shower?"

"You're done now, aren't you? Hurry it up, girl. Eva and some of her cheer friends want to go out, and we can still make karaoke."

I crossed my arms and peeked around the corner to see Mac standing in the middle of the locker room with his eyes clenched shut.

"Message received, Mac, now get out."

He hesitated then cracked one eye open, spotting me immediately. "Isn't Shaw in here with you somewhere?"

I glanced back to see Parker fully dressed. He took a step toward the lockers, and I sent him a death glare that stopped him in his tracks.

"Don't you dare go swaggering out there," I hissed.

Mac took my hesitation as an answer. "RJ, I don't care what you and Shaw are up to. Just give him the message, okay?" His footsteps retreated to the door, and he left with a final bellow. "We're celebrating tonight, baby!"

I eyed the impressive bulge in Parker's sweats. "We could try talking him out of it."

He shook his head with a laugh. "Good luck with that."

As much as I wanted to get Parker home to finish what he'd started, Mac had the right idea. We'd had a big win tonight, and the team deserved to celebrate. They'd expect their captain to show up.

Besides, I could use the cool down time to consider what Parker had said. *Was* I holding myself back by denying our connection on the field?

18

Parker

Mac, Noah, and Eva met us outside the locker room, and a small contingent of cheerleaders huddled farther behind them near the entrance to the tunnel.

Riley glared at Mac. "Why didn't you send Eva in, jackass?"

He shrugged. "Shaw was in there, I figured you were covered up."

I pinched the bridge of my nose. "Do me a favor. Don't follow me into the women's locker room under any circumstances." He opened his mouth, most likely to make a smartass comment about emergencies, but I wasn't in the mood after his cockblocking. "Under *no* circumstances."

Mac nodded and offered a snappy salute. "Yes, Cap'n. Sorry, RJ."

She smiled at him. "At least you announced yourself first."

Eva watched the whole exchange with a feline smile. "What were *you* doing in there, Shaw?"

I licked my lips and sent her a grin back. It was all the

answer she'd get. Technically, everyone in our little group knew about my relationship with Riley, but sound carried in the tunnel.

Eva fanned herself and turned to Mac. "Can you give us a ride? I want to change before we had over to Johnny's." She pointed her chin at the dwindling group of cheer-leaders and hooked her arm through Riley's.

Riley frowned. "I'm not really in the mood to get fancy."

It was a solid try, but there was no way Mac and Eva would let Riley out of partying on karaoke night after she'd scored us the game-winning touchdown. The entire bar would be buying her shots.

"Suck it up," Eva said.

Mac nodded along. "You can't leave Noah hanging. He's been looking forward to this for at least fifteen minutes."

Noah rolled his eyes and grunted, which could have meant either Mac was right or Mac was talking out his ass. Hard to tell with Noah. Harder to tell with Mac.

Riley sighed. "Okay, but I don't want to stay out long."

"We're going out to celebrate!" Mac whooped and tossed Eva over his shoulder, running toward the other girls as she laughed.

Riley followed at a slower pace, turning to shrug at me. I met her eyes with an apology in mine. She knew my rules. If Mac was going out, I went with him.

We only made it as far as the parking lot before fans stopped us. Mac wagged his eyebrows as he ushered the cheerleaders and several of his own fans away to his car, but I stayed back. I was used to dealing with fans, and I didn't want to leave Riley alone.

She blushed a pretty pink as several coeds gushed about how cool it was she played football, and a skinny guy with glasses asked us both to sign his TU shirt. Riley graciously thanked them, and when they moved away, a middle-aged lady approached with her hand on the shoulder of a little girl.

I wasn't a good judge of kids' ages, but this one reminded me of when Jaina was going through her 'I'm a grown ass woman' phase at around eleven. She had that condescending look in her eye, but she wore a pink shirt with Riley's number on the front and Jones written across the back in careful block lettering.

The older woman, in jeans and a generic sweater, held out her hand to Riley. "I'm Marian Kelsey. It's so nice to meet you. This is Alyce. She's a huge fan."

The little girl rolled her eyes, but a telltale blush turned her ears red. Neither woman addressed me, so I stayed quiet.

Riley shook Marian's hand and smiled at Alyce. "Nice to meet you both. Did you enjoy the game?"

Alyce shrugged. "It was okay, but the ending was the best." She eyed me up and down, then returned her attention to Riley. "He should have been throwing to you all along."

Riley laughed. "Maybe, but he figured it out when it counted."

Her eyes met mine, and I crossed my arms over my chest to keep from reaching for her. "Sometimes you have to wait for the right moment."

Alyce held out a wrinkled sheet of notebook paper and a Sharpie. "Will you sign this for me?"

The easy smile returned. "Of course." Riley scrawled her name and handed the bundle back to Alyce.

"Thanks. One day when you're famous, I'm going to sell this and buy a Tesla." She stuck the paper in her jeans pocket and patted Marian's arm. "I'm gonna go wait in the car."

It wasn't a request. She just turned and walked back to a dark SUV a couple of spots down from where we'd stopped.

Marian shook her head as the confident kid climbed into the backseat. "Sorry about that."

"At least your daughter knows what she wants," Riley said.

Marian laughed. "She's not my daughter, but I understand why you'd think that. I run STEM and Sports, a non-profit that supports girls interested in historically male-dominated fields like the sciences and athletics. Alyce begged to come watch you play—she earned the money for the tickets herself, but her mom works long hours and couldn't come. I offered to take her as long as she let me pay her for the ticket."

Riley's expression softened. "That's really nice of you."

"I admit I had an ulterior motive. Would you be willing to come spend some time with the girls—maybe talk to them about your experience in sports?" Marian pulled a card out of her back pocket and handed it to Riley. "Take your time to decide. Look us up. I'm happy to answer any questions you have."

A pensive look crossed Riley's face. "I'll think about it. Thanks for the offer."

"You're welcome, and congratulations on the win." This time she looked at both of us. "I enjoy watching you two play together. It's like a dance."

With that strange comment, she waved and walked back to her SUV. I glanced at Riley, but she was turning the business card over and over in her hand, staring after the woman.

"You should do it."

Her gaze jerked back to me, as if she'd forgotten I was there. "I said I'd think about it."

"Why are you hesitating?"

"My schedule is crazy right now what with all the studying." She sent me a pointed look.

I grinned, not one bit sorry for taking up her time. "Sure, but this sounds like a perfect opportunity for you. Don't you want to inspire leagues of future female football players?"

"Yeah, but I'd planned to focus on my own playing for the next couple of years. The inspiring wasn't supposed to happen until *after* we won the championship—twice."

I laughed and fought the urge to kiss her right there in the dark parking lot. As if she could read my mind, her lips curled into a slow smile. The air between us heated, and I took a step toward her.

Mac let out a sharp whistle, shattering the moment and saving my ass from a huge mistake. "Let's go, RJ. I need time to primp before I take the stage."

"You could ride with me," I reminded her.

She waved at Mac and sighed. "I think Eva wants to play dress up. Why don't you head over there with Noah and get us a table?"

I actually *had* forgotten Noah, who'd followed us outside and stood lounging against my car. A cold wind blew Riley's scent to me, and the control I'd gathered while dealing with the public disappeared. I'd never be able to visit the showers without hearing her come all over my face.

An unfortunate situation considering I showered with a bunch of guys who would *not* understand.

Riley laid a hand on my arm, and I realized I'd zoned out, probably because all the blood in my head rushed to my cock.

"You okay?" she asked.

I cleared my throat. "Yeah. I'll take Noah and meet you guys at Johnny's. After..."

Fire heated her eyes, and she nodded. "After."

————

JOHNNY'S WAS a dive bar on the outskirts of town, but they served the best pizza... and they didn't look too hard at IDs. To Mac's eternal joy, they also hosted karaoke on Saturday nights.

As usual the place was packed, but I'd called ahead on the drive over to let them know we'd be coming in with a group. Way back in my freshman year, Soren had worked out a deal with Rebecca, the manager. If we came in regularly and played nice with the customers, she'd give us the big table any time we needed it. All we had to do was give her fifteen minutes of warning.

At first, I'd felt guilty kicking people out of their seats, but they were always excited to hang out with TU's football players. Well, almost always. There was that one time when a couple of assholes on the hockey team came in and tried to swing their dicks around, but they'd been outnumbered and wisely found another bar to ruin.

They may be skilled—for hockey players—but this was Texas. Football was king.

I left Noah at the table, with instructions to order several pizzas, and stepped outside to wait for the others. Night had fallen, but Johnny's had plenty of outdoor lighting in the form of beer signs.

My phone vibrated with an incoming text, and I smiled at Eva's warning.

Coming in hot. Get your eyeballs ready.

I idly wondered if she knew the reason Mac insisted on

coming tonight was because he didn't want anyone messing with her. He loved singing, but I'd bet he'd watch Eva like a hawk all night. One day, those two would admit their feelings for each other, and I'd have to move into Riley's place to avoid seeing them naked together.

Which also meant I'd have Riley all to myself, all the time.

The sign behind me buzzed loudly, and I grinned at the thought. She'd lose her mind if I suggested moving in—not that I'd blame her. We already spent most nights tangled up in bed at my place or hers, usually mine because her bed was a joke.

Luckily for us, no one seemed to care about the comings and goings in our respective apartments. Mac, Noah, and I made ourselves at home in their place, and Eva had her own chair in our living room.

On the occasional night we were apart, I found myself waking up over and over again reaching for her. The world around me quieted while I let the thought settle. I liked the notion of my bed being the only bed she slept in, maybe too much. Riley and I hadn't talked about the future, but I didn't think she'd considered living together—being together—beyond the current football season.

Mac pulled up in his Jeep with the passenger window down and leaned over Eva in the front seat with a big grin. "I got a present for you, Shaw."

I frowned at him, and he laughed as Eva swatted him off of her. The window rolled up, and I squinted at the tinted glass blocking my view of the back. He'd left with Eva, Riley, and three cheerleaders. Had they all squeezed back there or had Riley managed to slip away?

Eva got out of the car first, in her usual party outfit of a tiny dress and stilettos, despite the impending snow. I shoved my hands in my jean pockets to ward off the chill, waiting for Riley to appear from Mac's giant excuse of a clown car.

The back door opened, and the three cheerleaders tumbled out in similar outfits. The last one pulled the seat forward, and my breath stopped. Riley carefully climbed through the opening, and I belatedly held my hand out to help her.

I felt like I'd swallowed my tongue. Like most athletes, Riley lived in workout gear most days. I had a special appreciation for the soft leggings she preferred during the clothes-on time in my room.

Tonight, she wore a shimmery black dress that barely hit the top of her thighs and tall boots that showed off her mile-long legs. With a raised brow, she ignored my hand to hop down the last bit. A gust of cold wind teased the bottom of her dress, making it dance *almost* high enough, and I couldn't drag my eyes away.

She shivered and tugged at the hem, but no amount of pulling was going to magically make the dress longer. I swallowed hard, jerking my gaze back up to her face. She'd done something dark around her eyes, but the smile was all Riley —and all for me.

19

Parker

"Y ou look beautiful," I mumbled like an ass.

Eva snickered somewhere behind me, but I didn't care how stupid I sounded. Mac could give me shit for the rest of my life if I got to see Riley all dressed up. Or lounging in pajamas. Or sleeping in nothing, with her hair spread across my pillow.

The need to touch her locked me up inside.

Riley took a step closer, then stopped herself like she'd momentarily forgotten we had an audience. "Thanks, Shaw."

She patted my chest as she walked past, and I had to clench my fists to keep from hauling her against me. Eva sent me a pointed look as the group of women went into Johnny's together.

"You are so fucked."

I spun at Mac's amused words to find him leaning on the building in the shadows. "Why are you creeping over there?"

He shrugged and joined me. "You and RJ were having a moment. I didn't want to interrupt."

I shook my head, pulling the door open. "It's not like that."

Mac snorted. "I know we don't talk about your sleep-overs, but it is *definitely* like that. I'm surprised I still have eyebrows after the heat you two threw at each other just now. You know I love RJ, but if you want to keep her a secret, you need to stop eye-fucking her in public."

My jaw clenched at the description. Not because he was wrong, but because I'd much rather be fucking her in private. The warning was probably apt too. I doubted the bonus cheerleaders saw anything in the dark parking lot, but I should put more effort into controlling my face.

Speaking of self-control. "Since you're well aware of what's happening between Riley and me, why did you follow me into the locker room?"

He sent me a pitying look. "Because the cheerleaders were getting antsy, and I didn't want one of them walking in on you guys. I waited a full ten minutes first. By the way, I'm not drinking tonight, so no need for babysitting duty. You know, in case you need to suddenly leave."

I nodded at him, mostly convinced he'd be okay on his own with Noah and four cheerleaders, and we walked into a crush of noise dominated by the entire bar singing "Bohemian Rhapsody".

Mac's face fell. "Aww, man. I missed the best karaoke song."

I gestured at the people vehemently singing around us. "It's not over yet."

"Close enough," he muttered.

Our table was full of women, not unusual with a group of football players. Ball bunnies loved to find us at the bar. This time, though, we'd brought the women with us.

Noah sat at the end of the booth, completely at ease as

he moved his head to the music and ignored the cheer-leader next to him sending him hopeful looks. The rest of the ladies took up the remainder of the booth, with Eva and Riley at the other end.

Mac pulled up a chair and straddled it backward in the sliver of space next to the table, leaving me to squeeze next to Riley. She scooted over to make space, but she still ended up mostly in my lap.

The flirty skirt flared out on my jeans, and even in the near darkness, I could see goosebumps pebble the skin of her thigh. I stretched my arm along the back of the booth, trying to alleviate the need to touch her without making it obvious.

"Cold?" I shouted in her direction.

Riley shook her head, and her hair trailed over my neck in silky ribbons. She went back to her conversation with Eva, but my gaze snagged on the scoop neck of her dress. Her breasts looked fucking spectacular.

Mac kicked me under the table and pointed to his eyes. Right. Eye-fucking. How the hell was I supposed to not stare when every move brought her scent in my direc-tion, and I'd been tongue-deep in her pussy not an hour before?

I grimaced at Mac, and he shrugged. No answers there.

In an effort to distract myself, I scanned the crowd. Writhing bodies packed the dance floor, moving to the fast-paced song. I couldn't see past the outer ring of people, and with the low lighting, everyone looked like the same human blur.

Karaoke night was always wild because some of the regulars were really good. Mac included. We hadn't been sitting for long when the DJ, Alex, clapped Mac on the shoulder. They talked for a minute, too quiet for me to hear, then Mac nodded. Alex left with a big smile on his face, and I leaned over to yell at Mac.

"What's going on?"

"He wants me to try something new he's been working on."

I raised my brows. "Like an original song?"

"It's a cover, so I'm not worried."

It wasn't the first time Alex had asked Mac to sing something for him. Alex was a music major focusing on production, and Mac's third love, after football and Eva, was singing. I kept expecting Alex to try to convince Mac to do some demos with him, but Mac swore he didn't have time with football and classes.

The momentary distraction ended when Riley dropped her hand on my thigh to tuck her leg under her. She lingered for a long second, but to anyone else, it looked like she ignored me to talk to Eva. I kept my eyes on Mac, despite every bit of my attention zeroing in on her hand. Maybe we didn't suck so bad at keeping things secret.

Mac thumbed over his shoulder. "Alex is waiting on me. Save me a pizza, okay?"

I laughed at his request because I wasn't saving shit. If he wanted pizza, he could stay at the table. He vacated his seat, and I immediately lost sight of him in the crowd.

Riley's hand slid off my leg, and the loss drove me to do something drastic. I leaned closer to her, trying to make myself heard over the pounding music.

"Dance with me."

She stiffened and scanned the center of the room. If people saw us, they might wonder, but at least I'd have a good reason to put my hands on her. Her eyes finally landed on me, considering.

The air between us became molten. Riley held my gaze

for a long moment, then nudged Eva.

"Let's go dance," she yelled.

Eva nodded, and I moved to let them out of the booth. She led Eva into the throng. At the last second, Riley sent me a final heated glance over her shoulder.

I knew that look—the one that dared me to push a little harder, take a little more. To follow her.

Seconds after they disappeared, the song changed. The slow sensual beat of "Black Velvet" pulsed through the dance floor, and Mac's low croon nailed the first bar. I pushed through the people who hadn't paired off as best I could until I caught sight of two blonde heads, one a foot taller than the other.

Riley and Eva danced together, swaying to Mac's voice. It wasn't quite a slow dance song, but the people surrounding us all seemed to feel the same visceral need to fuck on the dance floor.

Eva spotted me first. She jerked her chin at me, and I saw enough of Riley's face to watch the smirk curl the edge of her lips. Eva's eyes narrowed as she figured out Riley's plan.

My girlfriend could be devious when she wanted to be. With a raised brow, Eva reached out to yank me closer to them. Riley ended up sandwiched between us, the bottom edge of her dress at my fingertips.

Under the cover of the sweaty mass surrounding us, I circled Riley's waist and spread one hand over the warm skin of her thigh. She shifted subtly and my thumb slipped under the material to stroke along the line of her panties. Her arms circled Eva's neck, drawing her closer, as Riley rolled her hips back into me.

My cock strained against my zipper, throbbing from the pressure of her sweet ass.

We moved to the music, me, Riley, and Eva. Most guys would have given their left nut for the chance to touch two beautiful women as they danced with each other, but I couldn't tear my gaze away from Riley.

She leaned back into my chest, letting go of Eva with one arm to wrap it around my neck. Her dress rode up another glorious inch, and I bit off my groan. Eva shifted to the side slightly, close enough to block the view of anyone looking.

Riley's chest rose and fell in shallow breaths. She widened her stance, allowing me access if I wanted to risk touching her.

Fuck, I could love this girl.

I couldn't help myself. I slid one hand to her inner thigh, pressing her clit with my thumb through her soaked panties.

Her gasp was drowned out by the crowd, but I felt it. I wanted to lower my lips to her neck, to suck on the skin there until I left a mark for everyone to see. My hand fisted the fabric of her dress, holding her against my aching cock while she moved.

The room around us disappeared. Football, the championship, our reputations, nothing else mattered but keeping her here in my arms for as long as possible. I lowered my head to brush the shell of her ear with my lips, the closest I could get to kissing her in public.

Riley shuddered, and her eyes closed for a beat. My fingers dug into the flesh of her thigh, grazing her clit one more time before withdrawing. As much as I wanted to, I couldn't touch her wet heat any longer and maintain my sanity.

All my senses were focused on her, heightened by the surreal feel of being completely alone in a group of strangers. Before I was ready, the song ended, switching to a fast-paced girl rock anthem that had the ladies in the crowd around us cheering.

Riley blinked and let me go, swaying toward Eva as if she were drunk. "Thanks for the dance, but I need to head to bed."

She directed her words at Eva, but they were meant for me.

Eva leaned in, close enough that I could hear her words too. "That was the hottest thing I've ever been a part of, and if you don't immediately leave and ride him like a prize pony, we can no longer be friends."

Riley snickered and sent me a loaded glance. "Give me a ride home?"

I nodded, more than ready to drop the façade. With Eva's blessing, I made space to let Riley and Eva move past me on their way back to the table. Surrounded by gyrating women, I sucked in a breath and tried to will my hard-on down enough for me to walk normally.

At the current rate, I wasn't convinced I'd get Riley to my car before I tore the underwear off her. And that train of thought wasn't helping.

I forced a litany of non-sexy thoughts into my mind. Math homework. Winter in the mountains. Sledding with my sister. The time my mom yelled at my coach for encouraging violent plays.

After another couple of seconds, I was reasonably sure I'd at least make it to the table without bending Riley over it. Fuck. Wrong image.

I hurried through the crowd and nodded goodbye to Noah and Mac, who was accepting accolades from the group of cheerleaders while Eva scowled at him. Riley stood at the end of the booth waiting.

She led the way out of the bar with my hand at her back,

and I guided her to my car. The cold air helped clear my head, which was good because I wasn't sure I should be driving while distracted.

Riley shivered under my hand again, this time, probably from the cold. The temperature had dropped while we were inside, and I could see my breath fogging out in front of me.

"I think I have a clean hoodie in the backseat," I offered.

She let out a snorting laugh. "That's the worst line I've ever heard for getting me into the backseat with you."

I smiled as I unlocked the door and tucked her inside. "I wasn't aware I needed lines."

"Apparently, you don't," she mused, but she didn't sound too pleased.

I leaned across her to grab the sweatshirt and drop it in her lap before shutting her door. By the time I'd climbed into the driver seat, she'd pulled the thick material over her body. Despite being super tall for a woman, my hoodie was big on her. It came down farther than the dress.

"We can't do that again." Riley didn't look at me as she spoke, staring out the windshield at the trees beyond the asphalt.

This was not the way I'd expected the drive home to go. That dance had been sexy as fuck, but I'd let my desire for her override my caution. It had felt like we were alone, but anyone could have noticed us. Eva's cover wouldn't work if someone took a second look.

I cranked the heater and pulled out onto the road before I responded. "I won't apologize for dancing with you, but I'll make sure it doesn't happen again."

She spared me a glance. "Any of it. The sexy talk in the game. The locker room. The dance. We're being reckless."

While I'd been daydreaming about moving in together, she'd been coming up with ways to keep us apart. My first reaction was to argue—to prove my point by pulling over and kissing her until she forgot everything but my name—but Riley continued before I could speak.

"You make me forget."

Her soft admission washed away the hard edges of my response. At least I wasn't alone in the feeling.

I reached over to cover her hands, clasped tightly in her lap. "You're right. Today was reckless. I keep hoping..."

She glanced at me when I trailed off. "What?"

"That something will change. Something will let us be together out in the open. I hate the secrecy."

Riley flipped her hand over to link our fingers together. "Me too, but we can't pretend the rules don't exist just because we don't want them to."

I kissed her fingertips. "What do you need me to do?"

She laughed. "Be less sexy?"

I pretended to wince. "Sorry, babe. Do you have a second option?"

Her thumb traced a vein on the back of my hand, and the sound of her steady breathing filled the space between us until she shook her head.

"I don't know. Football used to be my whole life, but..."

It was her turn to trail off, and I didn't push her to finish her sentence. I understood. Nothing had prepared me for the feelings she evoked. They'd hit me hard and fast, and the stupid risks we were taking should have scared me.

They didn't.

What scared me was fucking up and costing Riley her chance to play. My intention to win the championship this year was within our reach with her on the field, and more importantly, I wouldn't take away something she loved.

I needed to remember that the next time I was climbing out of my skin with the need to mark her as mine.

20

Riley

"I know you're not sleeping, Lorelai, but I'm happy to play until you open your eyes."

Parker lay curled around me, and his silky words brought me fully awake. I didn't open my eyes because he was inventive in the way he played. I'd been dreaming about him, kissing me in the snow on a bitingly cold morning. The reality of a warm bed was much better.

His tongue swiped lazily across the erratic pulse in my neck, causing a rush of liquid heat straight to my core. I tried to squeeze my thighs together to alleviate the ache, but Parker slipped his leg between mine.

He brushed my breast, teasing the sensitive flesh without touching the tight bud. I made a disappointed noise and tried to shift into his touch. Parker chuckled and kissed his way over my shoulder.

"Open your eyes." His hand slid down my stomach, then farther, infuriatingly slow.

I leaned against him, and his cock spread wetness across the small of my back. Parker pressed his palm lightly on my clit, making me shudder. I lifted my hips, chasing the rush.

He pressed a finger into me, and I let out a low moan which he matched with a groan. His tongue flicked over my nipple, making me gasp. This deliberate torture was killing me. He withdrew his fingers as if he had all morning, and I clenched the sheets in a fist.

"Open your eyes, and I'll make you come," he whispered against my skin.

God, I could wake up like this every day.

Our battle ended when he added another finger with the barest hint of contact on my clit. I opened my eyes to meet his scorching blue gaze, like glaciers lit from within. He smiled, triumphant, then kissed me while he played me in earnest, driving me higher with his hand.

I shuddered with an orgasm, and he swallowed the sounds I made without stopping. The burning need never abated, convenient because I wanted him inside me.

Parker groaned when I circled my ass, making him pause long enough for me to roll over. I shoved his shoulder until he lay propped against the headboard, then straddled his lap. With one long slide, I sank down onto him. We both groaned at the pressure, and Parker's fingers dug into my hips, locking me in place.

"Fuck, baby, you need to hold still a second."

My muscles trembled at the hoarse order. I wanted to move. Instead, I dropped my forehead to his, and we breathed together for a moment until Parker's thumb stroked across my hipbone.

I smiled as I leisurely rose and fell. He let me set the tempo, running his hands over my body, teasing my breasts, whispering dirty words of praise in my ear. I could spend the rest of my life caught in the gossamer threads of pleasure we built, each moment drawing us closer.

Parker's name sighed out of me, and he moaned into my

neck—low and rough—as his control shattered. His hips snapped up, shattering the languid pace. One hand tangled in my hair, and he devoured my mouth. My short nails dug into his shoulders as I held on in a wild race to the end.

I collapsed on top of him, breathing hard and utterly spent. Parker's chest shook under me as he laughed.

"What's so funny?" I asked his shoulder.

"I was just thinking about Mac."

I sat up with fake concern. "Do you always think about Mac during sex?"

"I only think about *you* during sex." He rolled over, pinning me beneath him.

This was my favorite version of Parker—warm, playful, relaxed. We didn't have a game on Thanksgiving, so I'd turned off my alarm and planned to enjoy Parker and his big bed for as long as possible.

"So just right *after* sex then? It's the cuddling, isn't it? I've seen you and Mac on the bus..."

Parker brushed his nose against mine. "I'd rather be cuddling you on the bus."

This wasn't the first time he'd made a comment about wanting to bring our relationship out into the open. I knew he understood why we had to keep it a secret, but he chafed at the restriction.

I couldn't fault him. In a perfect world, I'd be able to play professional football, and no one would bat an eye at me dating a teammate. Unfortunately, our world was far from perfect, at least outside this bedroom. On the plus side, he never made me doubt how he felt about me.

"I know." I didn't have an answer for him. My favorite place in the world outside the football field was in Parker's arms, and I'd love to spend the long bus rides to other schools curled up with him.

Parker's stance relaxed, and he lay on his side next to me. "My mom made a good point to me the other day."

"And here I thought this conversation couldn't get any weirder after you brought up Mac," I deadpanned.

He tickled me, and I squirmed around squealing. "She said the football season will be over soon enough. Once it's done, the university can't make rules about who we *fraternize* with."

My heart stuttered at the hope in his eyes. "What about next year?"

"What about it?"

I shook my head and tried to resist his appeal. "We both have another year of eligibility after this one, and I plan to use mine. If we announce we're together, how do we go back in the closet for next season? Besides, the university's rules are the least of my worries if our relationship gets out. You know my reputation would be shot, and yours would take a beating."

He tucked a strand of hair behind my ear. "I'll take a tarnished rep if I get you."

The heart stutter turned into a full-on melt, but I couldn't allow myself to be distracted by the warmth spreading through my chest. "You already have me. Why do we need to tell the world?"

"It's not about the world, Lorelai. It's about holding your hand at lunch and dancing with you at Johnny's and kissing you before a game." His lips teased mine. "You deserve a life outside of football, no matter who you choose to live it with."

Words failed me, so I cupped his neck and pulled him down for a real kiss. "Why don't we make it through the season first, then discuss this again?"

Parker didn't agree, but he didn't argue either. With the

sun streaming through his windows, neither of us thought we'd go back to sleep, but I was willing to give it a solid effort snuggled next to Parker's warm body. Until my stomach rumbled from hunger.

Friendsgiving would start in a few hours, and Eva was probably already in the living room watching the parade. I knew Parker and Mac had filled the kitchen with food because I'd spent the evening watching some dance movie with Eva while he'd been at the store. Now was the best time to grab provisions before the horde descended.

It took another twenty minutes to convince Parker to feed me. Or let me feed myself. We almost ended up back in bed, but my hunger prevailed.

I grabbed Parker's sleeve before he could open the door. "Wait, what was so funny about Mac?"

He grinned. "He developed this theory that the longer the door is locked, the kinkier the shenanigans inside the room."

I thought back to the day before when we'd locked the door in a tangle of flying clothes sometime around noon. And all the other times we'd rushed into his room desperate to let loose after hours of holding back. I hadn't noticed anyone in the living room, but I'd been understandably distracted.

"How did he develop this theory?" I asked.

"Knowing Mac, creeping outside people's doors, but he can be sneaky and inventive when the need calls for it." He tugged me into the hallway, closing the door in question.

"Think he was talking about us?"

"Oh, yeah." Parker nodded to prove his point.

I grimaced. "Great. Now I can never look him in the eye again."

"You asked," he reminded me. "I'm going for a run before everyone shows up. Want to come?"

Normally, I'd say yes. Running was my jam, but we'd stayed up most of the night. I needed water and food before I exerted any more energy. "Nah. I'm going to get breakfast started."

He kissed me, lingering on my mouth until I shoved him away. If he kept that up, we'd spend the rest of the day in bed too.

"Stop distracting me and go run before I get hangry."

Parker chuckled. "See you in a while. Remember, I like my bacon crispy."

I rolled my eyes at his retreating back. As if I could forget. I liked my bacon well done too, but his version of crispy tasted like salty ashes. We still disagreed on doneness every time bacon was on the menu, which was not often considering our comprehensive nutritional plans courtesy of the TU football program.

Another perk my previous school hadn't included. I'd balked at first, but Kelly, the nutritionist, was super nice and really knew her shit. She also knew the players wouldn't stick to a strict eating plan without luxuries like bacon thrown in.

The living room was empty, but I found Eva in the kitchen blowing on a cup of steaming coffee.

"About time you two lovebirds got up. Mac's at the store getting last minute stuff, and I'm not sure I should have let him go alone."

"What about Noah?" I asked, grabbing a cup for myself and switching the coffee machine to hot water.

"Still locked in his room."

I blushed thinking about Mac's door lock theory. Before I could share it with Eva, a rustle in the hallway had us both peeking around the corner. Noah had the door across the hall from Mac, and I'd never been in his room, never even seen inside, not that I'd tried.

Usually when I was going down the hallway, I had a very specific destination in mind and Parker had his hands on my ass.

Noah liked his privacy, but this time, he stood in the doorway with his arms crossed as a brunette in a slinky dress trailed a finger down his bare chest. She said something to him, too low for me to make out, and he shook his head.

He didn't look happy to be having the conversation, but sometimes it was hard to tell with him. Noah had resting blank face.

"Who's she?" Eva whispered to me.

"You don't know?"

Her eyes narrowed as she stared at the girl. "She looks like Chloe... if Chloe were desperate and Noah had a death wish."

"Who's Chloe?" I asked, invested despite myself.

"D's sister. Used to visit a lot more when D and Soren lived here. Is this girl a regular in Noah's room?"

"How should I know? I don't live here."

She stared pointedly at the mug in my hand, my favorite one that I'd started keeping at Parker's. "Answer me this. How long ago did you stop packing a bag to stay the night?"

I opened my mouth, then shut it again when I realized I couldn't answer her.

"Honey, I love you and I'm glad you're still paying half our rent, but you live here now."

I stuck my tongue out at her, and we both turned back to the brunette, who pouted at Noah's stony face before tucking her heels under her arm and sauntering out of the apartment. She didn't slam the door, but it was close.

"I can see you." Noah's dry comment made us both jump.

He didn't wait for us to respond before going back into his room. The distinctive snick of the lock made me break out into laughter. Eva spared me a pitying glance as she plopped down in her chair.

"Are you making food, or should I text Mac to bring home breakfast burritos?" She tuned into the parade and held her phone up expectantly.

Not a tough choice. "Burritos."

"Done."

I grabbed a banana and eyed the weird mix of snack foods spread across the counter. Cut veggies and pre-made snacks were scattered among a truly obnoxious amount of fancy cheeses. My tea bags occupied their normal spot in the cabinet, wedged between a giant container of onion powder and a wok.

As far as I knew, Friendsgiving was an excuse for us to get together and share our favorite junk foods with each other while watching football all day. It sounded glorious, except Parker's friends Soren and Vi would be here too.

Our roommates knew about the arrangement between Parker and me, but the others would be wild cards. Despite Parker's words earlier, I wasn't willing to expand the circle of people who could screw us over.

With a sigh, I dunked my tea bag in my water and joined Eva in the living room. "How long until Soren and Vi get here?"

Eva's eyes were glued to a performance in front of Macy's. "An hour, maybe"

"I thought you knew everything?" I teased.

That pulled her gaze away from the dancing for a split second. "Don't be ridiculous, RJ. I can't control the traffic patterns. Though I did send Vi a better route than the one on the GPS. She said she'd tell Soren, but he'll probably take the slower roads just to spite me."

Her attention returned to the screen, and I smiled into the steam from my cup. Soren sounded like someone I could appreciate. I knew who he was, of course. Former tight end at TU, drafted by Houston in the second round.

He was the one who'd taken down the last coach, with Parker's help. Without them, and Coach Gordon, I wouldn't be here now. I had a lot to thank him for. Parker too, though I suspected my gratitude would make them uncomfortable.

The last thing I wanted was to make Friendsgiving awkward, but I wasn't sure what role I wanted to play. Friend or lover? Parker hated holding back, and I'd lived so long with my secrets I had trouble sharing the smallest part of myself.

I'll take a tarnished rep if I get you...

But would he if he knew how much I hadn't told him?

21

Riley

I vegged in the living room with Eva until Parker came in the door arguing with Mac, laden with bags hung over his arms.

"—sharks aren't the same. You can't make that comparison."

Mac swallowed the food he'd been chewing and pointed his burrito at Parker. "It's a hypothetical. Obviously, you wouldn't want either choice. It's about deciding which you'd hate less." He dropped the groceries on the floor in front of the door and pulled something out of the last bag.

Parker spotted me on the couch, and his grin widened. My heart sped up, and I almost missed the foil-wrapped burrito Mac threw at me. I unwrapped the food and the scent of eggs, bacon, peppers, and cheese wafted up into my face. Parker flopped down next to me while I tried not to shove half the burrito in my mouth.

Mac wound up like he was going to toss a burrito at Eva, but her laser-like glare convinced him to walk across the room and hand it to her. I needed her to teach me that skill. Maybe Professor Declann would finally get off my ass.

I'd made a lot of progress since our weekend meeting, again, thanks to Parker, but she still looked down her nose at me every time I dared to open my mouth in class. We only had a few weeks left, and unless I royally screwed up, I'd end up with the B I needed.

Parker absently laid his hand on my thigh as he finished his argument. "I'd hate them equally, so I choose option C. Nothing."

Mac shook his head in disappointment. "Nothing doesn't teach you anything about yourself."

I strongly disagreed, but voicing my opinion would mean I'd have to stop eating. The burrito easily won that battle.

Parker's thumb rubbed my leg in tiny circles, and I realized how comfortable we'd gotten touching each other inside his apartment. And Eva had been right, we spent almost all our time here, where we didn't have to hide.

My anxiety over the upcoming festivities sky-rocketed— my heartrate picked up, and a band of uneasiness squeezed my chest. Parker and I hadn't discussed how we'd play it in front of Soren and Vi, but maybe we should.

I finished eating and balled up the foil to throw at Mac. "How much do I owe you?"

"They're on me," he mumbled around his second burrito.

Shouting came from the screen and Eva sighed. "They're wasting their freshman talent if that's the best they can offer on national television."

I glanced over to see a cheer squad performing, but the stunts didn't look nearly as complicated as the ones I'd seen her watching in our living room.

Mac snorted. "I could do better than him."

On cue, the guy holding up the cheerleader bobbled her,

and she almost smashed her face into the ground. Thanks to Eva's influence, our little group erupted into criticism, including Parker, and I saw my chance to escape.

"I'll be back." No one responded when I got up and walked into the hallway.

I leaned against the wall next to Mac's door in the dim light and took steady breaths. Parker would find me soon enough—I wasn't exactly hiding—but I wanted a quiet minute to gather my thoughts.

Today would be our first real test since the night at Johnny's a few weeks ago. I frowned as my adrenaline didn't spike with the acknowledgement. Yes, I was concerned about being outed, but Parker trusted Soren and Vi. The risk there was minimal.

Still, my chest felt heavy, and I couldn't relax.

A burst of laughter from the other room made me jump, and the knot inside me pulled a little tighter. What the fuck was wrong with me?

As if he sensed my presence, Noah stuck his head out the door. "Do I smell burritos?"

I pointed back toward the living room. "Better hurry. I'm not sure how many Mac bought, but I think he's on number three."

"Motherfucker," Noah grumbled under his breath.

He came out and closed the door behind him, then gave me a second glance instead of heading into the living room. "You okay? You're looking a little green."

I tried a smile, but it felt awkward. "I'm fine."

Noah narrowed his eyes at me. "You're not, but I understand wanting to get away from Mac. I should warn you, I'm going to send Shaw this way."

"I'm already here," Parker said, joining us in the small hallway.

My whole body relaxed as he slipped an arm around my waist, and I was able to smile at Noah for real this time. "Mac's going to eat your burritos if you don't get in there."

A silent message I didn't understand passed between Parker and Noah before the big man sauntered away. Within seconds, I was calm enough to handle the rest of the lead up to Friendsgiving, but I still needed to talk to Parker about all the touchy-feely.

I hesitated again, trying to find the best way to bring up the topic, but nothing good came to mind. Blunt honesty would have to do.

"Does Soren know about us?"

"Is that what we're doing in here?" he asked, turning me to face him.

"You didn't answer my question."

Parker let out a resigned sigh. "No. He doesn't know. I haven't told anyone. Mac and Noah are aware because they live here, and I assume Eva knows for the same reason."

Warmth filled my face, and I dropped my head to his shoulder. "Eva knows because I told her."

There was a small chance Parker wouldn't react well to finding out I'd sort of broken our agreement not to tell anyone, but he held me loosely, pressing a kiss to my temple. "I trust them, and I trust Soren. You're worried we'll mess up with them around today?"

Relief at his understanding washed away the embarrassment. "I'm so used to acting a certain way with you in your apartment. This is our safe space to be with each other. The only way Soren and Vi aren't going to figure it out is if they're both suddenly struck blind."

He tipped my chin up. "Would them finding out be so bad? I don't like lying to my friends."

I let out a groan. "This is going to bite me in the ass."

Parker chuckled. "How about a compromise?"

Stupid hope lifted my head. "What kind of compromise?"

He played with the ends of my hair curling over my shoulder. "You could call me by my first name."

"Everyone else calls you Shaw. In public, you're Shaw to me."

He stepped closer, not enough to cross any lines, but almost. "In private…"

I flattened my palm against his chest. "We're not in private."

Parker nodded, his eyes hooded. "That's the compromise. We bring a little more of the private into the public."

"That is not a compromise, *Shaw*. That's you getting your way by using your sexy voice. A compromise requires give and take."

"Semantics. Here's what I think we should do. Act like we normally do in front of Soren and Vi, who will figure it out anyway, and trust them to have our backs. You can call me Parker or Shaw or Big Daddy—"

"I'm not calling you that," I interrupted him.

"Your choice. Then you can come home with me for Christmas."

My mouth dropped open. "Are you insane? The playoffs are over Christmas."

He skimmed his hands up and down my arms. "Not actual Christmas. I'm going home in mid-December for a couple of days after finals. I want you to come with me. So does my mom."

Another weird turn in a conversation I was barely following. "Why is your mom involved?"

"I was talking to her about you, and when I told her you

had no family to spend Christmas with, she insisted I bring you with me."

My brows rose. "It wasn't even your idea?"

"I would've gotten there eventually. She wants to get to know you better."

"I thought you didn't tell anyone about us."

"She figured it out before I did. Remember the first game when she ran into you?"

I did. The pretty older woman with the cute bob had plowed into me in the tunnel right before the game. She'd introduced herself as Gina, Parker's mom and biggest fan, then promptly invited me to dinner. It was surreal because I'd been trying to calm my nerves about playing my first game at the DI level, unsuccessfully. She'd patted my arm and told me I was going to be great.

Boom. Nerves gone. I blamed her mom superpowers because anyone who'd raised Parker clearly knew what she was doing.

"Yes..." I drew the word out because I wasn't sure I wanted to know any more.

"She planned the whole thing. Mom has a scary intuition when it comes to me and Jaina. She took one look at my face and decided you were the one."

I heard the undertone in his words—he didn't believe her any more than I did. Would his mom have seen that on his face if it hadn't already been there? I'd met his eyes in the tunnel, and all I'd seen was heat.

Parker tugged me a little closer. "I want you there, Lorelai. We have three whole days off, and I don't want to go a single one without you. The drive isn't that long, and have I mentioned the weight room we have set up in the basement? You could get your fix in without even leaving the house."

Temptation arrowed right through me. Parker knew my weaknesses and had no problem exploiting them.

"What about people seeing us together?"

"It's totally normal for me to drive to Colorado with my teammates. I brought Noah home last year, and Mac the year before."

Frustration sharpened my voice. "Except they won't see a teammate if I go with you."

"Then we make it as low-key as possible. My parents live in a small town on a couple of acres. We don't have to leave the house if you don't want to. It's not like the paparazzi follow us around."

He was right. After the first media push about a female receiver, we'd only gotten slightly more coverage than the other winning teams. I felt myself weakening and tried to be logical. Did I *want* to go?

Yes. No question. I liked his family, what little I'd gotten to know of them at the beginning of the semester. I wanted to see where he'd grown up—what had molded him into the man he was now.

I wanted to spend time relaxing with Parker in a place he loved.

"Okay, if we can make it work, I'll go with you. But I'm not calling you Big Daddy. You have to earn that one."

He trailed a hand up my arm, and I shivered. "That's fair, but you're going to regret throwing out that challenge."

"Prove it," I doubled down.

With a dark promise in his eyes, he backed me against the wall. "Your smart mouth is going to get you in trouble one day."

"You love my smart mouth, especially when it's on your—"

Parker silenced me with a kiss, and I made a throaty

noise encouraging him. His hands flexed on my hips, and I thought for a second he would haul me into the bedroom despite Friendsgiving starting soon.

His hands slipped around me to grab my ass, and I lifted a leg to curl around his hips. Unfortunately, a noise behind him penetrated my Parker-induced haze.

"Oh, shit." A woman with short brown hair and great arms stood in the hallway staring at us.

Parker glanced over his shoulder and echoed her curse. I considered trying to wiggle out of his embrace, but what was the point? The huge grin spreading across her face said she'd seen plenty.

"Later," Parker said to me under his breath. He adjusted himself and turned to face the woman, keeping his arm locked around my waist.

She held out her hand. "Sorry to interrupt. I'm Vi Malone, Soren's fiancé. You must be Riley Jones."

I nodded and took her hand in a firm shake. "Yeah, everyone here calls me RJ. Nice to meet you."

Parker reached out to examine the shiny diamond ring sparkling on her finger. "Congratulations. Nice to know Brehm didn't fuck it up."

Vi rolled her eyes and pulled her hand back. "I missed you, Parker."

He sent me a pointed look that clearly said *See? Some people call me Parker.* I ignored him to try to glance around the corner into the living room.

"Is Soren here?"

She pointed over her shoulder. "He's organizing the food so we can actually eat it. I came in search of a bathroom, but this situation is a lot more interesting." Her gaze darted back and forth between us with what I could only describe as glee. "Soren owes me twenty bucks."

Parker raised his brows at her. "You bet against me?"

Vi snickered. "I bet your control would snap when you met the right woman. You were putting too much pressure on yourself to lead the team after the shit last year. Now, you look happier, and the team is kicking ass. RJ is the best thing that could have happened to you."

I snorted quietly. "Damn straight."

"Shut it, Lorelai," he murmured.

My spine straightened, and his gaze jerked to me. Yet another example of why we couldn't let our guards down around other people. Vi's eyes narrowed, but she didn't comment on the slip.

"I'm going to assume Noah and Mac's bathroom is a disaster. Can I use yours?"

"Of course, Vi."

She patted his chest as she walked past, and I breathed a sigh of relief. My full name wasn't well known since my dad made it a point to keep me out of the media. If we hadn't reacted, she probably wouldn't have even noticed.

Parker watched her go into his room, then shook his head. "Fuck, I'm sorry. It just slipped out."

"It's okay. Honestly, I'm surprised you lasted this long without saying it in front of someone else."

He tucked a wild bit of hair behind my ear. "I'll be more careful. At least we can relax today now that the secret is out. Come on, I want to introduce you to Soren."

Parker took my hand to lead me into the other room. For a brief, insane second, I was nervous to meet Soren. He wasn't just one of Parker's best friends—he was a rising football star, at least according to his stats this season with Houston.

I'd met my fair share of professional players, but they were always presented as Dad's friends. Only later did I realize what they did for a living, and how many other people would kill to be in my shoes.

Soren smiled at my hand linked with Parker's, cocked his brow at Vi, then started giving Mac shit for not saving him any burritos. The sharp bite of nerves faded away when Eva threatened to bar him from the next Friendsgiving if he didn't bring Vi around more often.

No one mentioned my relationship with Parker, and since I wasn't willing to give him up any time soon, I'd have to accept we couldn't keep our relationship quiet from everyone. We'd just have to make sure the few who knew understood the importance of silence.

An hour later, after we'd had second breakfast in the form of a charcuterie board made almost entirely of cheese, I found myself alone with Soren in the kitchen.

He leaned against the counter with his arms crossed over his chest. "So you and Shaw."

I nodded, unable to read how he felt about the news. "Technically, we're breaking the university's fraternization rule, so we have to keep it a secret. He says we can trust you not to say anything."

"Is it serious?"

I didn't know how to answer that. Every time Parker looked at me, it felt serious. He wanted to take me home to spend time with his parents, but we hadn't talked in detail about the future. Parker's grin when I agreed to go with him flashed in my mind, and I couldn't help a tiny smile. He made me happy. Even at the beginning, he felt like home.

"Yeah, it's serious," I decided.

Soren nodded. "I've never been big on following the rules, but Shaw takes his role as captain seriously. He loves this team, and he's going to bring them to a championship...

if nothing trips him up. That said, I think you're good for him. I'm not sure he's good for you."

He understood more than I'd given him credit for.

I paced the length of the tiny kitchen. Five steps, turn, five steps. "There's a solid chance TU is only letting me play for the positive publicity. If I mess that up for them—for instance by dating the star quarterback and proving myself nothing more than a ball bunny—I could lose this opportunity."

Soren scoffed. "You're playing because you're a damn good receiver. If Coach Gordon didn't think you could cut it, you'd be riding the bench."

I stopped pacing to stare at the leftover cheese scattered across the counter, and he let me have the moment to consider. "What was it like being drafted?"

Soren let out a surprised laugh. "Terrifying. And exhilarating. I wasn't convinced any teams would take me."

I shot him an incredulous look. "Are you kidding me right now? You and Derrick Asher were football elite. I can't believe I'm playing for your same team. Hell, I can't believe I'm sitting here talking to you."

He eyed me as if judging my sincerity. I must have passed because he shook his head and grabbed a water out of the fridge. "D was elite, for sure. Don't talk like you aren't just as talented."

I snorted. "Yes, but my pesky vagina gets in the way."

Soren nearly spit out his drink. "No wonder Vi likes you."

A warm feeling filled my chest. Not only did I like Soren and Vi, but a professional football player thought I was as talented as a first round draft pick. Or maybe a second round draft pick if he was talking about himself. Either way, I'd take it in a heartbeat.

As if karma knew my life had peaked, Vi let loose with a triumphant shout in the living room. Soren shrugged, and we followed the noise.

"RJ's dad is Jed Jones?" Mac asked as we entered the room.

I stopped in my tracks. He, Vi, Noah, and Parker stared down at a phone clutched in Mac's hand. My stomach lurched violently as dread stole my breath.

"I knew I'd heard her name before," Vi crowed.

In that moment, I hated her, and I hoped Parker would forgive me.

He watched the screen a moment longer, then looked up and met my eyes. As always, he'd known exactly where I was. Fear trickled through my system as his brows drew together.

Parker grabbed the phone from Mac and held it up. "And you lectured *me* about trust?"

So he had been listening at practice. I wanted to reach out, assure him it wasn't a big deal, but even *I* knew it was. I'd been fooling myself thinking there'd be a right time to tell them—or hoping they'd never find out. Parker tossed the phone onto the coffee table and headed for the front door.

"Shaw, wait." I hurried across the room after him. He didn't slow, but I wasn't about to give up now. "Parker."

His shoulders tensed, but he stopped and turned with a sardonic twist on his lips. "This is what it took?"

The challenge in his eyes warned me that I didn't want an audience for the rest of our exchange. Only a few seconds had passed since Mac spilled my deepest secret, but to my surprise, Soren helped clear the room.

"Let's go for a walk." He held out his hand to Vi, and she nodded at the other three.

Out of the corner of my eye, Eva sent me a questioning look, but I waved her off. Mac ushered her out the door, and the room emptied around us as Parker and I sized each other up.

I'd only seen him angry like this once before, when Williams had been talking shit in the locker room. It sucked being on the receiving end.

I opened my mouth to say something—I didn't know what—but he slashed the air with his hand.

"What else did you lie about?" he asked quietly.

"I never lied to you." Simply held back key information in a stupid attempt to protect myself from the wrong person.

Parker crossed the distance between us in a blink, leaning down close to my face. "Lies of omission are still lies, Lorelai."

I refused to flinch, though inside I was a mess. The thrill of looking up into those blue eyes never got old, but the warmth I'd grown to love was missing. He looked at me like I was a stranger—worse, a disappointment.

22

Parker

J ed Jones. Linebacker. Two-time Super Bowl champion. Hall of Famer. Riley's father. No, Lorelai's father.

At this point, I wasn't sure they were the same person. I wasn't sure who she was at all. A hint of caution whispered through the back of my mind, but I was too hurt to heed the warning. Riley should have trusted me enough to tell me.

We stared at each other across the living room, with the low buzz of a football game as a backdrop. How appropriate.

She'd told me about growing up in Wisconsin, about the problems with her uncle, about her struggles playing a game that skewed heavily male—she'd even told me about her dad, in general terms. In any other circumstances, her dad's job wouldn't matter in the least, but she was football royalty... and she hadn't told me.

My dad had a lot of money... Well, no fucking shit. He'd been paid millions to play, and Riley owned that estate now.

I turned my back on Riley's defensive silence to pace from couch to couch. My mind wouldn't stop sifting through all the things she'd revealed, examining them in this new light. No wonder she had such a solid grasp of defensive strategies. Her dad was a legend until he retired and disappeared from the public eye.

Now I knew why, I guess.

The crowd cheered on the TV as someone scored, but I wasn't in the mood. I grabbed the remote on my next pass and turned the game off. Riley edged into my view as I dropped it back on the couch.

Her chest rose as she sucked in a huge breath. "Okay, I know you're pissed because I didn't tell you, but who my father is has nothing to do with you."

Intellectually, I knew she was right, but her words didn't penetrate the wall of hurt that came with the knowledge. Growing up with Jed Jones had clearly influenced her, and she'd let me believe she'd developed a love of football all on her own. Worse, doubt crept in on the heels of the realization. If she'd hidden this, what else could she hide from me?

She must have read the look on my face because she inched closer. "I wasn't keeping it from *you*—I was keeping it from everybody."

Frustration pulled at my skin. "That's not better."

She propped her hands on her hips. "I can't have secrets? Should I prepare a report detailing all the things I haven't told you yet? Spoiler alert, it's going to be girthy."

"Dammit, Riley, I don't need all your secrets, but this one is huge. I see the guilt on your face. You knew this would be important, and you went out of your way to keep the secret hidden."

Riley lurched forward, reaching for me, but I side-stepped. I couldn't let her make contact. If she touched me now, I might say something I regretted. Even with the resentment and frustration coursing through me, I didn't want to hurt her.

I pressed my lips together until I could think straight enough to consider my next words. Mac, Eva, and Noah had found out along with me, but none of them seemed upset in the slightest. Why couldn't I get past it?

Because I expected her to feel comfortable enough telling me anything—and she didn't. The anger drained away, leaving a knot in my chest.

"You don't trust me," I said quietly.

"I do." Riley took my hand, and this time, I let her. "Parker, I do. I've shared more with you than anyone else in my life. My *entire* life. I'm not a risk-taker, but here I am with you, despite the rules and the potential for our relationship to blow up in my face."

She pulled me closer, wrapping my arm around her waist. "I'm sorry for the way this played out, but I wanted to be accepted for who I am, not what I am—not as a girl player or the daughter of a legend. I'm sorry this hurt you. I never wanted that."

My arm tightened of its own accord, and I dropped my forehead to hers, tired of fighting the urge to touch her. "I don't hide anything from you. I don't hold back. Every part of me is yours for the taking."

Her eyes closed for a second. "This is all new to me. I don't talk about him. Yes, I keep it a secret out of habit in the hopes I won't be judged by my DNA, but I didn't purposely keep it from you. I haven't had someone important in my life since he died—until you—so it hasn't been a problem. The habit of secrecy is hard to break."

The admission helped smooth over the last of my knee-jerk reaction. I pulled her down on the couch, cuddling her in my lap. "Tell me now."

A tear spilled out, running in a glistening stream down her cheek. "He was the greatest man I knew. It hurts to think he'll never see me play at TU. He'll never know how good you and I are together." She wiped the moisture away with a frustrated huff. "He believed in me—always—and I wanted to live up to his legacy on my own terms. Give him a reason to be proud. Show him his daughter isn't the mascot or the team slut. If I fuck it up, at least they'll only drag my name down, and not his."

Her voice cracked on the last word, and the pain I'd felt at the shock of learning the truth faded in the face of her despair. She was breaking in front of me, and I was sitting there like a jackass, making the situation about me.

"Lorelai..."

Riley shook her hair back from her face and tried to take a deep breath, but it didn't help her control the sobs.

I cupped her head and held her as she cried. Now that I'd calmed down, I could see the similarities between her and Jed in her eyes and the shape of her mouth. The resemblance was subtle, and I suddenly wanted to see a picture of her mom.

Between hiccups, Riley wiped her face on my shirt. My girl wasn't a delicate crier.

"I'm sorry," she mumbled as she dabbed at the wet spot.

"Cry as long as you need. I'm not going anywhere."

She nodded, but her tears stopped falling. "I just wanted him to be proud of me."

"How could he not be proud of you, Lorelai? You've worked your ass off to get to this level, and you're the best receiver on the team. Don't tell Mac I said that." I tilted her chin up so she'd look at me. "I throw to you because I know you'll catch the ball. Coach starts you because he thinks you deserve it. What happened to the woman at the beginning of the season who knew how good she was?"

She gave as sniffly laugh. "She's going through some stuff. I blame her boyfriend for making her get all emotional."

"That asshole."

"Thank you for listening, and only being a jerk for a little bit."

I winced as a pang of guilt hit me. "We all have our dumbass moments. To be clear, I will always support you, and not only because I like spending time with you naked."

A half-smile curved her lips. "But partly because you like spending time with me naked."

Just like that, I was hard under her again. I couldn't get enough of Riley, and my dick had noticed we were alone in the room. Horrible timing, since the others would be back any minute. I had one more thing to say anyway.

"I'm sorry for overreacting. You have no obligation to tell me things, but I hope you will. I'll try not to stick my head up my ass the next time."

The half-smile bloomed into a full grin, and she pulled my head down to kiss me. With effort, I kept my hands where they were on her back. As much as my dick wanted to abandon Friendsgiving for another round of naked time, Mac and Eva wouldn't allow it. No amount of locked doors would be enough to stop them.

On cue, Mac gave a cursory knock, then walked in with a hand covering his eyes. "Everything good in here or do we need to take another lap?"

"We're clothed. The coast is clear," I answered.

Behind him where we couldn't see her, Eva shouted, "I swear to God, Shaw, if you're making her cry, I will make you watch every rom-com I own to teach you how to properly grovel."

I shuddered at Eva's threat and waved them in before they made any more of a spectacle. Mac made a beeline for the kitchen, but the others joined us on the couches.

"So," Soren nodded at Riley. "I hear you're faster than Mac."

She laughed, and I marveled at Soren's ability to ease the tension in the room. I blamed Vi for that newfound skill.

Mac came around the corner with his mouth full of chips. "That hasn't been confirmed by any third-party evidence."

Noah raised a brow. "We all saw the ending of the race."

"The race was a tie," he said.

"Sure." Noah waited a beat, then turned to Riley. "Want to prove him wrong?"

Riley shook her head. "Nah, I'm good with the tie."

Mac studied her face, slowly putting the chips down. "Holy shit. Did you fix the race?"

A smile washed away the last of the sadness in her eyes. "I might not have run as fast as possible at the end there."

Mac motioned for her to stand. "Up. Let's go. We're doing this."

She rolled her eyes. "Why? We're on the same team. It doesn't matter who's faster."

"It's the principle," he insisted.

Riley hesitated, and I knew she was trying to salvage Mac's pride by finding a way out of racing him again. Luckily, Mac's pride didn't need any help.

"I'm going to be so damn proud of you if you beat me, RJ. Come on. Show me up."

She sighed and stood. "I'm not dressed for this, and we didn't warm up."

"We'll do a quick lap around the block at a jog." Mac ushered her out of the apartment before she could change her mind.

Soren eyed the door then me. "Should we follow them?"

"No, we have at least ten minutes. Riley absolutely refuses to run without warming up."

"Smart girl," Vi muttered.

Soren wrapped his arm around his fiancé, tugging her closer. "D said to tell you he's sorry he and Nadia can't make it. He's flying his family out to New York so they can spend the holiday together."

Noah shook his head. "That first round bonus must be nice."

Eva tossed a throw pillow at him, missing entirely and hitting Soren. "Don't be bitter."

He shrugged his massive shoulders. "I'm not bitter—D earned that money. With his sister at that fancy private college, I'll bet his parents are thrilled to get a vacation they don't have to pay for."

Soren threw the pillow back to Eva. "Speaking of Chloe... she's transferring to TU for the spring semester."

Noah stiffened next to me, but before I could ask him about it, all our phones buzzed and chimed at the same time. I checked the screen to see Mac had sent a group text to get outside or miss the show.

We filed out the door, and I promptly forgot Noah's weird reaction at the sight of my girlfriend stretching her mile-long legs. The tight leggings she wore showed off every muscle, and for once, I let myself stare.

"Full sprint from here, around the parking loop, and back to the big man." Mac jerked his chin at Noah.

Riley nodded and took her ready position at the imaginary line. "Parker, count us off."

A warm buzz filled my chest when she said my first name, but now wasn't the time for PDA. I gave them a four count, and they both took off. Watching Riley run had to be one of my favorite pastimes.

She took an early lead, and it only increased as her stride lengthened. We cheered as they circled the parking lot, disappearing behind the detached garages and appearing again on the far side. Her eyes locked on to Noah, who hadn't moved, and she put on a burst of speed at the end that she'd held back during the first race.

Mac had no chance. He was the fastest guy I knew, maybe except for Soren who could fly when he wanted to, but Riley put him to shame. She crossed the Noah-shaped finish line a full two seconds ahead of Mac.

She slowed to take a bow, then slapped Mac on the back as he hunched over wheezing. "Come on, slowpoke. Cool down lap."

"Damn, girl," Mac panted. "How'd you get so fast with a linebacker daddy?"

"My mom was an Olympic sprinter. That's how they met."

Mac groaned. "So unfair."

Riley chuckled, heading for the loop again, and Mac followed her at a much slower jog. With the excitement over, Eva dragged Vi and Noah back into the apartment to get first dibs on the pie Mac had brought home.

Soren came to stand next to me, rubbing his chin. "She's seriously fast."

"She can catch too. Knows the game inside and out. Reads the defense like they took out a billboard." I watched her pace herself to Mac. "I think I'm in love with her."

Riley chose that moment to look over her shoulder. She

met my gaze with a smile, and even from a distance, I could feel the spark.

"I think the feeling is mutual," Soren said quietly. "Does she plan to keep going? Try for the draft?"

I shook my head. "She won't talk about it. Every time I bring up her plans after college, she takes her top off."

Soren nodded sagely. "A fine distraction technique."

They rounded the garages again and headed back toward us. After her admission about her dad, I had a much better understanding of her reason for not discussing it. Probably the same reason she hesitated to call the non-profit lady about hanging with the kids.

She'd been taught to fly under the radar, and she couldn't do that if she was in the spotlight.

Soren lowered his voice. "If she's as good as you say she is, you still have another whole season to convince her to try for the draft."

He sauntered away, and Mac peeled off to meet him. Riley threw her arms around my neck with a grin.

"Now that I've proved my dominance, what do I win?"

I gave her a quick kiss, well aware that we were out in the parking lot where anyone could spot us and took her hand to lead her back to the privacy of the apartment. "Cheese. So much cheese. And whatever pie is left after Mac demolishes it."

Soren's words circled in my head, but now wasn't the time to bring them up. Riley had been through enough emotional crap for the day. The long drive to my parents' house would be soon enough.

23

Riley

"Are you still pouting over that catch?" Parker changed lanes around a slow-moving lumber truck, and I huddled deeper in my burrito blanket.

"The catch was solid, Shaw. I fucking tripped and dropped the ball."

"You've never fumbled before?" He reached over to palm my thigh, and I didn't have the heart to snap at him.

"Not since high school." And certainly not in a conference championship game.

The trees whizzed by outside my window, lit by the crescent moon hanging low in the sky. We'd left campus after Parker finished his last final, scheduled for Thursday night. Coach had given us Friday through Sunday off, and Parker's family planned to celebrate Christmas a couple of weeks early on Saturday.

Parker let me stew in my silence for the first part of our journey. We'd won our post-Thanksgiving game, going into the conference championships with a single loss. Luckily, my fumble hadn't cost us the game, but it had garnered me some time on the news cycle.

I didn't have a good explanation for the mistake either. One second, I was catching a short pass, the next, I was face-planting onto the grass and the ball was loose. My face got hot thinking about it.

Parker cast me a quick glance. "You can't be perfect all the time, Lorelai."

"Thanks. That's very helpful," I replied dryly.

He laughed quietly, a low, dangerous sound that sent goosebumps dancing across my skin. "If you want me to be helpful, I could pull over and distract you with something else."

"We have…" I jabbed at the touchscreen in his car until the map appeared. "Almost six more hours until we get to your picturesque small town. Think un-sexy thoughts."

"Impossible. Your blob-like form in that blanket is too much to resist."

Eva had given me the blanket when I refused to get out of bed on Sunday after the Incident during the game. She'd planned to give it to me for Christmas, but she claimed I was too pathetic for her to wait any longer. Parker rubbed the nubby material over my leg, and I sighed. If he kept touching me, I might actually give in, despite our attempts to be less reckless the last few weeks.

Nothing like being caught naked with my team captain on a lonely stretch of highway a few weeks before the end of the season. Speaking of being naked with my team captain…

"Are we going to be sharing a twin bed in a teen boy's room covered in posters of football legends and swimsuit models?"

Parker shook his head. "Nah, I never had a twin bed, and

my mom remodeled my room after I left, though I can ask her to put the swimsuit models back if that's what you're hoping for."

I snorted, glad that my less than stellar mood wasn't dragging him down. It wasn't just the fumble bothering me. Right before we'd left, I'd received a serious-looking letter from George's lawyer in the mail.

He didn't usually use his lawyer as an intermediary, preferring to harass me in person, despite orders from the court. Dad's lawyer, like his former manager, had checked out as soon as the money was handled. Turned out a college kid from the middle of nowhere didn't have a lot of options about lawyers, even with a multi-million-dollar estate backing her.

Without access to the money, I had to make do with what I could afford on my stipend, then that dried up too. Honestly, Dad kind of fucked me with his estate planning.

Coming on the heels of a fumble and the damn human sexuality final that I passed with a razor thin margin, I chose to wait on the letter. George's harassment could resume after I'd had some down time.

Parker's hand on my thigh reminded me I hadn't told him yet. I planned to, when I opened it, but for now, I wanted to pretend the envelope sitting in my bag didn't exist.

He ignored my lack of response to his joke and hummed along to the jaunty Christmas music playing softly over the speakers. I liked seeing Parker like this—relaxed and happy. We'd won our conference, but he had higher goals.

The College Football Championship.

With playoffs starting soon, he'd been laser-focused on any little mistakes that could cost us during the next four games. Except for my fumble. Rightfully, he should have been all over my ass for the mistake, yet here we were driving to his parents' house with freaking Christmas music playing like some Hallmark movie.

How the hell did he even find Christmas music in the middle of nowhere? My brows drew together as I realized we never listened to the radio. Parker always cued up something from one of his playlists. My gaze landed on the AUX cable illuminated by the blue light from his console. I sat up, letting the blanket pool around my waist.

"What playlist are we listening to?" I grabbed his phone from under the bag of chips between us and scrolled through. "This is your Chill the F* Out playlist? The one you listen to before every game?"

Parker flushed slightly, and suddenly, my bad mood was gone. He shrugged. "I like Christmas music. It brings back good memories of home. You'll see."

His chill playlist was the only one he hadn't shared with me, and this had to be why. Being a good and loyal girlfriend, I didn't bring up his reaction to finding out my secret. Admittedly, they weren't the same level of serious, but it was hard to resist the chance to tease him.

Christmas wasn't a big deal to me. Without Dad, I'd basically stopped celebrating. He hadn't cared all that much either, but he'd put in an effort. No point in muddling through for only myself.

For Parker, though, I'd do my best to be excited.

I yawned, suddenly exhausted. It wasn't late, but we were cocooned in the warm car, I had my burrito blanket, and Parker's touch filled me with delicious low-key tingles. Carefully, I set his phone back in the console.

"You're a surprising man, Parker, and I'm glad I'm here with you."

He turned the volume down to a low murmur, then

caught my hand and kissed it. "Sleep, Lorelai. It's a long drive. I'll wake you up if I need you to take over."

I curled onto my side with Perry Como crooning in the background and watched him drive until my lids got heavy.

————

"Baby, I need you to wake up. I'd love to carry you inside, but I'm fucking exhausted." Parker's voice pulled me from the quiet darkness of sleep, and I cracked open my eyes to a less quiet darkness.

The rumble of the car's engine had stopped, but water burbled somewhere nearby. Parker crouched in front of me on the passenger side of the car, his hair sticking up in places from him running his hands through it.

"There we go. Almost there, just a quick walk to the house and up the stairs." His voice sounded tired, and I tried to kick start my brain.

"We're here? Why didn't you wake me up to drive?" He wasn't the only one exhausted. Sleeping in a car wasn't exactly restful at my height.

"Didn't need to. I've done this trip plenty of times. If you can talk, you can get your ass inside."

I focused on the house mostly visible through the windshield. Pine trees surrounded the driveway, a mass of dark shadows, but pale pink light tipped the horizon behind the two-story modern farmhouse. A perfect rosy glow haloed the house, and for a second, I wondered if Parker had waited until that exact moment to wake me up.

But Parker wasn't looking at the cute house, he was watching me, waiting patiently for me to get out of the car so he could go to bed.

I stretched my arms above my head, and a chill hit me

through the open door. Fuck, December in the Rocky Mountains was cold. I wouldn't risk my Wisconsin cred by saying so out loud, but I couldn't stop the shiver that took root in the base of my spine.

Parker offered me a tiny smile and tucked the burrito blanket back around me. "Come on. It'll be warm in the house. We can leave everything here until later."

I let him pull me from the car, and to my embarrassment, he had to catch me as I crumpled. My left leg was asleep from hip to toes. Together, we hobbled into the house, which appeared to be unlocked.

The interior felt big and airy, but I missed the details while I tried to wiggle feeling back into my foot. We crept through the quiet hush inside the house, our steps silent on the carpet. Parker led me upstairs to a hallway of closed doors and ushered me into the second on the left.

I sighed when I spotted the king-sized bed. It crossed my mind his parents might not want us sharing a room, but by that point, I didn't care. I just wanted to sleep horizontally, preferably curled up next to Parker.

Apparently, he had the same thought because he didn't even strip down like he normally did to sleep. He toed off his shoes and unwrapped the burrito blanket from around me, tossing it onto a shadow on the other side of the room. I stood there swaying slightly until he threw the covers back and gently pushed me toward the bed.

I didn't need any more prodding, and Parker climbed in right after me. A low hum of contentment rumbled in his chest as he pulled me back against him. I didn't bother trying to keep my eyes open any longer.

Surrounded by Parker, I relaxed as a warm curl of happiness spread inside me. Deep in my mind, a hazy dream formed of going to sleep like this every night, without worrying who might see us when we woke up.

————

THE NEXT MORNING, sunlight streamed through the sheer curtains, and Parker had buried his head under the pillow. I knew from experience he'd sleep until his body had refueled, so I got up and stretched.

Parker grumbled at the empty spot where I'd been, making me smile. I could always go back to bed—we almost never got to sleep in—but I wasn't tired any more.

Besides, the clock on the wall said I'd already slept in. In the daylight, the room matched the feeling I'd gotten from the downstairs on our stumble through in the dark. Big and airy. Light wood furniture paired with a soft blue and gray color scheme.

I peeked out the window and caught my breath. Snow sparkled on dark green pines under a bright blue sky. I was right when I'd called it picturesque. Behind me, Parker rolled over, then settled with the blankets over his head.

God, he was cute. The temptation to climb back into bed and wake him up was almost stronger than the urge to shower after sleeping most of the night in the car. Almost.

I grabbed my shoes and decided to take advantage of my non-showered state to check out the weight set-up he'd promised me in the basement. Best case scenario, I got my work-out and shower in before anyone spotted me.

In my socks, I tiptoed down the stairs, but my luck ended when I passed the kitchen. A black, brown, and red speckled cat raced past me with something long and fuzzy in its mouth. I had to stop suddenly so as not to step on it, and a frustrated grunt came from the kitchen.

I leaned forward to peer around the corner, and Parker's mom caught sight of me as she wiped up spilled coffee on the counter. She blew her hair away from her face and offered me a warm smile.

"Good morning, Riley."

As much as I wanted to slink away, my midwestern upbringing wouldn't allow that kind of rudeness. "Good morning, Mrs. Shaw."

She waved a hand at me. "Call me Gina. I wasn't expecting you guys up for another couple of hours."

I pulled at the hem of the cropped tank I'd worn in the car, wishing I'd put on something more appropriate for spending the morning with my boyfriend's mom in her kitchen. While I fidgeted, the cat darted back into the kitchen and leapt onto the counter, sliding to a stop next to the spill.

Gina propped her hands on her hips. "Dammit, Fiona. This is *my* coffee. You're a cat. You don't drink coffee."

The cat sniffed at the liquid, then meowed at Gina, clearly demanding something. She shooed the sleek little animal off the counter and finished cleaning the mess. "I swear that cat is part demon. Coffee?"

"No, thanks. I don't drink coffee either, but I'd love a glass of water. I was hoping to check out the basement and maybe get a workout in before Parker wakes up."

Her blue eyes, a softer version of Parker's, lit up. "I'll show you. It's a full gym with a walkout and a hot tub on the patio. Parker taught me how to use the equipment, but I have to say we get a lot more use out of the hot tub than the weights."

Gina grabbed a water bottle from the fridge and led me past the entry to another door on the opposite side of the stairs. Despite her description, I expected a small, cramped space with low ceilings and a couple sets of weights.

I was so wrong.

The stairs led down into a bright, open space with an entire wall of windows on one side. Through the glass, I spotted the hot tub she'd mentioned. A full rack took up one corner along with yoga mats, balls, hand weights—anything I would need for a home workout—and the wall opposite the windows was all mirror.

I could live here. Seriously, the setup rivaled the home gym my dad put in at our house in Wisconsin. I circled the room, touching the metal, letting the memories wash over me.

Gina showed the same capacity to read people as her son. She leaned against the wall at the bottom of the stairs and gave me a minute. When I frowned at a small bookshelf tucked beside the bathroom door, she laughed.

"Jaina likes to use the space to read when Parker's not here." She pointed at the expanse of glass. "Those are accordion doors. They fold all the way back so we can enjoy the outside during good weather."

I glanced at the small piles of snow under the trees. "What's considered good weather?"

"Anything above forty-five degrees basically. The patio is east-facing, so the room gets plenty of sun. There are more waters in the mini fridge down here."

Gina handed me the bottle she'd carried down, and I opened it to take a swig. I hadn't expected to conversate before brushing my teeth. My breath couldn't be all that great after the amount of sour cream and onion chips I'd eaten on the way here.

Gina climbed the first step to go back upstairs, then hesitated and faced me again. "I think I understand why Parker wants to keep your relationship a secret, but why do you?"

My brows shot up, and I choked on my water. She waited with a serene expression on her face until I stopped coughing.

I chanced a tiny sip to clear my throat, extremely curious about what she thought Parker's reasons were. "If it got out that I was dating one of my teammates, people wouldn't see a football player, they'd see a slut. My vagina would become the most important part of my body while the whole world speculated on who else I'd slept with to get to where I am."

She frowned. "I can see why you'd be worried about that, but surely the coaching staff and administration would support you."

A laugh caught in my throat. "Coach would, but the administration wouldn't. They made a new rule this year against team fraternization. I'm pretty sure the rule was because of me, and I doubt they'd appreciate me actively disobeying it."

Gina tapped her chin with a finger, and I could see the wheels turning in her head. "Historically speaking, fraternization prohibitions in large organizations are never enforceable. There are too many variables to control."

"With all due respect, they have the power. If they want to enforce it, I can't fight them. Honestly, I just want to play for as long as I can." And I wanted to be with Parker for as long as we could make it work, but I didn't tell her that part.

She refocused on me with determination in her eyes. "You have more power than you think you do. Your story resonates with people. Have you watched the coverage you're getting?"

I pressed my lips together as I shook my head. In general, I avoided any sports news about myself, but the number of fans waiting for me after games grew each week. Then there was Marian Kelsey, the lady who wanted me to come speak to the kids in her organization. I hadn't called her back yet because I'd been so busy with the season—also because I wasn't sure if I'd do it.

Gina nodded up the stairs. "After you're finished, come see some of the highlights."

"You have highlights of me?"

She laughed. "Of course. You're making history for women in sports. I'm hoping to show my grandkids some-day." She winked at my wide-eyed expression.

Parker and I hadn't talked about what to do for next year, let alone after college, but she'd very clearly implied that I'd be involved in those grandkids. Horrifically, the thought didn't scare me as much as it should.

I'd always assumed I'd have kids—someday. I wanted a family. Recently, I'd been thinking a lot about my relation-ships with people, not just Parker, but Mac, Noah, and Eva too. They'd given me the sense of family I'd been missing since my dad died. That didn't mean I was ready to reveal my personal life to the world at large.

"Umm, highlights would be great, but maybe hold off on the grandkid talk."

"It's okay," she reassured me. "Parker knows where I stand. It's been obvious from the beginning, at least to me, that he's totally gone on you, but I hope you're getting as much out of the relationship as he is."

I hadn't thought the conversation could get any more awkward. Gina waited expectantly for a response, and I surprised myself by blurting out the truth.

"I like him—a lot. Enough that I'm willing to risk my scholarship and my chance to play football to be with him."

As I said the words, I realized I was still hedging. Playing football at TU lost a lot of its appeal if I couldn't have Parker. My chest squeezed at the thought. I loved football, but I loved him too.

She nodded, completely unaware of what she'd led me to realize. "If you don't mind my saying, it sounds like your life would be a lot easier if you stopped hiding and simply hired a PR person."

A great suggestion, if I had access to my dad's money. Then again, when had I ever let a little hardship stop me from pursuing what I wanted. I wanted Parker, so maybe I should do a little research. After the playoffs.

Without another word, she climbed the stairs, leaving me staring after her.

24

Parker

Every time I came home, Jaina took joy in interrupting my sleep by bouncing on my bed, so I was surprised to wake up in a dark room with no kid sister in sight. No Riley either, which was a shame.

I crawled out from under the covers, intent on finding my errant girlfriend, and nearly tripped over our bags. They were piled up on my side of the bed with Riley's clothes spilling out of hers. I shook my head with a grin as I grabbed a clean set of my own.

Riley wasn't at all interested in keeping things neat. She took care of her gear, and her locker area was spotless, but her room was a disaster. In the last few months, she'd transferred some of the disaster to my room, but it was a small price to pay to have her there.

As soon as I opened the door, the rich scent of tomato sauce and garlic bread made my stomach grumble. A breakfast sandwich before dawn wasn't enough to fuel me for a whole day, even if all I did was sleep.

Jaina came out of her room and stopped short in the hallway at the sight of me. She'd grown another inch since they came out for the game, putting the top of her head at my shoulder. Her dark hair was scraped back in a ponytail, and she wore her usual stretchy pants and hoodie.

A big grin split her face as she launched herself at me. "You're up! Finally. We were starting to wonder if you were getting too old for the drive."

"Brat," I teased, squeezing her skinny form gently. "I could snap you in half at my advanced age. You need to eat more."

A sly look entered her blue eyes. "That's not what Korben said."

"Who the fuck is Korben?"

"A guy in my class. He's cool. Doesn't make me want to dunk his head in a toilet when he talks."

I curled an arm around her neck, fighting the urge to go into full protective big brother mode. "He's respectful?"

She rolled her eyes. "Yes. Otherwise, I'd definitely dunk his head in a toilet."

"My little sister, master of bullying techniques. Anyone else you're harassing at school these days?"

"Not anyone I'd tell you about." Jaina wrinkled her nose and squealed, wriggling away. "Ugh, you need to shower. Your man stank is overpowering."

I let her go. "Nice to see you too, sis."

She smelled the shoulder of her hoodie as she hurried down the stairs, mumbling, "Now *I* might need to shower."

A quick sniff test confirmed Jaina was right, as usual. I smelled like stale sweat and Riley's sour cream and onion chips. Not a winning combo. As much as I wanted to hunt down Riley and suggest she join me in the shower, I detoured to the bathroom instead.

The bathrooms in our apartments were nice—they had hot water and good pressure—but my parents knew how to do luxury right. Namely, multiple body jets to work out the lingering soreness from a long time in the car.

The only thing that would make the experience better was my girlfriend naked and wet in there with me. I stroked my hard cock a couple of times, but why use my imagination when the woman herself waited for me downstairs?

I got clean in record time and hurried to the kitchen. As expected, Mom stood at the stove stirring her red sauce while Jaina pestered her with questions. Riley sat at one of the island stools, staring down at her phone with a crease between her brows.

My heart did a curious little flip at the sight of her— barefoot, blonde hair draped over her shoulder, fitting perfectly into the scene. I could see her here with me forever.

As if she sensed my eyes on her, Riley looked up and met my gaze. Heat flared between us like it always did, doing nothing to relieve my hard-on. I pushed away from the doorway, took her face in my hands, and kissed her.

From a distance, I heard a gasp, but I was busy savoring the taste of Riley. She wrapped her fingers around my wrist, holding tight as she kissed me back. I'd missed her when I woke up alone, missed her in the shower, and now that I had her in my hands again, I wasn't sure I could let go long enough to eat dinner.

She sighed against my mouth, and I reluctantly pulled back.

"Hi," I said quietly, brushing my nose against hers.

"Hi," she replied with a grin.

My mom fanned herself with the potholder. "Jaina set the table in the dining room."

Jaina's brows drew together in surprise. "Why?"

"Because we have a guest, and I don't want her to think we're entirely without class. Also, I want to talk to Parker."

Riley hopped off her stool, kissing my jaw as she passed. "I can help. Jaina, show me what to do."

The two of them left the room giggling like they'd known each other forever. I took Riley's seat and noticed the basket on the counter covered in a thin towel. My turn to be surprised.

"Did you bake bread?"

Mom sent me a look that questioned my intelligence. "Don't be silly. I heated up frozen garlic bread and made it look pretty."

Curious, I lifted the towel, but she smacked my hand away. "Wait until dinner."

Bereft of a snack, I leaned back and crossed my arms over my chest. "Where's Dad?"

She eyed me, then returned to the stove. "In his workshop. I'll send Jaina to get him in a minute. First, reassure me you're being responsible with her."

Not Jaina. Riley. My mom was asking about my sex life. "Are you interfering again?"

"Yes. It's part of my job description as your mother, but this is mostly for Riley's sake."

I relaxed a little at the direction of her protective instincts. "Yes. We're being responsible."

"Good. I'd hate to see you ruin that girl's life because you're messing around."

"Since when is a baby the end of someone's life? You didn't quit grad school when you got pregnant with me, which you've told me many, *many* times."

She rolled her eyes. "I'm pretty sure you can still play football if your girlfriend is pregnant. She doesn't have that luxury."

I leaned forward, completely serious. "I'm aware of that, and we're being careful. She's everything to me."

"Good," she repeated.

"Could you imagine though? With these genes? We'd start a football dynasty."

The sparkle in her eye, and the direction of this conversation, told me she'd considered the idea of giant football playing grandkids. While she'd been alone with Riley all day.

My eyes narrowed. "Did you mention this to Riley?"

Her chin went up, a sure sign she'd been causing trouble. "Yes, of a sort."

A shout of laughter came from the other room, and I leaned closer to lower my voice. "Can I talk to you about something?"

She turned the fire off and set the spoon down, giving me her full attention. "Always."

"Riley's dad died and left her a lot of money tied up in a trust she can't access until she's twenty-five. Her uncle has been using the legal system to take advantage of her and try to get a piece of the estate."

Her eyes sharpened. "Does she need legal help? If so, I should be talking to her."

I glanced toward the doorway that led to the dining room. "I don't think she'd be willing just yet."

"Then *you* shouldn't be talking about it. End of discussion."

"You just said 'always', and you're a lawyer."

Mom let out a breath through her nose. "I love you, son, but sometimes you're an idiot. When Riley is ready to talk, I'm happy to listen and help. You can't solve her problems without consulting her."

I got up from the stool to walk off my frustration. "I hate that he has any influence over her."

She leaned back against the counter to watch me pace. "You love her."

"Yes." No question. None.

"And you want to protect her."

"Yes," I said again. Riley was my future. I hadn't convinced her yet, but I would.

A smile crept onto her face. "Then she's going to be fine. Talk to her about your concerns. She's got a lot going on right now, but we'll take good care of her until she's ready to fight another battle."

Some of the tension in my chest cracked and fell away knowing my family had Riley's back as well as mine. I nodded, unable to speak past the lump in my throat. Mom sagely turned away to strain the noodles.

Dinner was loud and largely uneventful. Riley sat across the table from me, and every time our gazes locked, a tingle of electricity zig zagged down my spine. Dad spent most of the meal asking Riley questions about her childhood in Wisconsin, and I paid attention to every word she said.

At no point did she mention who her dad was, but it wouldn't have made much of a difference. Dad wasn't a big football fan. Still, she chose her words carefully, and I didn't like the wall she'd built.

After the last of the garlic bread had been devoured, I nudged her leg under the table. "Want to go for a walk?" I wagged my eyebrows at her, only half kidding.

The distance left Riley's eyes as she laughed at me. "It's dark and cold outside."

"I'll keep you warm," I said softly.

Her breath hitched, and I knew I had her. "We should help with the dishes first."

Mom waved us off. "Go. I cooked. Dad and Jaina can clean."

Jaina groaned, but Riley sent my mom a small smile.

"Okay, let's go for a walk," she agreed.

We bundled up, and I led her out the front door to a short trail that followed the little creek on our property. I'd walked this path so many times I could do it blindfolded, but I slowed my pace for Riley.

She sent me a warning look. "Before you get any ideas, I'm not into outdoor sex."

I hadn't actually planned to seduce her, but my dick fully supported the idea. Any time we were alone with Riley, my dick had high hopes. Not this time though.

"I want you to talk to my mom about George."

Riley stiffened under my arm but kept walking at a steady gait. "Why?"

"She's a lawyer, and..." I stopped myself from making the same logical arguments I'd made before. Riley had heard them already, and they hadn't swayed her.

Instead, I pulled her to a stop in a patch of moonlight and let my emotions lead. "I hate that George has any control over your life. I hate that I can't do anything to protect you from him."

"It's not your job to protect me."

"I want it to be. I love you, and I want you happy and healthy and naked as often as possible. I want to play football with you until we both have so many concussions we don't remember who we are, and then I want to fall in love with you all over again."

She let out a shaky laugh. "Parker..."

"You don't have to say anything back, but I wanted you to know how I feel. I'm not playing games with you. This is—"

Riley slapped a gloved hand over my mouth, mercifully

stopping my tirade. "You're insane, and I love you too. I want a future with you, preferably without the concussions and George's interference, so I'll think about talking to your mom."

I tried to say something, but she leaned her weight into her hand.

"After Christmas, Parker. I'm not going to let my drama ruin your time with your family." She lowered her arm, replacing the heat of her hand with the cool press of her lips.

I pulled her close, deepening the kiss with a growl. Riley loved me. This perfect girl wanted a future with me, and I'd do anything to make it happen.

25

Riley

P arker had a ridiculous number of cousins, mostly male, and they were all as cocky as him. After spending early Christmas with the Shaws, I'd come to several conclusions. My dad had done his best, but I'd missed out on the joy of a large family, and Parker had come by his football talent naturally.

Despite not following Parker's career—or college football at all, apparently—the cousins insisted on a backyard football game. They grudgingly allowed me to join, and I took great joy in smoking all of them.

Coach would have given us his worst disappointed speech if he knew we were risking injury by playing backyard ball, but I *loved* proving people wrong when they underestimated me. Besides, they couldn't hurt me if they couldn't catch me.

Late Saturday night, after all the festivities were done and the cousins had left, I talked to Gina. Normally, I'd rather run over shaved glass than let a relative stranger know about George and his bullshit, but Gina didn't feel like a stranger. Thanks to Parker, she understood parts of my life I couldn't put into words.

I told her the entire fucked up story.

After, all three of us—me, Parker, and Gina—sat around her kitchen table with tea and leftover garlic bread while I opened the letter from George's lawyer. The single page of typed correspondence made my stomach cramp with dread. I laid the paper flat on the wood so I wouldn't have to read it aloud.

The heater kicked on with a hum, the only sound in the room other than rustling paper and my slow breaths. I scanned the message, understanding the gist of the lawyer speak as anger tightened like a fist in my throat.

He wanted more money. They were petitioning to increase the amount he received every month due to my unwillingness to maintain the house myself. I glanced over at Gina, relieved to find her frowning down at the letter.

A second piece of paper was tucked inside the first with George's tiny handwriting scrawled across the page. He'd included not so subtle reminder that he'd been "generous" thus far with his knowledge of my poor decisions and he'd hate for the information to affect my current standing at the university. The disgust on Gina's face warmed a part of me I'd thought long cold since Dad died.

Parker scoffed quietly next to me, but he stayed silent otherwise, letting me lead the show.

My first instinct was to burn the letters and let George do his worst. Not a great response, legally. With a sigh, I pulled out my phone to call my usual bargain lawyer. As usual, he didn't answer, so I hung up without leaving a message.

"Asshole," I muttered under my breath.

Gina pressed her lips together for a long moment. "Your lawyer?"

I set my phone carefully on the table. "He's basically useless, but he's cheap."

She took my hand. "Let me act as your lawyer, pro bono. I'll work with a Wisconsin lawyer on the initial ruling and see what options you have."

I couldn't look at her. Shame and resentment for George knotted in my chest, making it hard to accept the lifeline she was offering. Parker's hand landed on my thigh, warm and reassuring. His touch pulled me out of the spiral, and I let out the breath I'd been holding.

"I'll think about it."

Gina's eyes crinkled as she smiled at me. "At least let me draft a response to this ridiculous request. You two go get some sleep. I'll have it for you in the morning."

She wasn't asking, so I simply nodded and let Parker pull me upstairs. With admirable restraint, he held his tongue until we were alone in his room.

"Lorelai…"

I shook my head. "I don't want to talk about it anymore. Please, Parker. I just want to enjoy my time with you."

"Done." He reached behind him to yank his shirt off, and I finally let the last of the tension go.

I followed his lead, tossing clothes into a pile until Parker wrapped his arm around my naked waist and hefted me onto the bed.

"I thought you couldn't carry me," I teased him as I stretched out on my back.

He levered himself above me, bracing himself on his forearms. "I didn't have the right motivation before."

"And now?"

His grin should have warned me. "I'm going to make you

call my name so many times that my sister will have to sleep downstairs."

"Parker…"

"That's a good start, but let's see if we can't turn the volume up."

A thrill of anticipation raced through my body. He took my mouth, and everything pulled taut. His hand roamed in a meandering trail over my breasts and stomach.

I bit my lip, letting out a quiet whimper.

"Louder," Parker whispered as he kissed his way down my body.

In the back of my mind, I was vaguely aware of his parents and little sister hopefully sleeping right down the hall, but when Parker's mouth landed between my thighs, I arched up off the bed with a moan.

Shit. I couldn't look his mom in the eye tomorrow if she heard me getting off to her son's tongue. That didn't stop me from doing exactly as he wanted and begging him for release, by name, loudly.

As I struggled to catch my thoughts, I grabbed a handful of his hair and tugged until he met my eyes. "Your family can't actually hear us, can they?"

Parker dropped a final kiss on my hip and crawled up my body. "We'll find out tomorrow."

His knees nudged my legs wider, lining the blunt head of his cock up with my entrance.

I dug my nails into his ass. "I swear to God, Parker."

He chuckled. "They all sleep with white noise. No one can hear you except me, but just in case…" Parker reached over to his phone and music spilled into the room.

"Another playlist?" I asked breathlessly as he returned, slowly filling me.

"My favorite playlist is the sounds you make when I'm

inside you, but this is my second favorite." He moved with careless abandon, a lazy rhythm that drove me relentlessly higher as he brushed kisses over my collarbone, my neck, my jaw. "My Lorelai playlist—the songs remind me of you."

My heart melted into a puddle of goo, to join the rest of me. I raised my knees, locking my heels behind his back, and he hit the spot that made me say his name over and over until the world went white.

"Again," he growled, gripping my thigh and lifting it higher.

The playfulness disappeared, and Parker fucked me like it was our last night together. Or our first. This Parker—the one who let go of his control—rarely saw the light of day, except in bed with me. I loved it. I loved him. And I told him when I came again, squeezing him so tightly I dragged him over with me.

Completely spent and boneless, I let Parker clean us up without moving an inch. He pulled the covers over us and snuggled me against him.

"I love you," he murmured against my neck.

I'd never get tired of hearing those words—or having the privilege of saying them back. "I love you too."

Tomorrow we'd make the drive back to campus, and for one more day, I'd enjoy the chance to be with Parker in the open.

———

"What the fuck? How can you still be sleeping?" Mac's annoying voice jerked me out of a dream I didn't fully remember.

Parker and I had arrived back at the apartment in the early morning, exhausted after taking turns driving. Judging from the sun streaming through the window, we'd slept through our alarms. I flung an arm over my eyes to block the glare and poked Parker's rock-hard abs.

"Mac is in your room."

"Our room," he mumbled, apparently still on his kick about me moving in with him.

He'd brought it up before we left his parents' house, but I needed time to think about it. The apartment had three bedrooms. There was no reason to assume I was sleeping with one of the guys living here.

Except that I was, and I didn't want to cause any rumors about team orgies. I sighed. No matter how hard I tried— how "perfect" I behaved—people were still going to talk shit. Maybe Gina had the right idea to hire a PR person, if I could find one who'd work for next to nothing.

"I can't believe you guys slept through this shit." The underlying panic in Mac's voice finally broke through my hazy thoughts. I moved my arm in time to see him toss his phone at Parker's midsection.

"What shit?" Parker mumbled.

Mac's dark eyes shifted back and forth between us, but it was his hesitation that made me sit up, pulling the blanket with me. He was never at a loss for words.

"Mac?"

"Dammit," Parker cursed softly next to me.

He tilted the phone toward me, revealing a close-up picture of us outside the apartment. Kissing. Or nearly kissing.

I squinted at the screen as my stomach dropped out. The picture had been taken at night, and I was in Parker's arms, staring up at him. The angle reminded me of the cameras Mac had installed over the doors.

Even with Parker's body blocking most of the shot, I

could feel the heavy tension between us. The first night he'd taken me to the camper, when he'd hugged me and told me my mom was an idiot. When he'd started calling me Lorelai.

Parker scrolled up so I could see the headline from a local Dallas paper. I snatched the phone from him to do a quick Google search. Yep. The news had made it to national coverage, but at least only the gossip rags had picked it up.

College football players sleeping with each other apparently wasn't front page news.

An icy brick lodged in my gut. Several pictures of me and Parker made an appearance, none of which we'd known about. Most of the shots were only interesting because of the context—us at practice or walking to lunch or getting in his car.

The one with him holding me was the worst. Our feelings for each other were on display for the soulless journalists to pick apart, well before we'd admitted them. My stomach clenched at the violation.

That moment was for us, no one else, and now we had to share it with people who would cast judgement without a single shred of understanding.

Fury melted some of the cold distance, but not enough. I handed Mac his phone. "How did they get that picture?"

He shook his head slowly. "I'm a dumbass."

"How so?" Parker growled.

"The door cam. We have access to your feed. Near the beginning of the semester, I got an email—"

Parker groaned. "Tell me you didn't click any of the links."

Mac frowned at him. "Nah, man. Well, just the one, but it went to the right website. Said I had to change my password. Standard security measures." He ran a hand through his hair. "Except now I'm thinking maybe it wasn't legit. I'm sorry, RJ. I was only trying to keep Eva safe."

"Mac—" Parker started, but I held out a hand to stop him.

I ignored the blatant invasion of privacy, choosing to let Eva deal with it, but I didn't understand how they'd known about the door cams in the first place.

"It's not important."

PARKER LOOKED as pissed as I felt. His jaw clenched tight as he threw off the covers to stroll naked into his closet. He came back into the room a few seconds later and tossed me some of my clothes before going to grab his own.

Mac lifted his brows. "Did she already move in?"

My gaze shot to him. "You too?"

Parker raised his voice in the closet. "I talked to Mac and Noah about it before I asked you. They live here too."

I shook my head and held up my clothes, glaring at Mac. "Do you mind?"

He stared at me blankly for a second, then realization dawned. "Right. Naked. I'll just be..." He pointed over his shoulder, then hurried into the hallway, closing the door after him.

Parker came out of the closet fully dressed and leaned against the frame with his arms crossed. I let the covers drop to yank on the underwear and sport bra in my hand.

"We should talk to Coach," he said. "As soon as possible."

I hated the idea. One of my worst nightmares was discussing my sex life with my football coach. Before I'd met Parker, it hadn't even been a consideration.

"How bad is it?" I asked.

Parker had spent more time looking at the article. I'd only read the headline and scrolled the pictures. His lips pursed as he watched me, and my fledgling hope that it was rumor fodder died.

"Bad. They know about you coming home with me, and someone told them about the dance with Eva. There's some speculation that you're fucking both of us."

I grunted in disgust and jumped out of bed. Fucking journalists with no sense of integrity. If I wanted to sleep with Eva and Parker and the rest of the fucking team, it should be my business and no one else's. I pulled on the leggings and a long-sleeved top he'd tossed me.

"I really don't want to talk about it, but you're right. Even if this blows over, we should tell Coach."

He pushed away from the wall and wrapped his arms around me, halting my aimless wandering. "Whatever happens, I'm here with you. The semester is over, and the season only has four games left at most."

Neither of us mentioned the spring semester or the potential problems for next season.

I wove my arms around his waist and let my head drop onto his shoulder, already tired of the shitty day. Deep down, I knew it wasn't going to blow over. The stories were already sordid and only sort of based on the truth.

Gina was right. I needed a PR person, even if I couldn't afford it.

The bigger problem was that we'd broken the administration's new rule. They might have been willing to look the other way as long as we stayed under the radar, but those articles painted the university in a negative light.

One of the headlines had brought up the last coach's harassment and seemed to be questioning how high the corruption went. If they'd planned my presence here as a publicity stunt, it had backfired spectacularly.

Mac knocked on the door. "Coach just texted me with a message for RJ."

My brows drew together, then I realized we'd put our phones in do not disturb mode before we'd passed out. No wonder we hadn't gotten any warning about the story breaking.

I pulled away from Parker and yanked the door open. "What did Coach say?"

His eyes slid past me to land on Parker. "He wants RJ in his office. Now."

I grabbed my phone from the nightstand, not bothering to check my notifications, and shoved it in my gym bag. When I tried to push past Mac, he pulled me into a quick hug.

"We got your back, girl. Unless you're secretly having an affair with Eva too, then I'm devastated you kept it from me."

I tried to smile at his joke, but it fell flat. "Thanks, Mac."

He released me into the hallway, and Parker followed. The cold in my gut spread as I stared at the front door. Nothing would be the same once we left the apartment.

Parker's warm hand on my back urged me forward as he took control. "Where's Noah?"

Mac's phone buzzed with another message, but he ignored it. "Working out at the facility. I was going to meet him there, but the shit hit the fan."

"Go meet him. If any of the guys ask, tell them I'll talk to them after we've seen Coach."

Mac nodded. "Damage control. Got it."

He slipped around us to leave, and suddenly, Parker and I were alone with my slowly increasing panic. We'd been caught, and now Coach wanted to see me. If we never left—

if we just went back to bed and woke up again—maybe none of this would happen. It could all be a horrible dream for us to laugh about later.

When I stopped moving again, Parker gathered me against him, brushing a kiss on my temple. "We'll handle this together."

From the depths of my mind, I realized Coach hadn't asked to see Parker. Only me. None of the headlines mentioned Parker unless they were referring to him as a stud quarterback. If there was going to be fallout, maybe I could spare him from some of it.

I pushed on his chest until he eased back. "You should go to training like normal."

He let out a dry laugh. "No way in hell, Lorelai. You don't have to go through everything alone anymore. I'm driving you."

Parker linked his fingers with my trembling ones and led me out into the bright winter sunlight, mercifully empty of anyone taking notice of us.

26
_____

Parker

"Wait outside, Shaw." Coach's tone brooked no argument, but if Riley hadn't given me a subtle nod, nothing would have kept me in the hallway.

I sat in one of the two visitor chairs outside his office, wishing there weren't blinds covering his windows.

Riley had been silent and closed down since she'd seen the news, but I trusted Coach to support her. It hurt a little bit that she'd shut me out along with everything else, but she'd developed thick walls to protect herself when she hadn't had anyone to lean on.

If I had my way, she'd never have to deal with bullshit alone again. George, asshole reporters, the administration—I'd be by her side for all of it if she'd let me.

I spent the next half hour responding to the constant stream of messages from friends and family, mostly agreeing with them about the articles being total crap. We'd been spared any follow up "journalism" this morning, but Eva texted to say there were vultures waiting outside the apartments now.

She asked if I wanted her to *accidentally* back into one of their cars, which brought out a smile. I loved Eva like a sister, and if she and Jaina ever got together, I'd probably have to go into hiding.

When I didn't respond, she took it as a maybe and saved the idea for emergency plan C. I didn't ask about plans A or B. Better if I didn't know.

I'd about reached the limit of my patience when Coach's door opened. Riley walked out, but she wouldn't meet my eyes, staring over my shoulder instead. What the hell had Coach said to her?

"You okay?" I reached for her, but my girlfriend fucking side-stepped me.

Coach's bushy eyebrows nearly covered his eyes as he leveled me with a disappointed scowl. "Shaw, you're up."

I didn't give a flying fuck. Riley was upset, and she came first. Always.

"Lorelai?"

She must have read the mutiny in my expression because her stiff posture softened. "Go on. I'll be fine."

My instincts screamed at me to ignore the grumbling coming from Coach and take care of Riley instead. But she clearly didn't want that. Riley liked to deal with her emotions in private, and the longer I stood there, the more I forced her to hold everything in.

"I'll be right out."

Riley nodded, and I followed Coach into his office. The door shut behind me with a finality I definitely didn't like. What was going on?

"Have a seat."

It wasn't a request, so I took one of the chairs in front of his desk. He shuffled the papers in front of him, finally sighing and setting them aside. With a lawyer as a mother, I'd learned never to be the first to talk in bad situations.

I itched to rush back through the door and whisk Riley away somewhere private, but I respected Coach's leadership. If he had something to say to me, I could wait longer than ten seconds. Not *much* longer though.

Finally, Coach leaned back in his chair with a loud squeak and crossed his hands over his belly. "You guys fucked up."

"What the hell—"

He held up his hand for my silence. "I'm going to tell you what I told RJ out there, and I want you to think long and hard about your response before you make it."

"I'm listening," I ground out, even though I dreaded what he was about to tell me.

"It's come to everyone's attention that there might be fraternizing happening between you and RJ. Despite the rule I was very clear about at the beginning of the season. I've been informed she's temporarily suspended pending investigation."

"What about me?"

"You've been cleared."

I reared back as if he'd slapped me. "They're punishing Riley and not me? Why? How is that legal?"

"Because they used the words 'pending investigation'." He threw up finger quotes. "The decision isn't final yet, but they're very focused on the playoffs. They want to make sure you're the one under center, not Williams. To make the whole situation worse, one of RJ's professors has been making complaints all semester, which pushed the final blame onto her. As far as they're concerned, RJ instigated any rule breaking that happened—"

"Don't you get a say as the head coach?"

He sent a pointed look at my clenched fists, and I forced my hands to relax. "In this case, I was overruled. The athletic director is concerned about the negative impact RJ could have on the team."

I fumed silently as I counted to ten. "She needs her scholarship to pay for her education, and no other school will touch her if TU disciplines her. Not to mention, she didn't start things between us. I did. If they suspend anyone, it should be me."

Coach scoffed. "It should be both of you idiots for not keeping it in your pants or at least not being better at hiding it. Any dumbass with eyeballs in his head could see you two were sparking off each other. I wasn't going to say anything as long as you kept it under wraps and it didn't affect your play. You couldn't wait until the season was over?"

I scrubbed my hands down my face. This was worst case scenario, and Coach wasn't wrong. "They shouldn't be able to dictate who I'm in a relationship with."

"Doesn't matter what they should or shouldn't do. They made a rule, you broke it, and now we all have to deal with the aftermath. RJ can't play while she's suspended. She can't even practice. I'm not revoking her scholarship for this year, but I can't hold her spot indefinitely."

Fuck. The look on RJ's face as she'd come out of the office made more sense now. I could be mad and rail at Coach, which wouldn't get me anywhere, or I could ask for help. "What do we do?"

The pinched expression left his face, and he nodded like I'd said something right. "The good news is this is all temporary, and you two can plead your case, which I strongly recommend. RJ is a hell of a player, which is why I pushed for her with the athletic director. He saw a chance to repair the program's reputation, and I wanted her catching for you.

Just not..." He made a vague circling motion with his hands. "You know, euphemistically."

I winced at the reference, but his other words caught my attention. "You pushed for her?"

Coach rubbed a hand through his wiry hair. "How the hell else did you think she got here? Fairy dust? I saw her play at SWU, and they were wasting her. Now, *I'm* wasting her because you couldn't resist your urges for five months."

I got his point, but I didn't regret one second of the time I'd spent with Riley. She was outside right now, probably freaking out, and I needed to get back to her.

Coach seemed to have the same thought. He nodded at the door. "Don't miss practice today. The last thing I need is something else to defend to the AD. He's worried about our reputation. Fix it. Get her back on the field."

"Yes, sir." I stopped myself from saying the rest of what was on my mind.

Namely, why the fuck Riley should bear the brunt of the publicity fiasco. I wanted to march down to the athletic director's office and demand equal treatment, but the sane part of my mind assured me the display wouldn't have the effect I wanted.

I'd led the team back to the playoffs, but taking out the quarterback along with one of our top receivers would guarantee we'd lose—Williams wasn't ready to take over. After last year, I'd promised myself I'd put the team first, and I'd failed.

My feelings for Riley threw everything into chaos, but looking back, I could see how my narrow focus on the championship, and my role in our loss, hadn't exactly been healthy. In the end, football was a game, one I'd dedicated my life to, but it didn't come close in importance to Riley.

Coach didn't say anything else as I left, and it took a

second to process what I was seeing in the hallway. Or rather, what I wasn't seeing.

The chairs were empty.

"Riley?"

No one answered, and I felt like an ass yelling down the hallway. I'd driven us here, so she didn't have a car. Normally, I'd assume she went down to the weight room, but suspended players couldn't work out with the team.

I didn't think the restriction would stop her, but she'd barely been holding herself together. Riley would never risk losing her shit in front of the team, especially not after the damn stories about us circling the internet.

She'd cling to her armor with everything she had— showing nothing but strength—until she was in a safe spot to let it go. Why wouldn't she wait for me?

Maybe she went to the bathroom? I grabbed onto the flimsy excuse for her absence. My heart raced, and a rising sense of urgency pushed me to hurry up and find her.

The ladies' room was by the stairs, so I backtracked, checking each of the hallways. With the semester over, the building had emptied of everyone but essential staff, which left no one to ask about Riley.

I eased the door open a crack. "Riley, you in there?"

My voice echoed off the tile walls, then faded into silence. I waited a few seconds, but the bathroom remained quiet. Where else could she be? Would she have called someone for a ride instead of waiting?

My mind blanked. This whole thing was my fault. All the warnings from my mom and Coach came rushing back, and I slumped against the wall.

I'd pushed her for a relationship. She'd warned me about the consequences, but I'd never really believed we'd be caught. Riley had known—and she'd known she'd be the one blamed. A jagged pain tore into my chest at the thought she'd run from me instead of letting me help.

In a last-ditch effort, I called Mac.

"Have you seen Riley?"

Weights clanged behind him. "Isn't she with you?"

Fuck. She was really gone. "No. Coach had to suspend her pending an investigation." I spit out the words, and Mac whistled low.

"Not you?"

"Not me. I'll explain the bullshit later. For now, I just want to find her."

"I'll rally the troops."

"No." I ran my hand through my hair. Riley wouldn't want that. "Just you and Noah."

"On it, Cap'n." Mac hung up, and I focused on my next steps.

She was stubborn enough to try walking back to the apartment. It was the only idea I had, so I made my way to the car. Practice wouldn't start for another couple of hours, but if she was still missing, I'd be spending that time looking for her.

Even if she didn't want to see me, I'd make sure she was safe.

The temperature had dropped from this morning, and thick gray clouds spit icy rain in a feeble drizzle. We didn't have umbrellas, so I hoped Riley hadn't tried to walk home. Or anywhere. Ideally, we'd find her in a corner of the facility taking her frustration out on a set of weights or a heavy bag.

A text from Mac came through while I was running to my car. *Found her. Camper.*

I frowned down at the phone, and my heart slowly dropped out of my throat. Why hadn't I thought of the camper? Stupid. At least one of us was thinking clearly. I grabbed a towel and an extra sweatshirt from the back of my car, then trekked into the woods.

Rain turned to sleet by the time I made it through the path. Mac met me at the edge of the clearing with his hood pulled over his head, still wearing his work out shorts.

He nodded toward the camper, and I spotted Riley curled into a ball on the steps. The tiny overhang didn't provide much protection from the crappy weather. I could see her shivering from where we stood.

"Why aren't you over there with her?"

Mac shoved his hands in the pocket of his hoodie. "She doesn't want me near her, and when my girl says no, I listen."

I reined in my sudden anger—it wasn't meant for him. "Thanks for checking out here. Go on back to training and get warm."

"You're welcome. Tell her I got her, whatever she needs." He clapped my shoulder. "You too."

Mac jogged the direction I'd just come, and I joined Riley under the awning. She didn't acknowledge my presence, simply stared down at the dirt with her arms wrapped around her knees.

"Lorelai?"

Slowly, she raised her face, empty of emotion except for the misery in her eyes. "I'm done."

"I know." I draped the towel on my shoulder and looped the sweatshirt over her head. "Raise your arms."

Riley did as I asked, moving mechanically. I pushed her arms through the sleeves and tugged the rest down. "They're using me as a scapegoat. That's all I ever was to them. A pawn. Worthless."

A familiar swell of rage flared up at her words, but my anger wouldn't help anything. The athletic director could go fuck himself—my focus was Riley, who hadn't asked me to leave yet.

"Come here." I took a chance and pulled her into the camper, settling on the tiny bed with her in my lap.

"Parker, I tried so hard, and I still lost everything." She curled into me, and I threaded my fingers through her wet, tangled hair.

"I know, baby, but you didn't lose everything. You have me. I love you and nothing will change that."

Her walls crumbled, and she sobbed in my arms. My heart hurt. I wanted to raze the administration to the ground for doing this to her, but guilt hit me with my own culpability. I couldn't be sorry for the way things played out because she was worth it. Maybe it made me a selfish bastard, but I'd take Riley over football any day.

She tucked her hands under my shirt, and I hissed when her icy fingers made contact with my stomach. Nothing in the world would make me move them though. In maybe the worst moment of her life, Riley had turned to me for comfort, and I'd sit there holding her for as long as she needed.

After a while, the tears stopped, but Riley didn't pull away. Both of us were soaked from the intermittent drizzle outside.

"Can I take you home?" I asked quietly.

"I just want to sleep," she whispered, closing her eyes and pressing her cold face against my neck.

I took that as a yes and scooped her into my arms. Riley wasn't light, but I could carry her to my car thanks to the adrenaline coursing through my system. She let me buckle her in, compliant and hollowed out.

Riley wasn't compliant. She pushed and demanded what she deserved. Without me, she'd be at training with the rest of the team, prepping for our playoff game. I turned the heat up in the car and studied her for a long second.

"Don't give up on me, Lorelai."

She had every reason to hate me, but Riley reached out for my hand. I swallowed past the sudden lump in my throat and kissed her fingers.

I may have helped fuck this up, but I intended to fix it.

27

Riley

I slept for almost a week, and it wasn't nearly long enough. Parker made me eat, bringing me food in bed and pestering me until I sat up. He held me when he wasn't at practice, and I hated the time he was away. If his arms were around me, I could forget about the way my life had taken a sudden turn to shit city.

Not once did he mention how ripe I smelled, but when he left for his morning training on the day of the first playoff game, I couldn't ignore the stench anymore.

I'd exhausted myself going over what-ifs and hypothetical situations. Maybe a change of scenery would get me past the closed loop of doomscrolling in my mind. The bathroom would have to do.

I didn't make it far past the scrubbing phase before the looming question mark of my future overwhelmed me. My heart raced, and I had trouble drawing in a full breath past the tight band across my chest.

With the warm water cranked, I fell back on the cool tile, sliding to the floor in a heap. Luckily, Parker liked his space tidy, so he actually cleaned his shower. I'd have to thank him later, when I emerged from my sloth phase.

With my knees bent up to my chest, I dropped my head and took several slow breaths, careful not to inhale any of the water streaming down my face. Part of me knew this was coming. As long as I stayed in Parker's bed, I wouldn't have to face the aftermath of my career going down in flames.

But my dad would hate seeing me like this. He'd raised me to be strong and face the hard parts of life. Like him dying. Like George's lawsuit. Like convincing people to take me seriously as a football player.

Especially the last one.

Of course, Dad would have ignored all those people and just kept going, working toward his goals. He'd tell me to do the same. I'd been pushing away my memories of him, hoping if I could just get a little more distance the reality of his death wouldn't hurt so bad. It turned out distance and walls didn't help, but Parker did. The others did.

I wasn't alone. Whatever my future ended up looking like, I wouldn't be alone.

The tightness eased a little and my shoulders relaxed. I planned to sit there until the water got cold, but someone knocked on the bathroom door.

I frowned. Parker wouldn't knock, and no one else should be in there. I could have sworn I locked the bedroom door anyway out of habit. Probably not a murderer as I assumed they didn't knock first. If I didn't answer, maybe they'd leave on their own.

I should have known better.

Mac called my name from outside the bathroom, and I groaned, not bothering to look.

"Go away," I yelled over the water. A second later, a towel hit the glass door of the shower.

When I raised my head, Mac stood in the doorway with his hand over his eyes. "You have ten seconds to cover up before I come in there. I'm no stranger to naked ladies, but I'd prefer if I didn't have to let Parker punch me for seeing your tatas."

"You could just leave," I muttered.

"Five seconds."

I didn't give a shit if Mac saw my tatas, but the towel was right there. I opened the door far enough to grab it, then draped it over my torso. Good enough.

"Why are you here instead of training?"

He dropped his hand and grinned at me. "Super secret spy mission."

"In Parker's bathroom?"

Mac raised his brows and nodded. "Where he'd least suspect."

I leaned forward to turn the water off, and his gaze jerked upward. "Come on, RJ. Are you trying to get me killed?"

"Are you saying Parker doesn't know you're here?"

"Yes. I was sent by another party," he told the ceiling.

"Eva?" I asked dryly.

"No comment."

"What do you want?"

He finally looked at me again. "You have to come to the game this afternoon."

I shook my head, perfectly happy to sit in a soggy lump in the bathroom until Parker got home. Well, not happy. I was pretty damn miserable and weirdly tired—and really, really, incomprehensibly angry at the whole situation.

Bitterness coated my words as I stared straight ahead at the white tile. "I'm fine here."

A sharp jab to my bicep earned Mac a wet glare.

He ignored my warning. "Get off your ass, girl."

I grumbled at him, but he hauled me up by my armpits. The serious expression on his face stopped the sarcastic comment on the tip of my tongue.

"I don't think the administration wants me around the football team at the moment," I said.

"They don't get a say. You know why? You're Riley fucking Jones. The fastest, baddest, scariest motherfucker out there. Why do you think they had to knock you down? Because your skills will burn their tidy little system to the ground. Come. To. The. Game. The team wants to see you."

I blinked up at him, astonished. Parker had brought up me coming to the game, but I'd shut him down. I didn't want a front-row seat to watch what I'd lost. The team hadn't been a consideration at all, and the guilt from that realization hit me hard.

Mac tucked the sagging towel tighter around me, gave me a pointed look, then left the bathroom. The bedroom door closed after him, and I hoped he hurried back to the weight room. Coach's 'training is the backbone of the team' lecture had gotten longer as the season went on.

The heavy weight of regret threatened to smother me, so I purposely didn't let myself dwell on Mac's pep talk. Who cared if I was fast and scary if I couldn't play?

I managed to pull on a sport bra and underwear before the door opened again. I spun around expecting Mac to come give me another round of his tough love. Instead, Eva sauntered in—already in full cheer gear—and dropped her TU tote bag on the unmade bed.

"Oh good, you've already showered," she chirped.

I threw my arms up. "Why is everyone just walking into my bedroom?"

Eva tilted her head at me with a tiny smile. "Does that mean you've officially decided to move in here?"

"Argh," I grunted and threw my towel at her cheerful face.

"Good to see you vertical. Have you had enough moping?"

"Fuck off," I grumbled, not in the mood to engage with Eva.

She tsked at me. "I see we've entered the anger stage of grief. For a while, I thought maybe you'd skipped straight to depression, but Parker assured me you just needed time."

I scrubbed a hand down my face and sat on the bed. "Then why are you here?"

"The same as Mac. You have to come to the game. Harper and Gina are meeting you there, so you won't be alone."

Gina was in town? It felt like a lifetime since we'd been in Colorado, but a lot had changed since then. Of course, Parker's family would want to see him start in the playoffs, and there was no guarantee there'd be another playoff game after this one. That didn't explain the other unfamiliar name.

"Who's Harper?"

"Soren's cousin. She's a PR genius in Houston, but she's looking to branch out to athletes. Soren called in a favor, so she's going to meet you at the game to discuss your strategy going forward." Eva sounded like she was reciting a speech from someone else, which made me highly suspicious.

"I don't have the money to pay for a PR rep."

"That's the favor. She's doing this pro bono to build her name."

I rolled my eyes, annoyed despite already having

decided to hire a professional. "I'm supposed to take Soren's word that she's good at her job?"

Eva joined me on the bed and reached for my hand, holding it between hers. "No. You take mine. Gina and I put our heads together while you were... incapacitated. She's here to support you, just like everyone else."

My brow furrowed. "She's not here for Parker?"

"She and Harper want to meet with you to discuss a publicity strategy and legal options."

A dangerous thread of hope coiled in my chest. They were here for me? After the trouble and secrets, my friends, Parker, his family—they'd all stuck. I didn't get it. History had taught me people couldn't be trusted because they all left eventually.

I collapsed back next to her. "Why would you do all this?"

"Oh, I can't take credit for this one—Parker started it all —and we're doing it because we love you. Family helps each other. Take the assist. Go to the game." She yanked a balled-up piece of red cloth from her bag. "And wear this."

Warmth spread through me like honey at the thought of all of them as my family. They'd rallied around me when I'd been trying my hardest to shove them away.

I snorted at the cliché gesture though. "Let me guess. I should show up in Parker's jersey? Send a message to the administration?"

"Fuck that." Eva smirked and tossed the silky fabric at me. "You're going to show up in your own jersey."

28

Riley

I wore the jersey.

Over several layers of clothes because the temperature was still ridiculously low, and I wouldn't be getting sweaty at this game. Gina texted me from the entrance to the stadium, and I found her standing next to a gorgeous blonde wearing jeans and a parka as if they were a business suit. I almost expected to see stilettos on her feet.

Gina hugged me, the same way she had when I'd left her house thinking everything would work out. "I'm so sorry, sweetheart."

I clung to her for a second. "Thanks for coming."

She introduced me to Harper, who shook my hand and eyed me up and down. "I can see why the news is having a field day."

My brows drew together at the comment. "I'm not sure how to take that."

Harper laughed. "Oh, this is going to be fun. People love an attractive couple, makes my job easier. You're beautiful, and Parker is even more beautiful—no offense."

"You should see him naked."

Gina let out a cough next to me, drawing both our gazes.

"I'm fine," she wheezed, waving us forward. "Let's find our seats."

Harper stayed next to me as we walked, lowering her voice. "I have to ask this, just to cover all the bases. If you want to push the story that there's nothing between you and Parker, I can do that, but you'll have to break up with him. It would go a long way toward lifting your suspension."

I didn't say anything for a long moment, weighing my words. The thought wasn't new. When I'd seen the pictures, I'd noticed that only one of them was problematic, and we could explain that one away... if there weren't any repeats.

Parker and I would have to stay away from each other, for real, until the playoffs were over—maybe longer to prove the point. I'd probably get to play, but I'd lose him.

I couldn't do it. Parker was the only bright spot in the darkest week of my life. He'd held me together when I broke, and I didn't regret a single moment I spent with him.

"No. However you do this, Parker and I are together."

She nodded, and I followed her into the crowd.

Somehow, I'd never entered the stadium through the public side. The reminder I wouldn't be playing stirred up the anger I hadn't entirely gotten past. Harper took the lead, and I kept my eyes locked on the back of her white jacket.

I had no urge to mingle with fans who might recognize me—even worse, I didn't want to know if I suddenly became invisible when I took off the pads.

Our seats were a few rows up right on the fifty-yard line. Premium placement, but I shouldn't have been surprised. A couple of people stood so we could scoot past them, and haphazard black marks all over their red shirts caught my attention.

I looked closer and realized they had my number

written all over in black Sharpie. Not just my number, but
my name, hearts, and a hashtag I had to squint to read.
#playRJ. Everywhere.

What the hell?

I raised my head and realized all the people around us
were watching me, wearing the same kind of homemade
tribute shirts. Some had their faces painted. Some had
written down their arms, braving the cold weather in short
sleeves. Gina dropped her hand on my shoulder, and when I
turned to her, she'd opened her jacket, revealing the same
messages.

A wall of sound overtook me as everyone started to
cheer, encouraged by the players on the field—led by Mac
and Noah—who were waving their arms and pointing in my
direction. I searched through the guys until I found the one
standing still, staring straight at me with a smile on his face.

Parker had written #play on one cheek and RJ with a
heart on the other. I shook my head, overwhelmed by the
show of support. He made a heart with his hands in front of
his chest, and the bitter lump in my throat melted away.

I didn't have a single doubt Parker was behind this
incredible moment. He'd done all this for me. A watery
smile bloomed across my face, and I mouthed thank you.

Parker mouthed back I love you. The cheers exploded,
drowning out the music, the announcers, whatever Harper
said next to me. My chest filled with joy, even though I
wasn't down there with them, even though I couldn't play.

Football had been my life for as long as I could remember, but if I had to choose, Parker would win. Every time. I
could live without football, but not without him.

Whistles blew for the coin toss, and our moment ended.
Parker jogged over to the refs with Mac next to him. I felt
dizzy from the life-altering realization that I loved someone

more than football. Luckily, Gina pulled me down in my seat before I could do something crazy like rush the field to kiss my boyfriend.

The game got underway, but fans continued to stop by and tell me how much they enjoyed watching me play. I couldn't believe this many people were on my side, wanting me to be reinstated.

Halfway through the first quarter, Harper nudged my shoulder during a lull. "How'd I do?"

I blew on my hands, wishing I'd brought gloves for the chilly wind. "If this is your idea of a tryout, I'm scared to see what you can accomplish with a dedicated campaign."

She laughed. "Yes, I'm very talented, but do you feel like there's enough support to fight the administration on their patently uneven enforcement of the rules?"

I frowned. "I don't want Parker punished. If I have to take the fall, I'm willing to do that for him."

"No one is taking the fall because I'm going to convince the world to root for you two using the oldest story in the book."

"What story?" I didn't entirely trust someone who wanted to put a spin on my life.

Harper sat back with a satisfied smile. "Love conquers all. College football's power couple bring a win to Teagan University."

My mouth dropped open. "Holy shit, you *are* good."

"Soren filled me in on the situation, and I can make TU look really good or make them wish they'd never gotten into football."

I gazed over the field, absently noting the defense was going to rush on Parker's blind side. "If I bring good publicity to the school, they'll look like assholes for suspending me, but if they reinstate me..."

She nodded once. "Exactly. They'll have done their due diligence by 'investigating', and they can easily find no wrongdoing by either party. I've already lined up a great speaking opportunity for you with Marian Kelsey at STEM & Sports. Parker sent over her information, and when I contacted her, she was ecstatic to have you in."

"Even after the horrible news articles?"

Harper nodded, her blonde ponytail falling over her shoulder. "Marian was adamantly on your side."

Gina leaned closer. "By the way, I did some digging on that uncle of yours, and it looks like he's had a private investigator following you for a while now, which explains why someone wanted access to the door cams. He didn't even need to be there to get the shots. Your uncle sold the pictures to the tabloid that broke the story."

My hands clenched into fists, and I promised myself the next time I saw him he'd have a reason to file assault charges.

Gina patted my arm. "Resist those violent urges I see on your face. I took care of him and his sleazy lawyer. Faced with a real legal challenge they backed down immediately. I'm also working on the sham of a case with your dad's estate. Did you know the ruling judge is an old golfing buddy of your uncle's?"

I stared at her in shock. She'd been involved less than a week, and she'd already made that much progress? I'd cut myself off as much as possible from George and his case, so it had never occurred to me I was being hustled.

"Okay. I give in. You two are clearly better than me at running my life." I faced Harper. "In your expert opinion, what do I do now?"

She met my eyes with an easy smile. "Just be yourself."

I laughed without humor and returned my attention to the game. "Sure. Any more clichés to offer?"

Gina tapped my wrist. "Let me ask you something. If none of this had happened—if you were just a girl here to watch her boyfriend play—what would you do after the game?"

"Besides give him crap for overthrowing that last pass?"

She smiled indulgently. "Besides that."

I sighed, forcing myself to move past the bitterness of not being on the field with them. These guys were my friends as much as my teammates, and I missed them. Despite the amount of time I'd spent with Parker the last week, I missed him too.

He'd done everything in his power to take care of me, including this ambush. It was time I showed up for him.

"I'd go down to the field and make it clear I'm proud of him—of all of them."

She sat back with a decisive nod. "Then do that."

We chatted while we watched the rest of the game, cheering with the fans around us. At halftime, a lanky teenager wearing my jersey and a besotted expression brought me a hot dog with a note from Parker.

Wanted to make sure you were keeping up your strength. Love you.

I slid the paper into my pocket and devoured the food. Harper and Gina spent the second half trying to convince me to confront the athletic director's office as soon as possible. I wasn't sure I wanted to put myself through the experience of some asshole executive telling me I couldn't play because I dared to be female and have a sex life.

Both ladies insisted the message had to come directly from me.

My resistance faded as the other team came back from a

shutout to within one score of winning. Acid churned in my belly as I watched helplessly while the clock ticked down, refusing to sit until they punted without scoring.

With less than two minutes left and the ball back in Parker's hands, I finally gave in. I wanted to be out there. Win or lose, I wanted to use my skills to help my team. If that meant turning myself into a spectacle, so be it.

The administration may only see me as a publicity stunt —a token woman on the team—but everyone here *knew* I could play. I could help us win.

I turned to my companions. "Let's do it. I want to fight."

Harper gave me a classy nod, but Gina whooped and jumped out of her chair. "We'll meet you outside the athletic director's office first thing Monday morning."

I shook Harper's hand, then hugged Gina. "Thank you both. I should have done this a lot earlier."

"No time like the present." Gina squeezed me tighter to whisper in my ear. "I'm proud of *you*."

Hot tears pricked at my eyes, but I refused to let them fall. I sniffed them back and lifted my chin as she moved away. A whistle blew from the field, and the fans around us jumped to their feet.

I glanced at the clock to see the game had ended with us ahead by six.

With my new notoriety, I struggled to reach the gate without being stopped every ten seconds. The show of support felt good, but I needed to get to Parker. After thanking the millionth fan, I gave up and hopped the railing.

The cold metal on my palm took my breath away, but then I was running. With the sixth sense we had about each other, Parker turned my way when my feet hit the grass. A smile lit up his face, and the rest of the people on the field disappeared.

Luckily, he'd already put his helmet down because I didn't slow when I reached him, just launched myself into his arms. He caught me with a laugh, bracing me with both hands on my ass.

I wound my arms around his sweaty neck and kissed him for all I was worth.

"You were amazing," I whispered against his mouth. "I'm sorry I got up in my head. Nothing could keep me from coming to watch you play."

He brushed my nose with his. "Except you playing with me. I love you, Lorelai Jones."

"I love you too, and I'll be out there with you soon enough."

"Where you belong."

It took me several seconds to realize the people around us were applauding. I unhooked my legs from around Parker's waist and dropped back to the ground. He anchored an arm around me ensuring I couldn't move too far away from him.

We smiled and waved for the cameras pointing at us, and he didn't let me go again until he had to go to the locker room with the team. As they filed past us, they bumped my shoulder or slapped my back. Every single one of them wore my name marked on their skin somewhere.

———

MONDAY MORNING, I got out of Parker's bed—I still hadn't decided about moving in with him—took a shower without anyone interrupting for once, and dressed in one of the few professional outfits I owned.

Parker wouldn't let me go to the director alone, or rather without him, since his mom and Harper were meeting me there. He drove us to campus, holding my hand the entire time, and parked in front of the administration building.

Gina and Harper waited at the top of the stairs, a world away from us in the car. My heart thundered away in my chest, and nerves made my stomach twist.

"Do you want me to come in with you?"

I shook my head. "If they need to talk to you, Harper said she'd come get you."

Harper lifted a brow and tapped her watch. Time to get this show started.

"Glory lasts forever," I muttered.

He tilted his head. "Did you just quote The Replacements at me?"

My face heated. "You weren't supposed to hear that."

Parker kissed me, quick and full of confidence. "You're going to be great."

I leaned against him a second longer, still getting used to being free to touch him in public. "You're the best thing that's happened to me, and I got to ride in Mike Taylor's private jet when I was nine, so the bar is *really* high."

"I'll keep that in mind later." He grinned, and the naughty promise in his eyes helped distract me from my nerves.

"No matter what happens in there, I'll be waiting for you out here. This isn't the end—this is our beginning."

"I'm glad I'm at this beginning with you." I hopped out of the car before I could convince myself to stay a little longer staring at my ridiculously hot boyfriend. Or turn around completely and drag him back to bed.

The cold air settled my stomach, and with my lawyer

and my publicist at my side, I walked into the athletic director's office with my chin high.

We met with Matt Delongio and two assistant directors. They listened while I pled my case, a speech I'd practiced with Parker and the others for hours the night before. As expected, they weren't open to negotiation until Harper showed them the school's social media feed.

She'd filmed me jumping on Parker after the game, and thanks to her scarily brilliant marketing, the video had gone viral the next day. My mostly ignored social media was exploding, we'd officially been dubbed college football's power couple, and #catchmenow was trending.

She'd done more for my career in the last two days than I'd done in two decades.

The real dealbreaker was when she pulled up Sports-Center so the three men in charge of my future could watch the sportscasters talk about the ground-breaking program at TU. When the analysts started speculating about my presence in the stands instead of the field, Harper only had to raise a brow.

I thought I might love her a little bit.

Matt folded. He had me sign a dubiously legal contract agreeing not to sue or badmouth the school during my time here. Gina gave me the okay, but I think it was because she knew she'd be able to tear it to shreds in court if she needed to.

I *definitely* loved her a little bit.

By noon, my suspension was lifted, and I was cleared to play. From the moment I left the administration building, Parker stayed by my side. Since we were there, Harper insisted on getting pictures and video of us walking around campus like a regular couple.

"Stop looking at me. More heart eyes at each other. Sell it." She shouted from the other side of the quad.

Harper had no problem bossing us around to get the right image, but I wasn't used to being vulnerable with someone in public. Parker released my hand, which he'd been holding as we strolled aimlessly, and wrapped his arm around my waist.

He pulled me against him, making my pulse pick up. "Ignore her, Lorelai. Look at me."

I raised my eyes to meet his piercing blue gaze, and like always, the rest of the world faded away, including most of my nerves. "Are you going to say something meaningful and touching?"

His wicked grin should have warned me. "No, I'm going to kiss you out here in front of all these people so they *know* who you belong to while you think about what I'm going to do to you when I get you home."

My breath hitched, and my body erupted into flame, but I managed to raise a brow at him. "Who belongs to who?"

"I'm all yours, baby," he murmured as he kissed me, staking his claim as promised.

EPILOGUE

Riley

Three weeks later…

"Say it," Parker murmured, his lips against my ear.

Despite the vicious need slicing through me, I knew exactly what he wanted. I grinned, prepared to win this particular battle.

"Make me."

After playing around in bed for most of the morning, I was confident his control would snap before I gave in, but he surprised me by thrusting deep. His hands linked with mine as he filled me, a slick glide that vibrated along all my nerve endings.

He kissed me, silencing my moans as he moved. His tongue mimicked his cock in a welcome invasion. I would never get enough of the way Parker made me feel. Sexy and dirty and loved.

My muscles tightened, on the verge of release, and he suddenly slowed. I made an unhappy noise, wild with need, and Parker stopped altogether. When I urged him forward with my heels, he held his position.

His mouth returned to my ear with a chuckle. "You're so close, baby. All you have to do is say it…"

I was going to kill him. Hopefully before I died from the pressure about to explode in my body. Parker buried himself a little deeper, a tiny movement of his hips that nearly made me weep.

He knew exactly how to get his way. Eventually, I'd get revenge, but today, he won.

I met his expectant gaze and surrendered. "Big. Daddy."

Parker made a rough sound of approval took me the rest of the way in a cascade of pleasure. He collapsed on top of me, then rolled us so I lay splayed across his chest.

"You know I'm going to repay you in kind," I muttered to his shoulder.

His hand threaded through my hair, tugging gently. "Can't wait."

Before I could come up with a truly evil retaliation plot, a crash came from the hallway, followed by a woman's voice cursing. We glanced at each other in confusion, and I climbed off of him to grab the closest piece of clothing I could find—his hoodie. The material barely covered my ass, but it would have to do.

Parker pulled on his sweats, and we ventured out of the room. Noah, the only one fully dressed, stood blocking the entrance to the living room with his arms crossed while Chloe scowled at him and Mac adjusted his grip on the towel around his waist.

"What the hell is going on out here?" Parker asked from behind me.

Noah didn't take his eyes off Chloe, who looked like she was wearing the same sparkly mini-dress she'd been wearing the night before at Eva's birthday celebration.

"Chloe tripped over Mac's gym bag and knocked the llama off the wall."

Soren had given the guys a picture of a llama—I still didn't get the joke—while D still lived here. They'd framed it and hung it in the living room until Parker moved it across the hall from Mac's room.

I looked back and forth between the three standing there. Despite the towel, Mac's hair wasn't wet, but it definitely looked like someone had been running their hands through it. I hoped, for his sake, he hadn't been messing around with D's sister, who lived across the hall now.

I'd officially moved in with Parker shortly after the first playoff game, with Eva's blessing. She'd forgiven the guys for their door cam shenanigans once Mac admitted the truth, and I'd convinced her not to hide any revenge potatoes in the apartment where I'd be living. She'd already lined up another roommate—Chloe. None of that explained why Chloe was in our apartment.

"Chloe, what are you doing in the hallway?" I finally asked when everyone else seemed content to stare at each other in silence.

Her green eyes flicked to me, then back to Noah. "I needed some help, so I came over here to ask. I'm sorry I bothered everyone."

I was ninety percent sure that was only a small part of the story, but I wasn't going to grill her with the guys all standing there. Besides, Eva would get the information out of her much faster than I could.

Noah nodded at Mac. "Looks like you're taken care of. I'm going back to bed."

Mac snorted. "What? No, man. I'm half-assed naked." We all stared at him until he rolled his eyes. "Like butt-assed naked but still got a towel on. Noah can help her."

He didn't wait for an answer, simply turned back into his room and shut the door. Mac never missed an opportunity to harass Noah. He probably had a girl in his room after all, just not Chloe.

Noah's jaw clenched. "Parker or Riley then."

Chloe sent us an apologetic glance. "They can't help."

Parker and I shared another look. Noah was the most introverted person I'd ever met, but I'd never known him to actively avoid someone before.

"Are you sure I can't help?" I ventured.

Chloe chewed on her bottom lip and shook her head. She sent Noah a look I couldn't read, and he sighed. Both of them were acting weird. I hadn't known her long, but she reminded me of Eva. Small and sharp, full of sass. Not this hesitant version of herself.

Noah ran a hand through his russet hair, making some of it stand on end. "Fine." He moved aside to let her pass.

I frowned as Noah followed Chloe into the living room, and Parker dragged me back into our bedroom.

"What was that about?" I asked him.

He shrugged. "I don't know, and I don't want to know because then I won't have to tell D."

I turned my frown on him. "You'd tattle on Chloe to her brother?"

"If she's in trouble? In a heartbeat. But I trust Noah to handle whatever she has going on."

The answer appeased me a little, but I couldn't help teasing him. "What if Noah *is* the trouble?"

Parker grimaced and flopped back on the bed, turning on ESPN. "I'm pretending I didn't see all the knowing glances they were exchanging. I'd almost rather she was sneaking in to see Mac."

I laughed and joined him on the bed. "I had that thought too. What would D do if..."

My name coming from the TV interrupted the thought. The sportscasters were rehashing the college football play-offs—which we'd won—and discussing the future of "college football's power couple". Harper was really good at her job, but I was still getting used to all the media attention.

Parker muted the TV and turned to me. "Have you thought about the draft?"

I raised a brow. "I thought we agreed to focus on next season."

He picked up my hand and kissed my palm. "You can focus on next season *and* consider your future at the same time. Hopefully a future with me."

"Definitely a future with you." I straddled his lap and curled my arms around his neck. "Harper says I have other options besides the draft. If I keep playing the way I have been, I'll be a front runner for the top receiver in college football. She suggested D's agent would be interested in me, and I could sign on somewhere as an undrafted free agent. I told her I'd consider it."

Parker skimmed his hands up my back, taking the sweat-shirt with him and pulling it over my head. "What do you want to do?"

I smiled. "I want to be with you, and I want to play—in that order—but I've been thinking about Marian's group. My dad always said I could do anything I put my mind to. How many other kids never get that message?"

He brushed a kiss across my collarbone. "You *can* do anything you put your mind to, including helping a bunch of kids realize the same thing. I'll support you one hundred percent in whatever you choose."

Saying the words aloud made me realize I'd already

decided. "Breaking barriers and playing professionally was never the point of football for me. It's a way to connect with my dad, and a sport I enjoy. I know I'm good enough, but I don't need to prove it just because I can. As long as I have you, I'm happy."

"You'll always have me." He brushed his nose against mine. "I love you, Lorelai."

"I love you too," I whispered, letting him pull me down next to him on the bed.

Any future with Parker was the future I wanted, but we had another year and a half of school to get through first—and a championship title to defend next season. Together.

———

Want more Front Runner?

Who doesn't? Get a glimpse of Parker and Riley's happy ever after when Fiona the demon cat causes trouble.

Click here for your free bonus epilogue!

**If you're having trouble clicking, go to http://www. nikkihallbooks.com/front-runner **

———

Want more of the TU Wildcats?

Turn the page to meet Noah and Chloe in Hard Hitter, the next book in the Wild Card series.

HARD HITTER

Noah

Chloe Asher would be the death of me. I was tired, bleary eyed, and awake way too fucking early in the morning to deal with her. The sun hadn't even come up yet.

I'd only been asleep an hour or two when a crash in the hallway had me running to find the subject of most of my fantasies standing outside my door. If she hadn't been D's sister, I'd have gone back to bed, preferably with her next to me.

Instead, Chloe's wide green eyes darted between me, my roommate, Mac, and the llama picture she'd knocked off the wall. Her dark hair tumbled over her shoulder in soft curls, and in the dim light from the living room, her tiny dress shimmered blue-green like the mermaid she'd been in my dream.

Not that I'd ever admit to dreaming about her.

At some point after I'd left the party last night, she'd ditched her pointy-heeled shoes, and I forced myself not to immediately scoop her up in my arms to protect her bare feet from the broken glass littering the floor.

"Don't move," I grumbled when she looked like she'd take a step toward me.

She scowled at the gym bag in the middle of the hallway. "Do you guys have to be pigs all the time?"

Mac, owner of the offending gym bag, shrugged. "I live here, and no one else complains. Besides, you're the one who made the mess."

He ran a hand through his tousled hair and glanced back at his door, a sure sign he wasn't alone in his room. We couldn't leave Chloe standing in the middle of the glass, but Mac only wore a towel wrapped around his waist.

I could reach her from where I stood, and I wouldn't end up naked in the process. With an internal groan, I beckoned her to lean toward me. Chloe's eyes narrowed, but she shifted her weight my direction.

Keeping my hands at her waist, I lifted Chloe out of the danger zone—she weighed next to nothing. I deposited her on glass-free carpet then backed away nearly to the living room, crossing my arms over my chest to keep from reaching for her again.

Riley and Parker, the last of my roommates, shuffled out of their room and stopped short. At least they'd taken the time to put on clothes. I didn't need another reminder that everyone was getting laid except me.

"What the hell is going on out here?" Parker asked.

I watched Chloe, surprised to see the slight wince. She wasn't the timid type, and honestly, breaking shit in someone else's apartment in the middle of the night was entirely on brand for her.

When she didn't answer, I gave him the only information I had, hoping she'd fill in the rest. "Chloe tripped over Mac's gym bag and knocked the llama off the wall."

Parker's brows drew together as he took stock of the

floor, Mac's lack of clothing, and Chloe's outfit from last night. I clenched my jaw against the unbidden urge to defend her. She was perfectly capable of defending herself if she chose.

Except she didn't.

Parker glared at Mac, I glared at Parker, and Mac edged closer to his door. None of us were in top form, especially since I was probably the only one who'd slept.

Riley broke the standoff. "Chloe, what are you doing in the hallway?"

Chloe's eyes flicked to Riley, then back to me, and I suddenly knew why she was hesitating. "I needed some help, so I came over here to ask. I'm sorry I bothered everyone."

There it was. The only reason Chloe paid any attention to me now—when she needed help. After spending hours watching her flirt with every guy at Eva's birthday party, I wasn't in the mood.

I nodded at Mac. "Looks like you're taken care of. I'm going back to bed."

Mac sputtered. "What? No, man. I'm half-assed naked."

I narrowed my eyes at him, willing him to take this one for the team, but Mac didn't get my telepathic message.

He rolled his eyes as if we were confused about his state of undress. "Like butt-assed naked but still got a towel on. Noah can help her."

In an act of friendship aggression, he went back into his room and shut the door without another word. The one time I *wanted* him to be loud and annoying. I chanced another look at Chloe. Her face seemed more expressive than usual without her glasses, pleading with me to help without making a fuss.

Or maybe I was still suffering from the weird-ass dream

where I'd had her naked in the pool with gleaming scales hugging the curves of her hips.

I clenched my jaw, unwilling to give in this time. "Parker or Riley then."

Chloe winced. "They can't help."

The couple shared a look I couldn't read, and Riley took a tentative step forward.

"Are you sure I can't help?" she asked.

I knew I liked Riley, and her soft question put her firmly in favorite roommate territory. Unfortunately, Chloe shook her head. Why was she so determined to make me suffer?

Chloe caught her full lower lip between her teeth, and a bolt of heat shot down my spine. As if she could sense my reaction, her gaze skipped back to me. The last time I'd showed up to help her, when the hockey fuckboy had abandoned her drunk at a party, she'd spent the entire drive home explaining in vivid detail how I'd missed out on the best blowjob of my life.

Sweat gathered between my shoulder blades just thinking about it.

I wasn't sure she remembered—we'd never discussed it —but I'd swear on Mac's signed Wonder Woman poster she hadn't been blackout drunk. Our gazes clashed and held, a battle of wills I was already losing.

Her fingers tangled together in front of her, and the image of drunk Chloe gleefully tossing her shirt at a hooting frat boy tightened the muscles in my back. How much worse could this situation possibly be if she was standing in front of me, barefoot and sober?

In the back of my mind, I knew it didn't matter. If she needed me, I'd be there.

I sighed and ran a hand through my hair. Fuck. I was going to regret this. "Fine."

A relieved smile flashed across Chloe's face, there and gone so fast I might have imagined it. I shifted to give her space to pass me, and she didn't spare the others another glance.

Parker's door closed softly behind us, and I found myself alone in the dark with her once again. Better get this over with. Chloe waited while I grabbed my shoes and keys by the door. Hopefully, sweats and a TU football shirt would be appropriate attire for whatever she needed me to do.

I dragged my gaze away from Chloe's perfect ass as she led me out into the cold night. "Where are we going?"

She nodded at the apartment she shared with Eva. "I have a small problem in my bedroom."

I frowned at her. "Chloe..."

She rolled her eyes. "I'm not trying to trick you into bed. Eva's staying the night elsewhere, and I can't handle this on my own. I'd hoped the problem would be resolved by the time I finished cleaning, but..." She trailed off with a shrug.

Guilt pricked at the thought of her picking up the huge mess we'd left in their apartment. I'd assumed Eva would hire a cleaning crew like she usually did.

I couldn't imagine Chloe cleaning in the tiny dress she was still wearing. Why wouldn't she change? Her massive wardrobe had to include something more comfortable than sequins. I didn't understand Chloe on the best of days, so I had no hope of keeping up while sleep-deprived and horny.

Goosebumps raised on my arms as the cold night air hit my skin. I was a furnace most of the time, so if I was cold, Chloe had to be freezing. Despite the frigid January temps, she hesitated outside her door.

"What's going on, Chloe?"

Chloe huffed out a breath. "I don't want you to get the wrong idea."

The guilt solidified into a hard knot in my stomach. My life would be a lot easier if I could write her off as a silly party girl, but I'd seen the parts of her she only let out when she thought no one was looking. When it came to Chloe, I was always looking.

"You came to me," I reminded her.

The edge of her lips quirked up, and she tilted her head in assent.

She led me through the dark apartment to her room. I expected a spider or broken furniture, but when she flipped on the light, my brows rose. Fury ignited, hot and fast.

A lanky guy with an unfortunate target tattoo on his back lay face down in Chloe's bed. Naked.

I almost turned around and went right back home. "You want me to get rid of your hookup?"

She groaned. "He's not my hookup."

I didn't want the details. The football season may be over, but I was pretty sure Coach would still make me run until I puked if I beat the shit out of a random dude in Eva's apartment. Don't ask me how, but Coach had a soft spot for Eva. Her influence was everywhere.

Despite my irrational rage at the guy, I tempered my voice for Chloe. "Need me to move him over so you have space?"

"Dammit, Noah. It's not like that. I don't know this guy, and I definitely didn't invite him into my bed. All I want to do is sleep, but I'm not about to lock myself in the apartment with a random drunk dude who may or may not murder me before morning."

It was on the tip of my tongue to offer her my bed for the rest of the night. Talk about bad decisions. Her eyes sharpened like she'd read my mind, or maybe my face, but even I wasn't that stupid.

I rubbed the back of my neck, markedly calmer knowing she didn't *want* the guy in her room. "Eva's not here?"

She sagged in relief. "No. Mysterious booty call. Can you please use your giant muscles to get rid of this guy?"

My jaw clenched, really unhappy with my role, but I moved toward the bed anyway.

What was I supposed to do with him? We couldn't leave him outside to freeze his balls off, and I definitely wasn't bringing him into our apartment with Riley and Mac's mystery girl there.

With some effort, I hauled the guy up by his armpits, trying my best to ignore the full frontal on display. He grumbled something about trolls, and his breath knocked me back a step. Once I blinked away the acrid tears, I got a good look at his face.

Thank fuck, I recognized him. Miller something. Second string kicker. Not really a surprise he was a football player considering Eva's social circle. He was a freshman, so he'd be living in the athlete dorm. I could drop him off in the lobby with a spare blanket.

Chloe held the doors for me as I muscled him out of her apartment and across the parking lot to my truck. He didn't stir as I heaved him into my passenger seat, and I made a mental note to scrub down the leather tomorrow.

As soon as the door closed, he slumped against it, snoring lightly. Chloe followed me around the truck to the driver's side, pulling me to a stop before I could climb inside. She searched my face, and my stupid heart took off at her close proximity.

"What are you going to do with him?"

I raised a brow. "Worried about *him* now?"

"D would never forgive me if you murdered someone on my behalf."

"Bold of you to assume they'd find the body."

She scowled at me, and I relented.

"He's a freshman football player. I'm going to return him to the athlete dorm where he can sleep off his bad decisions in public."

The breeze picked up, and she shivered. "Do you want me to come with you?"

"No. Go back inside, put on something warm, change your sheets, and get some sleep."

Chloe wrapped her arms around herself, shifting her weight from foot to foot, finally gracing me with the wicked smile I expected. "Always a pleasure watching you manhandle another guy."

"Chloe," I growled, now completely sure she remembered the night with the hockey asshole.

I may have given him a helping hand out of his car when I spotted him in the parking lot with another girl. Not my fault he tripped and fell face first onto the asphalt with his pants around his ankles.

Chloe patted my chest. "If you ever need help in the bedroom department, give me a call."

My dick went from half-hard to rock solid in the span of a breath. Thank god the dark parking lot didn't reveal a lot of details.

"Not interested," I lied.

"You made that very clear when you turned me down the first time. In this case, I meant if you ever need help removing a lady from your bed, I'm your girl."

I grunted, forcing myself to climb into my truck instead of leaving her unwanted visitor here and taking his place. "Get inside before you freeze."

She gave me a finger wave and hurried back to her apartment. Alone. I'd give my left nut to be the one keeping her warm, but a relationship between me and Chloe would never work. She wanted a temporary fun time, and I wasn't built that way.

I suffered in silence because I wouldn't disrespect D's sister by treating her like a disposable party favor. I wouldn't treat any woman that way, but especially not Chloe. D was closer to me than my family, and he'd trusted me with his sister.

Chloe was off limits, and I'd kick the ass of anyone who touched her.

———

Did you enjoy your first chapter? Snag your copy of Hard Hitter today!

A NOTE FROM NIKKI

Thank you so much for reading Front Runner! Riley has been living in my brain for years, just waiting for the right hero to come along. Thank goodness Parker was up to the task. And his family of course. They love Riley as much as I do.

This book was a wild ride ending with the championship, but what happens to the guys when they're in the off season? Chloe happens, that's what. D's sister is a hot mess heroine, and Noah can't escape the chaos. I can't wait for you to read their story!

If you have a second, please consider leaving a review. Even better, tag me with the review so we can be besties. You can find me on Facebook or TikTok. Finally, if you want updates on future books and other fun stuff, join my newsletter. I promise not to bite.

ACKNOWLEDGMENTS

I'd like to thank (in no particular order):

- Nicole Schneider, Liz Gallegos, and Jolene Perry, they make the words go
- Angela Haddon, for another beautiful cover
- Every female football player, ever—they pave the way
- M. Guida, author and friend, for convincing me to wait
- Shay Archer, author and friend, for convincing me to try
- Coffee, you get me
- Ted Lasso, for the joy and the sport

ALSO BY NIKKI HALL

Wild Card series

Game Changer

Rule Breaker

Front Runner

Hard Hitter

Play Maker

ABOUT THE AUTHOR

Nikki Hall is a smart-ass with a Ph.D. and a potty mouth. She writes stories that have spice and sass because she doesn't know any other way. Coffee makes her happy, messes make her stabby, and she'd sell one of her children for a second season of Firefly. She also writes paranormal romance under the name Nicole Hall.

Want to find out when the newest Nikki Hall book hits the shelves? Sign up for her newsletter at www.nikkihall books.com/signup.

FRONT RUNNER

Copyright © 2023 Nikki Hall

Cover designed by Angela Haddon

Edited by Jolene Perry, Waypoint Author Academy

Printed in Great Britain
by Amazon

28810784R00169